Brat out of Hell

By

Paul Lubaczewski

Paul Lubaczewski

A HellBound Books LLC Publication

Printed in the United States of America

Acknowledgments

First off thanks to the folks at HellBound for making sure this latest tome has gotten to your hands.

I also want to sincerely thank my beta readers on this, my wife Leslie, Reed Lazaro, Edward Mignot, Brian Strenko, Steve Knol, Sab Grey, John Hicks, Mike Strobl, and Jessica Charles, always thank beta readers, they keep you from looking as stupid as you really are. I'd also like to thank the folks that make the horror community possible, and the friends I've made along the way doing this, online or at signings and cons. And finally thanks to all of you fine readers out there who love horror, but realize it can be pretty funny too. Actually, Leslie should get two thank yous here, she has to look at me before I've had coffee.

Brat out of Hell

Chapter 1

"How long will I even be gone? A week at most!" - B.
Baggins

Danasdius was bored. Not only bored, but bored and deeply dissatisfied with everything to be more exact, which often go hand in hand. Both could be had separately, which was why it was important to clarify that this was a twofer malaise instead of the more common singular bummer. He often found himself feeling this way these days, even if he tried to hide it. He was also angry at everything that he felt was wrong with his life that made him feel that way, which somehow didn't alleviate his boredom any. Nothing in his life seemed fair, and to be fair to him, in his case he was right, nothing was, and it was that way by design.

This wasn't the normal angst the young males of any species feel about their surroundings no matter what they are. His being correct about his circumstance was a special case, it isn't normally the reality for a male on the verge of adulthood, normally it's just the confusion caused by having a body full of hormones and too much free time and too little life experience to find somewhere to put all that energy. If you could understand beaver as a language, you would be able to hear the younger male beavers complaining, "Why trees? Let's go to a lumberyard for the love of God, the wood is all ready to stack, it'd be so much easier! You're just old-fashioned, Dad, stuck in the forest!" Danasdius wasn't feeling that understandable youthful rush of misery, he wasn't even sure if he had hormones for one thing.

No, in Danasdius' case, since he lived in hell it was the de facto reality that nothing was fair, it was practically in the definition of the place. Eternal souls were tortured here...well, eternally actually, it was the place that gave the phrase "eternal torment" its bad name. Probably should have checked how we started that last sentence in our head before it got redundant like that. But anyway, in such an atmosphere the tender feelings of a demon prince coming into his birthright were not exactly going to be respected much more than anyone else's was. His fellow demons ignited or ate each other for pranks, souls were tortured, evil was plotted, so the idea of keeping your dad out of your room and respecting your privacy was something that had no shot whatsoever.

Thankfully his dad was his dad. "Moraspus the Not Very Nice At All, No Really, Most Unpleasant," or, as he was also known, Moraspus the Bad, which is what he usually went by at court since it was shorter. He was also called Murray but only by his closest friends, of which he had almost none, so most people didn't know this. Moraspus was the definition of a distracted father. He had his business on his mind and his mind on his business at all times. That business was trying to figure out ways to get ahead of other demons. Technically it was supposed to be tempting and tormenting humans, but since humans are pretty easy to tempt and torment that gets old over time. The real juice was finding new ways to damnation, of doing evil in a way that would vault you over your fellow demon Kings, Dukes, Lords, and Earls in the eyes of the big cheese himself.

Satan was also a bit of an absentee Dad, Moraspus knew that better than anyone, and the big Kahuna spent most of his time tormenting himself about losing the love of his father, and writing songs so depressing about that loss that the echo of their playing eventually wafted up to earth and inspired bands like the Cure, the Twilight Sad and Joy Division, among many others, who hear the echo in their souls and try and write something similar. Hell was just massive Daddy Issues with brimstone and pitchforks if you had to live there.

Danasdius was not totally alone in hell at least, having someone to complain to always helps. He had his tutor provided by his father, a lost soul named Girolamo Gentili to keep him company, or as Danasdius had always referred to him, GG. He had called him GG since he was a little boy demon when he couldn't pronounce either Girolamo or Gentili. Eventually, the poor put upon man had just given up on trying to get the small demon to stop igniting things long enough to pronounce it correctly and had just accepted his fate.

The man had been an alchemist when alive, not a particularly good one, but still, a learned man, and his father automatically equated that to tutor/babysitter. The man who would be cursed to be known as GG ended up in hell after he had pledged his soul to darkness one night in a fit of frustration over a relatively simple conjuring, and here he was. Danasdius' Dad had put as much thought into designating him in charge of the boy as he did most things involving his son. He knew he had an alchemist around somewhere, in his mind that meant someone smart enough to teach the boy something. Past that it was no business of Danasdius' father, the demon just assumed education would happen in there somewhere. Or, equally possible, the little boy demon would torch the tutor into smoldering ash, which would not only be amusing but a good life lesson for the lad. A soul you torch today is a soul you don't have around to torment later so don't be wasteful.

GG tried his best to teach the young demon about the world above, he really did. Someone needed to, so that when he was deemed ready by his father, the young Prince could go forth and do some serious tempting on his own with what he had learned. It was hard to do without going topside for field trips, but GG did his best. Hopefully, with his help, the boy would one day achieve the kind of tempting that keeps the Globe, the Enquirer, and all the other tabloids in business. Which brings us to this moment of boredom for Danasdius as GG was trying to impart that kind of wisdom to his charge.

"So, you see, young sir, it is not enough to woo the young woman, she must be left a ruined woman. That is to say, a woman who has lost her virtue and her chances of marriage, and her worth to herself and society," he repeated a lesson given many times before. Irritation flitted across the middle-aged Italian face for a moment before he said in a much more parental-sounding tone, "Sir? Are you quite yourself?"

Danasdius paused in twisting the limbs of a doomed soul long enough to say, "Sure, I'm fine, continue with the lesson GG."

GG attempted a smile, though it looked sickly in the flickering light dancing on this plain of hell at the moment, "Well, that leads us to what you're about right now, Sir. You're just twisting the limbs off. Yes, it's terribly painful at the moment, yes, the man will be screaming in agony for the time you're doing it, but those limbs will have grown back tomorrow. You will have left no wounds deep down in his heart where they'll last. Now if you were to torment his psyche instead, he might remain in torment for all eternity. If you twisted his limbs in a manner that wounded his self-image and left it lingering..."

"Why don't you just mind your own damned business?" the man who was having his arms torn off snarled at GG. Turning his sweating, tear-streaked face to his tormentor he gasped out, "Don't listen to this little creep your demonship. You're doing a great job!"

"So, you see? Even he knows you could be hurting him much worse than you are," GG pointed out.

"You know, I ever see your ass around the puss pits buddy, ain't no demon gonna have to torture you! You are all MINE," the now one-arm and one-legged man growled.

"C'mon, I'm bored," Danasdius sniffed throwing the soul away towards a pile of offal.

"You and me geek, when the Demon ain't around to hide behhhhhhiiiiinnnnnnd," the soul faded away as it traveled out of sight.

"Where do you wish to go my lord?" GG asked as he scrambled to keep up with Danasdius who had shrunken himself down to the size of a common soul by this point to make conversation a bit easier.

"I want to be alone; I mean with you of course, but apart from that, alone," Danasdius replied not bothering to see if the soul of his tutor and all-around babysitter was keeping up, he knew GG was. What his father would do to the damned soul if wasn't able to keep up with the young demon didn't bear thinking about. Although, GG spent a lot of time thinking about exactly that, especially since the boy had given him the slip on more than one occasion, and probably even more times GG didn't know about. You could tell when GG was thinking about what would happen if Moraspus ever found out by the way his eye twitched and he let out the occasional involuntary whimper.

"Well, you know that would be rather difficult I'd think," GG gasped as he jogged along to keep up, "there's an awful lot of souls and demons here." Nor was he mistaken in that in any way, souls had been pouring down to hell since time immemorial, so even with filtering out those souls who were awaiting judgment, it was still relatively packed on this particular plane. The various planes of hell being thought of as something along the lines of countries, this particular one could be considered on par with maybe India as far as population density. And it was that full despite the fact that it stretched almost for eternity. Something occurred metaphysically that allowed for limitless expansion, while at the same time ensuring miserable overcrowding. No one knew who had thought of the idea, but quite a few demons who had to oversee this mess wished to discuss it with them, at length.

"Still, not impossible."

"Oh no, we aren't going climbing again, are we?" GG moaned.

"Yep, good thing Father never asks after me, it's going to take a moment," Danasdius actually smiled as he made that particular proclamation, which showed there was some demon in there after all.

They were talking about the Putrid Mountains. Literally, massive mountains of garbage, which was why they were called Putrid, it was pretty self-explanatory really. Wherever you stood in this part of hell you could see them looming. No one knew why there was so much trash in hell, at least none of the souls condemned there, nobody told them anything. Even many of the demons themselves had no idea where it came from, but Danasdius and by proxy GG were privileged to know. The mountains upon mountains of refuse, the cities were even built from earth's garbage, were a specific punishment tailored to the souls dwelling here. When you want and lust for everything, well, trash was certainly something.

Trash wasn't all this plane of hell offered though for vistas. There were real, natural-looking mountains as well, each slope dotted with some classically styled mansion far from the sights and smells of all this refuse. That was where you got your mucky-mucks who could stay out of the muck like Danasdius' father and by extension Danasdius himself and by further extension of the extending, GG. The section of hell they were in today only had the worker demons calling it home, and thanks to the difference in living standards, those demons knew their place. They only had to look up at the only natural mountains they could see to figure it out.

Danasdius grew up in, and lived in, one of those wonderful mansions, which meant that even by being here he was slumming. He suspected he was spending time with his mother's people when he came here, if she was even still alive that was. If she was, she had been cast back down to the ranks of succubi she had been plucked from for the mating that produced him. His father had thought it would be amusing and right to have an heir here in hell one night while high on vapors from the abyss. Before he had sobered up, he had already set about doing the necessary things to make it happen. Once Danasdius was born and suckled, his mother was no longer considered useful to Moraspus so she was discarded in some manner. Soon after that, Moraspus' own interest in his heir waned, and GG was plucked from the ranks of the damned to suffer a torment almost as awful as the tortures afforded other souls, cursed for eternity to be tutor to a noble demon child.

The same child who was now almost a full demon on his own, and was dragging his tutor up one of the Putrid Mountains, Mount Stench to be exact. They moved as well as they could up the steep slope of trash. Time and other curiosity seekers had worn what could almost be a path up the slope of old grocery carts and Chevy Vegas. Not far below their current location multi-hued towns and cities had sprung up that used earth's forgotten treasures for building material. Climbers were not discouraged by the demons in this area, it was considered good fun to let them get close to the summit before sending winged homunculi to harry and worry at them until they plummeted back to the streets of the damned below.

GG followed as close behind his charge as he could manage, it was harder for GG than it was for Danasdius to make good time. Not just for the obvious reasons, one was a demon with all the power thereof, and the other was the soul of a man who had become a scholar because it let him stay inside a lot and avoid heavy lifting and callouses. There was the additional issue of only of them was desperately attempting to touch as few of the handholds provided by Tickle Me Elmos, Commodore Computers, and rotten fruit as was possible. For every easy movement Danasdius made, GG was forced to contemplate whether it was better to grasp the lava lamp firmly or see if he couldn't get a purchase on the mold-covered beta max cassette players, all while trying to not get anything on him. There were safer and more stable slopes comprising of things that had just failed to catch on back on earth, still in their boxes, but the demons watched those more closely.

They had reached a slightly less steep spot when Danasdius called a halt in front of a 1980s Plymouth K-car. "This is as high up as we go," he said raising his hand, "what we want's in there."

"In where? Wait, what do you mean 'what we want'? I thought what we wanted was to be alone?" GG protested as he pulled himself level with his charge.

"Well, we'll be even harder for my father's spies to find inside," the young demon replied as he stuck a key into the lock of the boxy-looking car. The door squealed as he opened it, not because of disrepair but because that was a standard feature on a K-Car, revealing only part of a tan interior, and the darkness of the heart of the mountain beyond that. "Come on then, let's get inside," Danasdius said and vanished inside one of the famous cars that saved MOPAR.

GG stood there contemplating the gaping dark in front of him. No matter how anything went after this moment, he was kind of in trouble here. When had the boy found this? He was supposed to be the boy's guardian, he was supposed to know his comings and goings. Unfortunately for GG, even in hell souls shut down so they could create the illusion of days here and rehabilitate the more minor wounds caused by even a normal mellow day in hell. A day was the measure of time used after a soul was through being dismembered for the day to judge when they would have their limbs and internal organs restored to them, ensuring they were fit as a fiddle for another day's torture and mutilation. Unless they were too far gone that was, and had to spend time being reconstructed in the pits. Had the boy been sneaking out on him while he slept? Whatever had happened during that time wasn't really his fault, his lord supposedly had guards, well, guarding his mansion on the mountains of hell at least. Why hadn't they spotted the boy and stopped him from sneaking out? Not that GG thought for a second that if they were found out Lord Moraspus would see it that way, when Moraspus was angry he had more than enough wrath to share it out for everybody, innocent and guilty and random bystanders alike.

Sighing mightily, Girolamo followed his charge into the darkened depth of the car's interior.

Which didn't end in another closed door on the far side of the seat. That door was open, and cool fetid air wafted up from the depths it led to. The put-upon teacher's soul humped across the tattered interior of the vehicle and found himself standing in a cool dark tunnel.

"Close the door! This place is supposed to be secret," Danasdius practically snarled from the inky depth in front of him.

Gulping, GG climbed back into the car and pulled the squealing door closed again, shuddering as he heard it click closed. "Could we maybe have some light? I'm afraid we souls don't have your abilities in the dark!"

"Just come out, and I'll take your hand. When we're well out of sight I'll turn the lights on, never fear," Danasdius replied, in a tone of voice that GG suspected heavily was laden with amusement.

GG fumbled his way out of the car and began waving his arms around the area hoping to make contact with anything to give himself some feeling of grounding. He started when he felt a hand take his own out of the dark surroundings. Danasdius' voice was right beside him, "Now just stay still, I have to close up the car." The sound the forgotten vehicle made in the dark as the other door shut was even more hideous than it had been in full light. He heard something else flop down, possibly some scrap of cloth to blot out any light from this side.

GG started to sweat as he heard footsteps in the dark, was Danasdius leaving him here as some demonic prank? Could he even find his way back out if he did? He must be able to, it was right behind him after all, it should be impossible to have gotten turned around this soon. At least he HOPED it was impossible, he secretly thought that not only was it possible, but it was also likely he could blunder around down here forever. What was happening? What was this all about? He was beginning to work up a good panic when he received his answer a moment later when a switch flicked and a dull light came on. GG let out a gasp of air that he had no idea he had been holding in this entire time.

GG gasped, not only because of the fact that he had been holding his breath and was about to turn a funny color if he didn't start breathing again but because of what he saw when the lights came on. In front of him was less a tunnel, than a hallway. That probably requires explanation. A tunnel looks dug, it's uneven it almost even looks naturally occurring even when it isn't. This did not look like that at all, it was squared off, it was lit, if only dimly, by individual bulbs strung out going off in the distance. If it wasn't for the fact that the walls were made out of the refuse of man above, you could easily picture people walking down it carrying stacks of papers containing sales figures. Ironically, a lot of the material that made up both the mountain itself and these walls consisted of pieces of paper containing sales figures, along with many of the products those sales figures related to.

"Well come along, we've still got to walk a bit. Sorry about the blackout, I tend to forget sometimes that humans have such limitations here with the light," Danasdius said crisply before turning and marching down the tunnel.

What does one do in a situation like this? There was some slight possibility, and one that GG was holding on to desperately, that this tunnel had already existed before Danasdius had found it. If his charge had made it, that meant a LOT of negligence on GG's part, and that meant...best not to think about what that meant now, GG would only start hyperventilating if he did. But if his charge had found it, how had he found out about it? The whole point of a place like this was to hide from the demons, which Danasdius definitely counted as.

Ironically there wasn't as much need to hide from the higher demon lords themselves, who one would think was the greatest fear. They only tortured for their own amusement and usually just ordered souls in to play with when they were bored. The royalty class of hell delegated everyday torments to the lower demons. Even that was not exactly accurate, that suggests some sort of organization to the whole thing. No, more what happened was there were an awful lot of subordinate demons around, and demon nature was to torture humans anyway. The lords and ladies of hell just let them get on with it as best as they were able on many planes of hell. Those who belonged to Satan's direct traceable lineage were expected to practice at it so as to be shown worthy of their position by dint of more imaginative and effective torture, but that was the extent that they did any real tormenting in hell. The real everyday eyeball plucking was done by those further down the food chain. Hell, as run by the Lords and Princes of Hell operated under the theory that if you had enough lesser demons and enough human souls around, massive amounts of torture would happen as a matter of course.

The torment of middle managers everywhere, most of which were doomed to come here, was to find out that with no real structure, or corporate mission, or scheduling at all it all worked far more efficiently than most massive corporations which spend most of their time bogged down in procedure and meetings. Meetings on this plane of Hell were far closer to three-day-long biker gang benders, but with the added bonus of no one going to jail for the hideous crimes against humanity that happened mid-party. If it was a good enough crime against humanity, they might even get a commendation of some sort. There was some organization, it couldn't be avoided, but the rulers were as hands-off as possible. They set up the thematic structure of each level, and let torture take its course. In the course of his duties for Moraspus GG had been to other levels of hell, including one that was nothing but a gigantic middle management office. Frankly, he preferred the easy-going dismemberment of home.

GG had so many questions he wanted to ask, but Danasdius suddenly looked much older than GG had ever thought of him and it quieted the tutor. He walked with the smooth gate of a full-blown demon in this place, no longer the little hoofed child who constantly had to be chided to stop chewing on his tail. "Danny boy...," GG began, using a name he only called the boy in private, and at his insistence. A sure sign of nervousness on the part of the tutor.

Danasdius cut him off by raising his hand. "Please," he whispered, "I will explain all when we reach our destination. No point doing it here where the sound may leak out to a passing imp."

With conversation cut off from him, what could GG do? He trailed along behind his charge like he'd been told to do. Part of him marveled at the tunnels, how could he not? How often could you really see construction of this caliber with salad shooters as a medium? He had heard of hidey holes like this existing in spots around hell, but what he had heard about were always described as slapdash affairs. Hastily dug and shored up with whatever material could be found before the demons found out about it. If the demons found out, they made no effort to announce themselves, they just blew the tunnel up with whoever was inside still inside. The thought of being slowly suffocating and being crushed to death sounded like a pretty nasty way to end up in the pits, so it seemed like good fun to the demons. It was that knowledge of what usually happened to these things that weighed heavily on GG's mind as he kept hoping against hope that this wouldn't all end with the tunnel itself weighing heavily against GG's body.

"Mind the Big Wheel," Danasdius turned and said softly, "the tunnel may be well made but things still fall out."

GG was thankful for the warning; he might have tripped over the toy in the dim light. He gaped up at the hole it had left in the wall and tried not to think of more things falling out. A moment later he was wishing that Danasdius' warning had included mentioning the Legos that littered the floor a little after that. GG was not allowed shoes by Moraspus, who said it made the tutor easier to find. All he had to do was just listen to the whimpers of pain or disgust depending on what was being stepped on. Danasdius and his cloven hooves probably hadn't even noticed the little toy caltrops masquerading as building blocks.

GG still had his hand over his mouth to hold in the muffled curses when Danasdius stopped in front of a door to the right that GG hadn't noticed through his tears. "Here we are, this is what I wanted to show you," Danasdius said drawing out a set of keys from who knew where upon his person.

The door unlocked not with the clank you would have expected from such a large lock, but more of a dull and muffled click. This might have looked like a hallway that had been built, but it was still made of compacted and dug trash, which thankfully softened any sound. When Danasdius pulled back the door, at first GG had to blink from the bright light that flooded out at them from inside. Danasdius stepped into the brilliantly lit room nonchalantly and beckoned his tutor to follow him.

GG stepped through the doorway and was awed. Somehow, under a mountain of filth and refuse, someone had managed to create a perfectly normal room for a teenager, only much cleaner than a normal teen's room. You could tell it was a teenager's room by the teenager that was sitting in the middle of it, who looked up at them from playing some kind of video game which was another sure sign. He was a boy of maybe fifteen, seventeen at the oldest. His cheeks still showed the roundness of childhood, his muscles lean without the filling out of manhood yet. In defiance of what was in actuality a very nice room, he was still dressed in torn jeans and a t-shirt.

"Hey Danno!" the cherub said smiling widely.

"Who?..... How?...." GG sputtered causing both of the young men to stare at him.

Danasdius chuckled, "This is who I wanted you to meet GG. This is Nathaniel Jordan, a soul of my acquaintance. Nathaniel, this is GG, my tutor who I've told you so much about."

"Charmed, I'm sure," the tutor said automatically.

"Yo," said the boy with an equal amount of thought, but less verbiage.

"But Danasdius, what is this all about? Some secret plan your father has you working on? Some deviltry of your own design?" GG's voice was filled with concern as he turned back quickly to his demon charge.

"Far from it! It could not be any further from it! Nate here has changed everything for me, and I hope he will for you too! He proved to me that I was not meant to just do as I was told, torture and maim for the rest of time without any thought, to just be a tool of evil. Nate has convinced me that I could be something more than that," Danasdius enthused.

GG drew himself up, "You most certainly *were* meant to do exactly those things, young man! If your father found out about what you were hiding down here! I mean that you even had a down here at all to hide things in....why I... why he...with a human soul no less!"

Danasdius shook his head, almost sadly, "Especially with a human soul my dear GG, especially Nathaniel. The boy dates back to the 16th century, and here he's been stuck all these years later to be tormented and rot in hell."

"Well, that happens to the best of us," sniffed GG.

"GG, did you even hear what you just said? 'Happens to the best of us.' That lays out the problem pretty bluntly! That there *is* a best of you for it to happen to. That it might be true that there are some that maybe shouldn't be here at all! And there are some who shouldn't be here, oh my yes there are! Do you know why some of those stuck in hell don't belong here? Because, my dear tutor, *the rules change!* They change all the time, Nathaniel, please tell my tutor why you're in hell?"

"Well, we couldn't afford a baptism nor confirmation y'know, and I was caught stealing bread for my mom," the teenager replied distractedly as his attention was already drifting back to the game he was playing.

"Well, those were the rules Danasdius, nobody said they were all fair."

The young demon snorted, "You know yourself that if you did it up there now, you'd be in heaven before your body got cold. It's capricious, it is needlessly cruel," his protégée snapped, before continuing, "So, anyway, how we met. One day I'm about to torture him, you know, get some practice in, and the thought occurred to me. 'I wonder why he's here?' Do you know in the entire time I've been torturing souls, unless it was a lesson from you in ironic tortures, I never once thought to check? Once he told me I just thought, well I can't do this. At first, I thought I'd make it up to him, bring him here, teach him how to be a real teenager. But as he's learned from the world above the way it is now and not just the slum of souls from his own era he was existing in, I've been learning from him."

"What could you possibly learn from a human Danasdius, you are a demon lord!" GG's temper flared for the first time in ages. And for good reason too, the boy was putting them both at intense risk of unspeakable torment just because he wanted to be nice to this snot-nosed thief. What was he thinking?

"How to be human for one thing."

"But...but I was human, I could teach you how to be...."

His charge held up his clawed hand to stop him, "No you can't GG, you've been teaching me the best ways to hurt humans for so long, you yourself have completely forgotten how to actually BE human!" The young demon smiled showing his fangs suddenly, "Maybe he can teach both of us! You can come with us!"

"Come with you where? We shouldn't even be here!"

"We're leaving hell GG, I've had enough. I want to see what it's like to live up there, I want to know what it's like to be human!"

"You can't take a human soul from hell! Well, not without permits and a lot of paperwork, and you can't possibly have those, your father would have told me! Nobody is even sure who's in charge of issuing them anymore!" the tutor spluttered, his face white with shock.

"Can, and am GG. That's why I brought you here, I want you to come along. I have the spell ready, we're leaving in a moment, as soon as I convince you to come. Think of it, to finally be free of Hell, to walk the earth and take in earthly pleasures. I bet you can't wait, right?" the demon enthused.

GG brought himself up to his full unimpressive height, "I shall do no such thing! Do you have any idea what your father would do to me if he found out about it? My suffering would be legendary! And neither will you. If you leave with me now and we got back to the palace, no one need know about this terrible lark of yours. I suppose it's admirable that you've shown the boy this kindness, and given him a place to hide, well he can keep doing it without you. I won't take that from you. I doubt any demon in the land would find this place, not when there are so many available souls for the picking on every street. Come Danasdius, we need to get out of here now!"

Danasdius looked disappointed and crestfallen from the speech, "If that's the way you feel about it."

"It is!"

"Well. Goodbye GG, "the demon prince said, before snapping his fingers.

Suddenly, Girolamo Gentili was very, very alone. Shaking, he went and sat down where the boy had sat playing video games. He sincerely hoped he was right about no one being able to find this place, and no one even trying. In that instant his world had completely changed and a new one become strikingly obvious to him. GG, Girolamo Gentili, member of the royal household, was fully sure of one thing right now. He would be living here, hopefully, if he was very lucky, for the rest of eternity. Thinking about being unlucky was to be avoided right now, it would only make him whimper.

Chapter 2

"Now how much would you pay? Too bad! It costs way more than that"- Ronald William Wordsworth Bartleby Dechets Popeil XXV

Dillon was looking forward to today and had been all week. But like many things in life, there were reasons that on the other hand made him less than enthusiastic. He was going to get to spend time with Hannah, so that counted as cool, very cool. On top of that they were going to New Hope, so that was pretty cool as well. Well, maybe not as much the New Hope part, that was mainly girlfriend going shopping territory and that had foibles attached to it. His mom kept telling him New Hope used to be cool, but other than the architecture he couldn't see how that had ever been. Hannah would like it though, of course why she would like it was because she would almost definitely have her dad's credit card. Considering it contained a tap that led to old family wealth, as in the Clymer fortune credit line, she would most likely do some damage with it.

New Hope was a shopper's paradise, provided you had expensive tastes. Dillon's tastes were much more "son of a single Mom, Rosenberger lack of fortune," tastes, instead of "signed the Declaration of Independence old money Clymer" tastes. So that meant he would mainly be a spectator to her shopping, and that was the not looking forward to it part of the day. But even then, Dillon had what was across the river to look forward to. Lambertville could still be well out of his price range in some shops, but it still had some of the weird shops that his mom swore New Hope had been famous for once.

He'd probably end up with something from one of the expensive shops as well, it was bound to happen at some point. Despite him telling her not to, Hannah would probably catch him ogling something with naked desire in spite of himself, and when he wasn't looking buy it for him. Once it was purchased, he'd find himself having to be appreciative, his mom had raised him right and all, he just didn't like it. It only served to remind him that he lived in a dirtball development that was built cheaply in the eighties near Dublin, and she lived in a VERY nice house near Buckingham. They might not have ever met or crossed paths in their entire life if they hadn't both signed up for the Anime class at the Michener Museum. The socio-economic gap between them was just something he forced himself to learn to live with, it wasn't like she lorded it over him. Today she would go into expensive shops in New Hope and spend amounts of money he didn't like to consider, and that was just what she was used to. But at least when that was over there would be time for what he wanted, spending a moderate amount of money at the Sixth Circle.

The Sixth Circle was an awesome used book store, in Dillon's mind the most awesome ever. What made it so specifically awesome was its total lack of a theme. Most used book stores you can get the idea of what the owner likes, or what gets read in the area it's located in that comes in on trade-in. Not the Sixth Circle, it was a place you could find the cheesiest pulp paperback horror books and an exquisite 18th-century treatise on military tactics all in the same trip. Their specialization was basically everything and nothing, and even when pressed, the couple that owned it, Danny and Nate, would never give you the same type of answer as to what was on their own bedstand that night.

Dillon carefully pulled the Beast up to the end of Hannah's drive and honked. He was no longer allowed to pull the Beast up that particular driveway since the time when his 1997 Ford Contour had a little accident involving a leaking hose on the concrete drive. Dillon tried to explain to Mr. Clymer that the Beast was sincerely sorry for his bad behavior, it was just so gosh-darned excited to be there, and it would never happen again, and that he had even smacked the Contour on the grill with a rolled-up Car and Driver as punishment, but to no avail. The new rule was that "that hunk of crap" (which was a hurtful thing to say with the Beast right there and all) was no longer allowed on the driveway.

The car door suddenly opened with a loud creak causing Dillon to spill soda on his lap as he jumped. "Hi, sweetie!" Hannah said as she dived in the now open passenger door. She gave him a quick peck on the cheek before adding, "Now drive Dominic! No Hope awaits!"

"On it, sweet cheeks," Dillon replied forcing the transmission into drive.

He guessed that her dad was giving her shit about him again, she always wanted to leave immediately when that happened. She didn't want to give her dad a chance to storm out with, "And another thing!" Dillon waited until he saw her seatbelt click into place before immediately taking his foot off the brake and hitting the gas. Her Dad could get up a hell of a turn of speed for an old guy when he wasn't done yelling about something yet, and Dillon didn't want to give Mr. Clymer a chance either since what that was, was probably him.

She turned immediately in her seat, her blond hair whipping with the force she did it with, "So! You looking forward to today?"

"Yeah, sure, of course, I am. But now on to the more important subject, why does your dad find me unacceptable today? Not that I can do much about it, but I like to have a full intel report in advance of the uncomfortable situation when I see him again," Dillon replied.

"Oh, it's bullshit, he still doesn't like the idea of us getting an apartment. I told him I didn't want to live on campus, and I sure as hell am not living in a hostel, so I'd need an apartment anyway. I told him the one we found would be perfect for both me to go to my classes, and for you to drive out to B triC for yours but...." it was funny in these conversations her blue eyes would always look worried, like he was judging her for her father being intolerant, instead of Dillon worrying he wasn't good enough for her which was the actual situation here.

"But he doesn't want you living in sin with somebody who isn't at least going to Temple because his grades aren't good enough for Penn where he would have been a legacy," he finished for her.

She was quiet for a second before replying, "Yeah, that seems to cover it." A nanosecond later, as she was wont to do, she dismissed the thought and perked right up, "Anyway, he can go to hell, we're doing it whatever he says. And I am not letting him ruin today, he isn't here, his credit card is, and we are going shopping!"

"Well, there we are then," Dillon chuckled pulling onto the main road and giving it some gas.

"So where do you want to go the most?" she enthused while unhooking his iPod from the cassette adapter for his stereo and hooking up her phone.

"You know where I want to go most, but it'll end up being our last stop."

"Those book guys are weird," she replied distractedly as she scrolled through her Spotify list.

Dillon chuckled, "Hun, it's a bookstore, if the owners weren't slightly weird, nobody would ever shop there. In fact, them being perfectly normal and running a bookstore, now THAT would be weird. Not to mention I bet the selection would suck."

"Well, you can spend some time in there as a reward, I know you hate clothes shopping with me."

"I never said that!" he protested.

"And I'm not stupid," she replied finally getting her phone to play, allowing Little Big to get thumping away to drown out his reply.

Finding parking was a struggle like always, but again, as always, Dillion's Mom had informed him that it wasn't anything like it used to be. According to her, once upon a time, you had to always park way up at the school on the edge of town and walk down. She said it was nice, there were always weird and interesting little shops opening up on the fringes of the town itself that you might not have found otherwise. Since they had put in additional lots, and especially if you were willing to spend Hannah's Dad's money on parking, it wasn't nearly so bad as all that. It still managed to be just more than exactly bad enough. After looking even for a little while for a cheaper spot on the street Dillon was happy to sacrifice Mr. Clymer's money on parking in a lot, being as Hannah more than fully intended to sacrifice some of it on shopping and he wanted the car close by so they could ditch all her new stuff in the car before they crossed the Delaware river to Lambertville.

This was going to be almost exclusively clothing so Dillon was happy to put his mind into neutral unless he was specifically needed for something. That's what he always did when he took Hannah shopping, he was sure she did it too when they went somewhere he specifically wanted. She'd ask if he thought things would look nice on her, and he'd say they would, because in his world most of what she wore looked nice because she was wearing it. Every once in a while, she'd slip something in that was absolutely butt ugly to trip him up, but he had gotten relatively good at spotting those traps before they were sprung on him and had tactful answers ready for when it happened.

This was the routine, first he would be allowed a brief stop in Farley's the bookstore that sold new books, Farley's was a little shop that had been there forever, and maybe purchase something there if something caught his eye. Other than that, and the comic shop, this side of the river was Hannah World. Dillon guessed that she and her dad must have had a pretty good fight, because she was really walking him all the way down the main street, with an option of side streets today. One thing that caught his eye was a new magic shop. These came and went all the time, there would always be one hard-core Wiccan place that had been there practically since the town had been built to give the town flavor with herbs and what have you, but this one looked more clothing oriented. Clothing-oriented meant it immediately caught Hannah's eye.

"C'mon, I want to check this place out," she tugged on his hand.

"Couldn't we go in the punk place instead? God Save the Qweens?" he protested to keep up appearances. This was part of the game. The more put upon he looked now, the longer she'd uncomplainingly let him explore the bookstore later.

Dillon wanted to object even further about this place, he wanted to reasonably say, "If you think your dad is pissed now, just try walking in the door wearing something from here!" But he nixed that thinking quick, that sounded like Dad talk on its own, not her cool young boyfriend talk. No girl on earth has ever been dating a guy and thought dreamily, "He sounds just like an overbearing authority figure I'd like to move out of home to get away from!" Well maybe some, but then again, some people paid good money to be spanked, so it just went to show, crazy old world out there.

Instead, what he said was, "All right, but then we drop all this stuff at the car and go over to Lambertville already, my feet are killing me."

The store they stepped into screamed, "Jill Stein voter." Its appearance warned of sandalwood incense, positive energies, and crystals. Dillon could only assume there was a Gwyneth Paltrow shrine in the back, probably something involving a stone egg. He was not positive that the older woman who smiled at them from the counter was stoned, but if she wasn't he would have been sincerely shocked to the point of taking it as a lesson not to be so judgmental of people. Considering her eyes though, and her Cheshire cat grin, he'd need a blood test before he'd believe it was just allergies and a healthy outlook on life.

This was not a place for people who were really hoping to do serious magic, that was the other place (assuming you believed in magic, Dillon didn't, but even he could tell the difference here.) This was a place for mainly older women, with excess finance, who needed something to do during the day other than joining a book club or any of the other things that rich women used to do during the day while their husbands were doing whatever their husbands did with their days. Golf was probably what the husbands did back then, these days it was probably rock climbing. The feminist movement had made a mark on these women, not in the sense of throwing off the shackles of being housewives and arm decorations for rich and powerful men, but more in the sense that they prayed to a goddess for Botox to work on these wrinkles instead of a man with a white beard up above to make sure nobody noticed the facelift.

Hannah was entranced, the other store freaked her out a little bit, but this looked to be perfect. Daring and father annoying without leaving a comfort zone. Here, she could find something that looked vaguely witchy enough to freak out her Lutheran father, while at the same time not really involving getting mixed up in the actual dark arts which seemed taking youthful rebellion a step too far to her. While Hannah was whisking through the store, plotting out what would upset her dad the most while at the same time leaving him with no proof that she was involved in any actual witchcraft or that she'd done this on purpose, Dillon drifted over to the jewelry cases just for something to look at while he waited.

Dillon was surprised to see something actually catch his eye. It was a little pentagram necklace. Not that there was anything special about a pentagram, not after the eighties satanic panic, that was for sure. Usually, he thought they were kind of hokey and the wardrobe choice for metalheads and Wiccans only. In this case, it was just neat how it was made, little silver-colored wires had been tightly woven together to build the thing up bit by bit. He could just make out through the glass the words 'sterling silver" on the tag, which left him out of its price range. Still, it was interesting craftsmanship.

"What's caught your eye?" Hannah demanded appearing next to him suddenly.

After Dillon swallowed his heart from surprise, he managed to let stumble out, "Oh... nothing, I just thought that necklace was kind of neat, but it's too rich for my blood."

She peered where he pointed for a second, and then smiled, "Well it's not too rich for my dad's. Especially if he's going to start a fight with me right before I go out." She looked up at the shopkeeper who Dillon only now noticed was wrapping something up that looked like a small statue, "This too please."

The woman came over slowly and with a smile so perpetually blissed out that Dillon assumed she kept a whole Tupperware container full of brownies for maintenance. "This one dear?" she asked Hannah.

"Yes please."

Rung up and back out into the wilds of Bucks County Pennsylvania, Hannah stopped, "One condition on your good boyfriend present."

"Oh?" his eyebrow rose warily.

"Well, you have to wear it obviously," she giggled, "here, let me help you clasp it."

"What if someone from my mom's church sees us?"

"Your mom only goes on Christmas and Easter. Anyway, what would they be doing in New Hope? Godheads think this place is Sodom and Lambertville is Gomorrah."

"Point."

What can you do in this situation? Nothing obviously, you let your girlfriend put the jewelry on you that she just got you, duh! Dillon was just thankful she waited until he was looking at something he kind of liked. He had friends, and he saw the results of the "meant well" jewelry purchase when a significant other misjudged him looking at something in mute horror and had mistaken it for being interested in owning it. Jewelry was touchy ground for the male of the species, and what was attractive for a male to wear as judged by the female of the species rarely found itself lining up with what the male of the species thought looked cool. This does not mean that men are any better about jewelry purchases, in fact, they are far worse, but many women usually have enough of the stuff kicking around, that the absence of the offending "he meant well" is hard to spot and it can vanish with less notice.

Newly branded with her mark upon him, they finally set out to drop this stuff off at the car. The town was relatively crowded today, so they didn't quite make the time they were hoping for heading back down the main street. Even if overall New Hope certainly didn't count as a city, it felt particularly long on the walk. This meant they got somewhat sweaty in the process, which facilitated a need to stop for ice cream along the way. They had to sit and eat that because they were too laden by that point to have a hand free for anything else. It went without saying that by the time they got her shopping stowed into the trunk of his car (which he kept clean specifically for these trips) Dillon more than felt the world owed him a trip across the river to get his bookstore on. And additionally, on the plus side, he'd gotten ice cream.

They weren't taking the car across the bridge, not because Dillon had any outstanding tickets in New Jersey, which could be considered an achievement for a PA driver, but more because he liked the walk even if he was a little hot and tired from toting bags. He enjoyed the rumble of the long bridge when cars drove over it and the sound made by the lapping of water from the Delaware down below. The view going off in either direction was one of the better ones in the area. It almost gave you some idea of the kind of beauty that made it cost so ungodly much to live anywhere NEAR the river on the PA side. There were too many people coming and going on the bridge to walk next to each other, but Dillon was able to let his hand trail back, and Hannah was holding it behind him. This meant that it was also a cute couple thing to walk over the bridge rather than drive.

Lambertville is like New Hope with its tourist qualities tuned down a few notches, or like Dillon's mom pointed out, "Like New Hope used to be." Its quirkiness wasn't as forced feeling as New Hope's was. New Hope was the Gen Xer who had been a punk rocker back in the 80s who would wear a special "cool" outfit to go out to a show to reminisce about the good old days. Lambertville was the Millennial who might have gotten a job in tech support, but he was still in a band, and still played RPG's at least once a week. Still kinda cool, and had not put his "cool clothing" in the closet yet, but had also grown up and had learned to adult to some degree.

Hannah at this point knew when to give a bit. They both knew that they were going to be exploring antique stores and other weird stuff on the way back to the car, but right now, her man wanted to get arm deep in the printed page. Dillon kept a little extra money out of his paycheck for these trips just for this book store. He didn't intend to spend it all there, but you never knew, really cool editions that were JUST barely in your price range happened, and if you didn't have the extra ten bucks, where would you be when that trumpet sounded? Looking at the empty spot on the shelf and crying because the moment had come and now it was gone. Because you knew when you were able to get back down there to buy it, it wouldn't be there, because anybody with half a brain in their head would know that something that cool doesn't just hang around waiting forever for you.

"It's cute," Hannah said as they power walked for the Sixth Circle.

"What is?" Dillon looked at her perplexed.

"It's cute how excited you get for the book store," she replied with a large smile on her face.

"How on earth is that cute?"

"First off, I never dated anyone who was excited to read anything. I've never known many people who even showed emotion about reading, except my dad, and only on days when he's reading the paper and his stocks did well. But you don't just get excited, you get little kid in a toy story giddy for a good used book store, especially this one," she explained.

"I don't know, I just like books," Dillon shrugged.

"You can get books anywhere, but you get really excited for a used book store. Any ideas on why?" she pressed.

Dillon had to actually think about that for a minute, and consider it from different angles. Finally, he replied, "I think it's the thrill of the hunt for one thing. It's the pawing through the racks until you find that special book. I mean if you just want to get a used book you can go online, but where is the fun of just clicking on a few things? Not to mention, while I can't afford the "really great books" the ones that go for a fortune online, sometimes you get lucky. You get to own something precious and rare, which we never had once my dad was gone. No antiques, no collectors' items, nothing really precious that I could appreciate except my mom's records which I was forbidden to touch anyway. It's a way I can hunt down something precious and own it."

She smiled, "Now that's a well-thought-out answer. But you didn't mention reading once."

"I thought that was a given," he shrugged.

"People have lots of books available in school, but they don't usually read them unless they're forced to."

The window to the bookstore looked perfect, exactly like it should belong to a bookstore. A large pane of storefront glass with carefully drawn 19th-century fonts declared that it was the "Sixth Circle Bookseller, Purveyor of Fine Literature Since 1997", with a slightly dingy sheen over the inside of the glass from all the dust inside. The bell jangled lightly as they entered, a proper bell, not some electronic thing beeping. Nate and Dan, the owners, were at the counter talking to someone when they came in, but they both made a point of looking up briefly and waving. By this point, they knew Dillon on sight.

The man they were talking to caught Dillon's eye and held it for a moment, Dillon tried hard not to stare, but how often do you see a purple pompadour? The guy was dressed to the nines in a very expensive suit, but it looked unnatural, the body that filled out that suit looked like an overgrown psychobilly kid. Dillon could even see the tattoos peeking out of the guy's collar and down on to his hands.

Instinctively he knew Hannah was about to say something, with the sixth sense of a boyfriend who has been here before. Now, while it was probably going to be complimentary, like "cool" or something like that, Hannah liked the new and unusual, it still would be causing a scene if she stopped and accosted the stranger. Bookstores are like libraries where the books are on sale, they are meant to be quiet mellow places, with emphasis on quiet.

Dillon grabbed her arm, "Come on let's go check in the humor section and work our way forward."

He had been intending to head for there anyway, but this gave him an excuse to hustle her out of the vicinity of the faux pas she was about to make. He knew her silence in this situation was a finite quantity, he was just hoping to get it to a more socially acceptable position before it ran out. His own experience with people like that was that they only wanted to talk to the world on their terms, not to have a stranger accosting them to find out where they got their hair dye from.

No sooner had they made the twists and turns to the dusty and poorly lit rear of the building when she burst out in what she thought was a quiet voice, "Holy shit! Did you see that guy?"

"Umm, how exactly do you miss that?" he whispered while beginning to scan over the titles.

"And here I thought this area wasn't cool enough for that anymore!"

"I wonder what he was talking to Nate and Dan about? Whatever it was, they didn't look happy," he replied, glancing back to the front of the store.

"Well, maybe a book deal or something. I'm gonna go look around, call me when you're ready," Hannah replied, leaning in and planting a kiss on his cheek. Dillon couldn't help but smile, it was a special girl who saw you had something you loved to the point of it almost being a vice and just let you have it. Most of the girls he'd gone out with in High School when you were with them things were only fine as long as you only paid attention to them and did what they wanted to do. Maybe it was because he was malleable and went along to get along, and their previous boyfriends had been control freaks, who knew? Whatever the reason, having your own world, your own thing, something that wasn't something anyone could intrude on, that was kind of verboten. Not Hannah, she read, but she understood that he was well past that, he collected. She'd probably find a book or two, and that would make her happy. He had to set aside an exact amount to bring along, otherwise, he'd spend far more than he could afford. In his wallet right now was exactly as much money as he could afford to spend, with the sure knowledge that he was probably going to spend quite a bit of it even if he didn't find that special must-have book.

Dillon had only been back there for a few minutes and had already grabbed a collection of old Doonesburys. He liked Doonesbury, because it gave an actual accounting of what was happening in the past, not the cliff notes, agreed-upon version you got from your parents or school, but what was actually happening at the time happening in real-time. That, and of course it was funny, there'd be no real point reading it if it wasn't worth a chuckle, he liked Duke in particular. On top of that, he grabbed a David Sedaris book, strictly for humor reasons.

Those finds were nice, but he had other fish to fry and he moved on from humor to more weighty sections. This was heaven to Dillon, digging through and looking for lost treasures, things that would mean far more to him than what the little stickers on the covers said Nate and Dan wanted for them, which was still often actually less than the book was worth. Dillon thought that the habit of underpricing some books was just for good business sense. They'd let a couple of "real steals" out onto the floor just to keep people like him coming in. Buy a heap of books from an estate sale, put a low-ball price on a few of them, and let people like Dillon find them. They weren't dummies about going rates, but if they could keep drawing you in with surprise bargains, sooner or later you'd be in their store drooling all over the really rare editions, maybe saving up for the day you could afford them, coming in every month or so and really learning to covet those books behind the glass cases. Which, actually worked, he'd saved up for months to buy that first edition paperback of "Weird Shadow Over Innsmouth" but it had been totally worth it. Something small, something he could afford, but something totally precious to him.

Chapter 3

"If I am known for anything, it for my unwavering loyalty"- Barry Arnold, Colonial Army stable boy

G G was concentrating on playing Tecmo Bowl. He had become addicted to the game in recent weeks since he had found the cartridge sticking out of one of the lower passages. Well, he was trying to concentrate on it and failing, to be more honest. He had things on his mind. Big, bad, and terrible things, and getting irritated at the game was not proving to be the distraction he'd hoped for. While he was definitely NOT THINKING ABOUT THOSE THINGS AT THIS MOMENT because he was playing Tecmo Bowl, Bo Jackson had just run for a touchdown on him. Again! He knew he should have played as the Raiders! He had been playing this game for almost a month now, how could he not realize that playing as the Raiders was the only viable option if you wanted the easy rush of winning? He had to wonder if he had self-destructive tendencies and a deep-seated need to suffer needlessly that had caused him to play as the Browns, it seemed the only logical explanation.

Cursing, GG threw down the controller and decided to examine what was bugging him so much, take it out into the open and examine the problem. He was pretty sure that the powers that be were no closer to discovering him than they had been on the day he vanished. He had become amazingly adept at keeping his head down and avoiding attention over the years. He was just being needlessly paranoid, but if you couldn't be paranoid in hell, where could you be?

The mountain of garbage provided all manner of amusement, so that wasn't an issue. As far as food, well it was a matter of wanting to eat more than needing to eat really. It was something you were accustomed to, and as Hell somehow had days and nights it was instinctive to feel that those days should have meals. He had discovered through necessity that hell had a thriving black market to provide a wide variety of food, all of which would be lacking and leaving one full but unsatisfied. All manner of creatures used the black market for all kinds of reasons. Demons who had decided that they were above torturing and torment, some that even had aspirations of worming their way back into the good graces up above, and a surprising number of souls who had somehow slipped the bonds of their torments by exploiting this plane of hell's slipshod bookkeeping and were now roaming under the radar, they all had things they wanted. Possibly those souls had slipped those bonds because of those demons who had set their pitchforks down for some copper wire that they shaped into a circle that they had buffed up and called a halo.

No, GG personally was fine, he was sure of it, well mostly sure, well, pretty sure at least. As always, this was still hell, the only certainty was torture if you got caught out in the open so the idea of safety was truthfully oxymoronic here. What really worried him, deep down inside, was that Danasdius might not be fine for much longer. Moraspus had discovered his progeny, and GG for that matter were missing. Word had reached GG through his various trading partners that after the old man had raged for a while, he had numerous seers and such search out the younger demon's aura on this plane of hell. GG already knew how their search would have gone. GG also knew it wouldn't end with just not finding him here, he doubted the old man would just let bygones be bygones and give up.

It would take a while to work out all the various permissions needed, but it was only a matter of time before Moraspus managed to conduct similar searches on the other planes of the abyss, and GG highly doubted he would find his son on any of those either. In point of fact, GG would be kind of pissed if Moraspus did. Here he had sat for all this time hiding out in this hovel, and his former student might be living it up on some other plane of hell? But that's the thing, GG didn't believe that Danasdius would do that to him for a moment, and that led to GG's own dilemma. While he was positive that his former student would never treat him so poorly as to withhold vital information like this, that loyalty worked both ways. How could he not warn him about his father coming for him?

There were ways to do just that. There were ways to get back up there if you were determined enough, especially if you were outside of the loop as it were. What the boy had done, well it must have been years ago now, that had been magic only available to one of the higher demons, but there were other ways to get out. Back doors that opened for the right price. This was not the first time GG had considered whether or not he might want to exit hell. After the heat of the initial argument with Danasdius had run out of him, GG had quickly realized that he might want to consider being able to make his own way out of here in a hurry sooner rather than later. The protections he had enjoyed for years had vanished with the boy. Even before this situation he had worked hard and greased the right talons just in case he had to flee back to earth and go join a monastery when the boy no longer needed him as a tutor. He figured running for earth was a foolproof plan as long as he was smart. Do not make the same mistakes up there, do not come back here at all, no reckoning with Moraspus. He knew that there was no way that a meeting with Moraspus would end up in the demon seeing GG's side of things, maybe exposing the ribs in GG's side, sure, but...

GG's conscience ate at him. No matter how much he told himself that he wasn't important enough to interfere, it wasn't about importance. Even a small man can hurl the rock that kills a giant. His first instinct driven by self-preservation had been to stay well out of it, wait until Moraspus was on another plane conducting his search, and flee to become a monk with all possible haste. It was a solid, reasonable plan, his former student had left him here, so why shouldn't he look after himself? He hadn't come back to check in all the intervening time, what did he owe the boy? Why should he give up his second shot at salvation and the grace of God? For a demon princeling no less?

Sighing, he turned off the TV and the game console. Because the boy was his friend was why. He'd practically raised him as his own, Moraspus certainly didn't have any interest in raising his son. Children assumed you were all right because you were their source of stability, you had to be all right. Going to warn the boy now was what friends did, they looked out for each other. Grumbling he got up to gather the various things he'd need on his journey to the mortal world, including various mystical weapons in case he got double-crossed along the way. Anyone who doesn't consider the possibility of being double-crossed by a demon is EXACTLY the kind of person who ends up here for all eternity. Fool GG once and all...

It had been a good haul, Dillon had six different books in his hands and was going to walk out of here coming in at around thirty bucks. Included in that stash was a Camus that was definitely meant as a "keep them coming back" bargain that his eye had caught. This '57 Knopf edition of "The Fall" should be going for a lot more than the 8 bucks that was carefully noted inside the cover, he knew it, he knew the booksellers knew it, he also knew it was bait to keep him coming back and he further knew that he didn't care. Bait or not, he was scoring a thirty-dollar book for under ten, and he would have been coming back anyway, so as far as Dillon was concerned, he had won this battle.

The weird guy was still at the counter talking to Dan and Nate, leaning towards them conspiratorially. All of their facial expressions had changed a bit, at least now it no longer looked like an argument was going to happen any time soon, so that was an improvement. Still, the guy with the weird hair's body language said he was annoyed, but was just way too cool to be showing it outright, while Dan and Nate still looked defeated and contrite. They might be smiling a bit at this point, but there was an undercurrent that even Dillon could pick up.

Dillon set his pile of books on the counter interrupting their conversation again, Hannah had already paid for her own couple of books while he was still browsing. The weird guy looked over at Dillon's pile, which consisted of a Doonesbury, the Sedaris book, a Clive Barker, a Roger Zelazny, a Jeff Strand, and the aforementioned Camus. He gave Dillon a once over with what could be considered a Grade A, adorable scamp, top of the heap, winning smile, "Nice find on that Camus, solid edition there."

"Ummm....thanks. How are things today?" he directed his question at Nate, the younger of the two booksellers, who he talked to more often.

Nate looked up from tallying up the stack with a wan smile, "You know, same old, same old, that'll be $29.50, and next time tell me if we underprice something as badly as we did with that Camus!"

Dillon looked up, a little shocked to hear Nate be that blunt, only to see him wink, a bit more animation coming into his smile. Dillon smiled back, "Well, I'll certainly try, but accidents happen."

"Accidents seem to happen a lot with you, young man," Dan added by way of joining the conversation.

"Oh?" the weird guy interjected, "The kid got an eye for books?"

"We lose money every time he's in here," Dan replied.

The weird guy turned and looked directly at Dillon while reaching into his coat pocket, "Here kid, take my card. You find something unique enough, I might be interested. I pay top dollar if it's good enough."

Dillon took the card gingerly, printed on fine linen stone card stock were the words, "Devin Morgan Purveyor of Rare and Unique Books." Dillon took out his wallet and slid the card in, "Umm, OK, thanks."

Hannah had been dropped off back at home and Dillon was back home. After the start of their day, and her massive shopping retaliation, they'd both agreed that maybe dropping her off early might be a better idea. They'd see each other tomorrow in Doylestown anyway, they were going to see a movie at the County Theater. The Theater was a grand old dame of a place going back to the thirties. Since it was the County Theater, it meant either an art film or a classic being shown on the big screen for the first time in forever. This was Dillon's own retaliation for all the retaliatory shopping today, the film they were going to was a showing of Alien which Dillon absolutely, desperately, and with a deep religious fervor normally reserved for snake handlers, wanted to see on the big screen. It was one that Hannah could take or leave.

Since his evening was free, and he was low on cash, he was hanging out with Zach. Zach was Dillon's best friend, had been since he'd punched Zach in elementary school for executing a slide tackle on him when they were playing soccer at recess. This is a weird thing about young males of the species, once they wallop each other, they either become mortal enemies for life, or they will team up to face the entire world together. Zach had tackled Dillon, Dillon had whomped him in the face for it, they both spent the rest of recess stuck standing in corners of the building as punishment. Since no one else had been available, they'd talked to each other and discovered they both liked the X-men. More well-known life-long friendships have been built on flimsier ground than that. Heck, trade relations between countries are often founded on flimsier ground than, "I totally agree with you, Wolverine is awesome."

They were over at Dillon's house today. A couple of years into High School, Zach's folks had moved to Coopersburg so they hadn't finished school together, but that hadn't really stopped them from hanging out since they both drove. Zach still lived with his rents, Dillon with his mom and while neither Dublin nor Coopersburg were considered a hotbed of activity, Dillon had something Zach didn't to recommend Dublin over Coopersburg. A brand-new copy of Facenommers IV The Search for Curley's Ear for X-box. Also, Zach's parents were Baptist and didn't approve of half the crap they watched on Netflix together. Dillon's mom on the other hand swore up and down she saw Nirvana on South Street in Philly, and would often make popcorn and sit with them if the film was gory enough. So, overall, they could chill easier at Dillon's place as well. They just told Zach's mom that they were playing Mario which she did not find objectionable in any way and had to deal with Dillon's mom saying, "COOL!" during exceptionally disturbing game deaths. Zach only prayed that his mom never ran into anyone hip enough to make a joke about all the mushrooms in Mario, or Dillon's mom would be getting a concerned phone call.

"So, her old man still pissed about you guys getting a place," Zach asked as he leaned sideways, in some way hoping that his character would do the same and therefore not die in a horribly mangled way.

"If I were a law student from a good family, she could come home with a black eye and it'd be fine," Dillon replied throwing a Cheeto at Zach's head.

"Class fuckers, all the same."

"She isn't though. I know everybody makes fun of the concept of "geek girls" and all, but I was playing this with her and she totally cleaned my clock."

"You let your girlfriend play before me?" Zach demanded as he backed up his character from the engagement, hoping Dillon's would save his ass which was in danger of being eaten. Somebody hadn't been checking their ammo and was in serious need of rescuing. "What's she got that I don't?"

"Do you really want me to answer that?" Dillon raised his eyebrow.

"Hey, I've got a cute butt!" Zach protested, "Speaking of which, could you save mine, I'm out of ammo."

"And I know that there's a certain someone on the football team that appreciates that butt, I noticed where you applied to college by the way," Dillon laughed. "On a side note, here, have some more ammo. Some of us stocked up at the last checkpoint."

"You are my savior, if you were gay, I wouldn't be applying to Kutztown."

"But I'm not and Caleb is, so enjoy Kutztown. Maybe you'll make some nice Amish friends out there English. I'll be staying here with my man, who just happens to have boobs and a vj."

"Just because you're moving towards the city and I'm moving for love to the middle of nowhere is no reason to be a bitch," Zach grunted with mock disgust.

"It is every reason," Dillon threw another Cheeto. "So how are things on the breaking it to Mom that you aren't exactly 'looking for a nice girl' front anyway?"

"Not well, she keeps introducing me to girls at church, awk-major-ward," Zach shrugged.

"How has she not noticed? You dressed up as Big Freeda for Halloween one year."

"Dude, she thought it was an Elton John outfit who she doesn't believe is really gay. She still wonders when Anderson Cooper will finally meet a nice young girl and settle down. My Mom's gaydar has a permanent short circuit," Zach chuckled.

Devin Morgan was trying very hard not to be pissed. This, was not an easy task. He was on Route 78, he was in New Jersey, and he was going home empty-handed, all of which had a high level of pissed off they individually could present him with. Ignoring time and money spent on this task was easy, books led him on all kinds of wild goose chases, it was the nature of the type of books that paid best. But in this case, it had meant driving through New Jersey. He hated driving in New Jersey, and God damn it if he was going to do that, life owed him the book at the end of it!

The damndest thing was, they had HAD the book, they'd sent him pictures of it and this was a case where you couldn't fake that. On top of that, he trusted them too much to think they'd try it. The book itself was small, and most surprisingly for a book that warranted a drive in New Jersey, clothbound. Devin had recognized the printing immediately; it WAS the book. It wasn't THE copy of "Lux Abyssum Irent" that would be priceless, but it was one of an ungodly rare series of printings that somehow got made of it in the 19th century. How they had even put the thing together boggled the mind, the block-making that must have gone into getting it on to the press itself... The rumor was that no one printer could work on the typesetting at a time lest they lose a printer to the madhouse of Bedlam. It must have cost an absolute fortune to print. Of course, the man who had it done, Sir Arthur Kenworthy, had a fortune to play with.

Kenworthy was the definition of a spoiled aristocrat. His family had made their money through trade and association with the East India Company, and he had been raised with every luxury available to him. And like spoiled brats all through time, having everything on earth available to him was insufficient, he wanted more than just everything the world had to offer. Which of course turned him to the black arts, which had always had a bit of a following in English Aristocracy anyway. The rumor was that he had the copies made for his buddies, which was mighty nice of him if you think about it. The book was intensely powerful, even rumored to have a spell that could hurl any demon short of Old Scratch himself back to the abyss without so much as a by your leave. Like not, "Get thee away from me, and where you go next is not my problem," more, "You go back to hell and you think about what you've done for the next century or two little Mister!" That's the kind of thing that's handy to have around if your pastime includes summoning demons and not necessarily having the clearest handwriting for the sigils around the circle of protection because of all the stuff you imbibed in.

It had other spells including one that was rumored to be one that could also serve as a get out of hell free card, which also sounded pretty handy if you boned the first spell. What became of Artie Boy's personal copy that was used as the basis for this printing got a little vague after he died in an opium den about a dozen years later. There were rumors now and again, but Devin figured if it still existed whatever billionaire owned the thing kept it under lock, key, laser, guard, pit bull, vault door, pyramid scheme offers, and poison gas. It was not resurfacing anytime soon is the point being made here. Even the copies Kenyworth had made were rare enough to reach in to the seven figures easily, depending on condition, i.e., scorch marks. What it would take to pry the original free defied numbers.

Devin was only thankful he hadn't put the word out that he had a lead on one. There were at least ten clients who had expressed an interest, "If you should ever find one available." There would have been a bidding war just to get to see it. Not having it after saying he did would have been some return phone calls that would have just about broken Devin's heart to make. "Hey? Know how you were going to pay me over a million smackers to give you a certain book? Well, I don't know, buy a Ferrari or something because the deal's off, I got no book. Yes, I do know how to delete a number from my phone, why?"

No point crying over spilled ink, the thing had been there, now it wasn't. There would be another book, there always was. At least now he knew one was in the states, he'd get it eventually, he always did. Those types of books often were just a waiting game, hopefully without scorch marks. Once he did have it in his hands, he would also, as a matter of course, photograph every page and assemble his own copy of it. You didn't spend as much time as Devin did hunting down that kind of book and not learn a thing or fifty about the subject matter. Devin had made it a pastime of his to help out people with those kinds of problems that required that kind of book to fix. He put special emphasis on those who got there through no fault of their own. Rarely did he help the actual conjurers though, you summon the thing, that's your problem bucko. But innocents get caught in the crossfire when magiks started getting toyed with. That banishment spell sounded damned ass handy to have.

He gave his custom 54 Studebaker Commander a bit of gas and cranked up Mad Sin, and tried to relax. He still had a lot of miles before he got home to the city no point in being miserable for every one of them. There would be beer at home, he felt like he deserved beer right now, also, maybe scotch, intravenously.

Moraspus was.... well, pissed was the right word for it, definitely pissed off. He had come back to his palace on this plane of hell to find it missing a key component he had come to expect when he came home, mainly his son. And not missing like, "just stepped out for a minute" but missing like nobody had seen him for so long that some of the newer servants had no idea who Moraspus was talking about, or that he even had had a son at some point. That his tutor was also missing was an interesting side note, but not entirely a surprise. If the boy had gotten into jeopardy, he had been trained from an early age to throw his tutor at it and run while whatever it was, was busy devouring the Italian. If the boy had run away from home, which Moraspus had explained to him by an adviser was a hazard of the boy's age, whichever age that happened to be, Moraspus couldn't be bothered to remember, he had probably dragged his tutor along as bait like the good boy he normally was.

Still, Moraspus was king in his castle, well not king, there was only one King in hell, but still, a pretty high-ranking mucky-muck Prince in his castle, so his rules were law. So, coming home and spending a little time with the boy, see how his studies were coming along, a bit of father-son toss the severed head, that sort of thing, was what he damned well expected to get. Not an empty palace and not even a note to explain why. Even the more trusted older servants had no idea where the kid had gone. He was sure they were telling the truth; he was a demon of considerable resource and strength and he could torture the hell out of someone (ha ha, get it?) for quite some time without even straining his intellect to think of new torments. After he had amused himself for some time doing just that while interrogating the servants, he finally told them to stop screaming already, he believed them.

At a loss as to what to do about all of this, he summoned some of his sniffers. That wasn't what they were called, but he called them sniffers because that was what they did. Moraspus was sure there was some lengthy tiresome real demonic name for them, but he could never be bothered to remember it. It was probably in Latin and any language that could take you from a nice hot sulfur bath to trapped in a pentagram by some weasel magician was not to be trusted. Even a demon Lord really only had so much memory space available to him, and if it was remembering what the damned sniffers were called or the address of where that absolutely exquisite blood orgy was going to be instead.... look, he had servants to remember what in the hell the sniffers were called. He wasn't going to let the servants do the things he could get up to at a good blood orgy for him, so he didn't remember trivial facts, it was for the servant's sake really.

The sniffers were somewhere trapped between souls bound for eternity and demons. They had been souls, they still retained some human appearance, but because of loyalty and devotion to their masters in hell, they had been blessed with demonic powers and the ability to even return above on missions for their lords. They served as the bloodhounds of hells for their masters. With a handler keeping an eye on them, once the beasts were put on a trail, they would not be dissuaded from it for anything. Their pale-skinned bodies would flood away on all fours, their mutated noses that looked more like muzzles trained to the air for any sign of the scent. In other words, sniffers, it suited them.

A group of sniffers was soon assembled. Ignoring them as cavorted the abominations they had for bodies around for the demon's amusement and appreciation, Moraspus called on one of his advisers, Mallocolic. Personally, he didn't like the slender little demon at all. The bastard reeked of being a "go-getter." Everything about him, from the designer suits he wore, to his carefully coiffed hair, spoke to Moraspus of a young demon that might not even take his hand off the blade he had just stabbed you in the back with even as you lay dying, just in case it needed an additional twist. In other words, perfectly suited to a damnably difficult job with a potential of danger. A guy, who if he failed, Moraspus would be fully justified in inflicting whatever wrath he felt like on the slippery bastard. Win-win in Moraspus' book.

"Yes, my Lord?" the demon oiled, appearing directly next to Moraspus' throne.

"My son, appears to have gone missing Mallocolic," the demon Lord said calmly.

"I have heard this might be the case, I am shocked at the audacity of the child, not waiting for his beloved father to return home. Especially seeing as you had only stepped out for the last century."

"Quite. As I'm sure you're aware my sniffers here are amazingly good at finding things, have a nose for it you see, but they tend to be a bit brainless. Something in the process of creating them, it's all we can do to keep them from pissing in the palace."

"Does my lord wish me to summon the handlers?"

Moraspus smiled, which most that knew him, knew to be a bad sign, "No my dear devoted Mallocolic, I want you to be their handler's handler. You are a smart young lad, with a bright future, at the moment. The exact kind of demon I want leading the hunt to find my son and to bring him back to me."

The younger demon's face went tight for a moment as if he was contemplating what failure at achieving this might mean to him, before his ingratiating smile returned, "Of course my lord. Anything to please you of course."

"Good, good, that's the attitude I like to hear from my majordomo," Moraspus replied before languidly tossing a human arm towards the sniffers, who immediately began to snarl and fight for possession of the severed limb. His last majordomo had been the first demon Moraspus had gone looking for when he'd found his son missing, it would take a long time to reconstruct him in the pits.

Chapter 4

"We'll be there before you know it!"- noted gastronome George Donner

It was a bright and sunny day. Which was a damned good thing since Dillon had talked Zach and Hannah into going with him to Quakertown and any place people need to be talked into going had damned well better be sunny when you get there. More specifically he had talked them into going to the farmers market there. Hannah had tried to point out that there was a flea market right in Solebury Township, and like every other time they had this discussion Dillon pointed out two key important points. The first one was that like everything else in Solebury Township, that flea market was way more upscale than what he was looking for. Even the people who went to the flea market were more upscale for that matter, and the shops that sold there knew their market and priced accordingly. The second, and Dillon thought this was FAR more important a point, the one in Solebury closed by one in the afternoon and he didn't want to have to rush around to make it in time.

The one in Quakertown still had some grunge to it, and loads and loads of outdoor vendors behind the place selling gods could only guess what on any given day, and for who knew how cheaply. People in that area often would have their yard sales by just renting a table for the day, thus saving them from the absolute worst part of having a yard sale. Namely, having the kind of people that go to yard sales knowing where you live, and what kind of taste you have. Not that yard salers are a criminal element, but they will start trying to bargain with you with a starting bid of one cent, then they will start trying to buy things that are not technically for sale, things that quite often you haven't paid off yet, like your car for instance. ("I'll give you 20 bucks for the Range Rover!) Much easier to have little price tags on things, and just leave them out on a table at a flea market to hope for the best while you ignored it all by fiddling on your phone.

Dillon loved the rustic outdoor atmosphere, and the chance that you might find some little treasure you couldn't live without at some insanely cheap price. The opposite could happen too, overspending for garbage could happen, in fact, that was probably more likely. Like the time that Zach paid twenty bucks for an early Pink poster with a crease in it because he was trying to leave a major hint to his mom. His mom had indeed complained, but only because she thought the girl was showing too much flesh in the picture. But, regardless of how it had worked out, Dillon still thought Zach had overpaid for that poster. Being sarcastic and subtly passive-aggressive could be had cheaper in Dillon's opinion.

Friendly complaints received from his friends, and ignored, Hannah and Zach were tucked away in the belly of the Beast heading for Q-town with him. Dillon actually felt kind of bad for Zach, the Contour was not exactly SUV spacious back there. It might not be fair to his best friend size wise, but girlfriend/boyfriend rules were rules all the same. On those occasions that Zach picked him up when he was with Caleb, Dillon would find himself crowded into the extended cab of Zach's truck which managed to be worse than the Contour. The significant other got shotgun, it was sacrosanct, it was law. Fair was only fair, and just, and right, and hell, at least Dillon had cleaned out the wrappers from Wendy's before they got in. So, in his opinion, he was definitely doing his best for Zach here.

The trip to Quakertown involved hills. Long, long, hills. This showed exactly how much Dillon really wanted to head up there today. The Beast was not the most powerful car on the market when it had been new, boasting a meager 4 cylinders under its hood. Those showroom fresh days when it had been a sprightly young powerhouse were a very long time ago for the car. The brakes were not exactly tip-top either, because frankly, Dillon had been putting off replacing them as long as possible for the very strong, valid reason of, he really didn't like getting that dirty. The brakes being one of the Beast's quirks was fine for this though, because one of his major strategies was to get up a serious head of steam on the downhills hopefully ensuring he didn't drop to below 55 until he was cresting the next hill saving the motor from undue misery.

They all made attempts to chat over the stereo but those efforts proved mainly unsuccessful. Dillon knew the volume being up was a stupid trap of youth, but was equally incapable of breaking himself out of it. Whoever was the first to suggest to turn down the music, would come across as no fun, and lose whatever cool points they had stored up with the rest of the group in that instant. You could only ask to turn it down if you had something really important to say like, "DEER!" or "POLICE! Or "HONEST TO GOD A CLOWN CAR!" Even then you had to be pretty sure that the vehicle was about to actually strike said animal, or police car, or clown car. If you just saw some deer up ahead near the side of the road that you thought looked sketchy and untrustworthy and you turned down the stereo and the thing didn't leap into the road you not only lost your cool points, but you became a wuss on top of it. There was another reason for not wanting to turn it down. If the stereo was turned up, Dillon couldn't hear any distressing expensive-sounding rattles coming from the Beast, and tinnitus was a small price to pay for that kind of peace of mind.

So, it was with ringing ears that they slowed down, at last, to make the big round right turn into Quakertown. Quakertown Pennsylvania was a former factory town that had never been able to make the leap into "quaint," like so many other towns in Bucks County had. It was just something in its basic makeup that held it back from the coveted "quaint" label. It wasn't the buildings themselves; it certainly had some decent architecture that could be considered colonial. Some actual history had even happened there, the Liberty Bell had been hidden there, Frye's Rebellion had been plotted in a bar that still existed. Yet something about the place's ingrained blue-collar existence still permeated the area keeping it from ever being the kind of town or ville that the well-heeled would want to flock to. Even extra *E's* pretentiously put on the end of words like "shop" and "old" and "town" never took hold there. While in say, nearby Buckingham, if you didn't name your new store right away, you'd go home for the night and find a sign over it the next day proclaiming it to now be the, "Ye Olde Towne Shoppe" and you needed a permit from the Borough to ever change it.

But that was all right. There needed to be a place for those that didn't actually own a horse, three expensive cars, a nice oversized house, and their own woods, and....well you get the point. For everyone else, there was

Quakertown and its pride and joy the Q-Mart. The Q-Mart was an ancient flea market and farmers market that had been there since roughly time began. Maybe even a bit before time began, time might have been started so that the Q-mart could have shoppers moving about inside. As creation myths go, it's not the dumbest. It was a huge sprawling warehouse of a place, filled on the inside with ever-changing and moving booths. This was in contrast to the back lot which had rows upon rows of tables selling everything known to man along with quite a few things man just didn't even want to know about.

Dillon pulled into the parking lot with immense care. The parking lot here was paved only in the most theoretical sense. The entire state of Pennsylvania is not known for its asphalt skills, flea markets just fit into the state's overall cratered pastiche. Efforts had been made to patch it, but it was fighting a battle against the commonwealth's general base state and overall war against smooth surfaces to drive on. At least there wasn't construction which was another hallmark of Pennsylvania roads. Dillon often wondered about that, you saw PennDOT working hard constantly, but you rarely saw any actual smooth and new roads. It was one of the great unsolved mysteries of the state, along with why beer distributors were closed on Sundays.

Dillon knew that if he was going to be allowed to successfully rummage out back in the flea market section for weird antiques, rare vinyl records, and books, they would have to do the tour of the farmer's market section in the main building. This was not vengeance is mine sayeth the teen daughter with your credit card shopping like New Hope had been, so it wouldn't be too bad. While it might not be her normal stomping grounds, Dillon was smart enough to know Hannah would at least want a look-see just in case something interesting came up. Not to mention, the one permanent bookstore inside had a comics section, so that should keep Zach happy. If you know that you're going to browse forever through what is mostly essentially junk out back, buy your friends off first by letting them check the other stuff, you get to keep your friends that way.

He parked the Beast where he could find a spot a few rows back from the front entrance, there was nothing closer. Going through the big ancient, squealing double doors, Dillon was reminded immediately why it was that if it had been just him, he would have parked out back and not come into this part. The place was packed to the gills. Malls might have had a great fall off in traffic with the advent of the net, but farmer's markets still packed them in for "great deals" and fresh meats and vegetables. In front of them were the entirety of the middle class and lower social strata ranging from every age and every body type milling through the halls. This was the 99% in toto. Thankfully Dillon had set aside the day for it because this was not going to be quick, you just couldn't move through a crowd like this fast enough for quick.

The first words out of Hannah's mouth were, "I want to look at the lizards!"

Inwardly Dillon groaned. She wanted a pet when they moved in together, he was hoping for maybe a dog or a cat, but Hannah was fascinated with reptiles. Every time she came here and dragged him into the pet store, he saw a future where he tried to find the cuddly side of a scaled and frankly bored animal that ate mice. He could only console himself that today would not be that day when she bought one. They hadn't moved in yet so they'd have nowhere to put it, he sure as hell wasn't going to care for it by himself. He blamed kaiju films for the situation.

"These are adorable," she squealed pointing to the baby iguanas.

"They get huge."

"So, we'll just get a bigger cage then. How about the snakes? Very masculine," she switched gears.

"Not when I scream like a girl when I see one, ruins the whole effect," Dillon deadpanned.

Hannah pouted for a second, before asking, "Well do you see any you like? I'm serious about getting a lizard for a pet you know."

"How 'bout that lil' fellah?" Dillon pointed.

"The Giant Plated Lizard? I haven't seen it move once," she looked at him incredulously.

"Perfect."

"We'll get a monitor lizard; you'll grow to love one!"

"No, it will grow huge enough to eat me."

"You'll see."

Zach decided to break up their Desi and Lucy routine to ask, "Hey can we get some food? I mean it's around lunch, isn't it?"

Dillon was glad for the respite. These conversations always ended with Hannah wearing him down to the point where he'd say, "I'll consider it." They hadn't reached that point yet today, so he was willing to consider that a win.

"Tell everyone what, why don't we get some grub, and head out back. The best stuff should be out on the tables by now, and then when we're done Hannah can see if there's anything she wants in here?" Dillon added quickly hoping to put some time and distance between his girlfriend and her love of things with scales.

Hannah flashed him a look, it mainly said, "You're lucky your friend's here protecting you, buddy, I was about to verbally mop the floor with you." Instead, her mouth said, "Yeah sure, that way I can actually linger in a few stores."

Ouch, shot across the shopping bow! It was worth it to get her out of the pet store though.

A little while later they were armed with breaded pork chops, which were finger food in the land of flea markets, and were munching on them as they finally made their way towards the set of doors in the rear. The doors were big metal monstrosities that would lead them back outside to where Dillon really wanted to be, the actual flea market section. Tables upon tables of what, you never knew, but he had no doubt he'd find something cool. He absolutely had to; he always did. Hannah and Zach often didn't agree with him on it, but he would assure them, "Dude, I'm telling you ten bucks for an East German Border Guard medal is a STEAL! Hey, now that I think about it, that guy did speak with an accent, you don't think he was the actual guard, do you?"

Already the first table looked promising, he could see magazines in a box, always good for a look through, a plumbing elbow joint, fishing gear, an un-exploded dummy bomb(he hoped it was a practice shell and not the real thing, but you never could be sure at these places) cassette tapes (nothing would be even slightly better than the Fat Boys, but since he had already bought that on vinyl from another flea market he wouldn't even bother to look), Readers Digest condensed bestsellers probably stolen from a dentist's office twenty years ago, and numerous broken 1980s He-Man toys. Dillon didn't even need to look at Hannah and Zach to see the disdain on their faces. To Dillon though, the randomness of the first table was a good sign, it meant the crazies were out today, and you never knew what one of them just might dig up.

Despite his fascination with everything, from the actually kind of cool, like the guy who had the Eisenhower campaign button, to the just weird, like the guy who had five Ronco inside the egg scramblers not one in a box, Dillon rarely actually threw his money around willy and or nilly when he came here. He'd look over every table, and then buy maybe one thing. There was always something worth taking a chance on, and he'd know it when he saw it. It might even be that Ike button, but something really cool, really unique, and surprisingly cheap was out here on these rickety ancient tables somewhere, it was just a matter of having the patience to find it. And that was the fun of it, the hunt, just as it was with a good used bookstore. If modern man could not hunt the mastodon anymore with spears as his instincts demanded, he could at least hunt for weird collectibles as a consolation.

Dillon was making his routine first pass when he froze in place. Lying on a table overseen by a weaselly looking guy wearing a Slipknot t-shirt a book caught his eye. It was small, clothbound instead of leather, but it looked like a legitimate antique. He glanced at the title and could just make out the words in gold leaf, "Lux Abyssum Irent" That sounded impressive, and expensive whatever it meant. He could just see the price tag of $60 on a sticky tab on the cover. Dillon quickly walked past the table and leaned over to Zach, "Dude, lend me twenty bucks until we get home."

"Why, what for? I thought you always brought money to these things," Zach replied as he handled an Extreme Dinosaur toy that had definitely seen better days.

"Guy has a book I absolutely want to buy; he wants sixty and all I have is forty."

"Talk him down," Hannah interrupted with an expression that said she was shocked he hadn't thought of that himself.

"I'm no good at that, look can either of you loan me twenty?"

Hannah let out an exasperated sigh, "Look, let me do it. If I can't get it for forty or less, I'll just buy it for you myself. What book is it?"

"It's the only hardback on his table."

"So, you want me to do this?"

Before waiting for his reply, Hannah turned and went back to the table. She looked it over for a minute before picking up the book. She opened it and began to thumb through the pages. She pretended not to notice that the guy who was selling it was practically leering at her as she examined it. Dillon thought she had to notice, from where he was with Zach, he could see a little drool coming down the side of the guy's mouth. Up close it was slimy halitosis city, it had to be.

Somehow the creep managed to find his voice, "That's a real cool book, I just got that a little while ago, good price."

"I don't know, I've got a friend who likes old books like this, but I don't know if I want to spend that much in case, they don't like it," she replied noncommittally.

The creep leaned in, Dillon figured she HAD to notice when he took a deep inhale of her perfume, "Well how much you got?"

"I could give you twenty?"

A look of disgust washed over the guy's face as he leaned back to make sure she saw it. Dillon spotted the bad acting even though both he and Zach, who were pretending to look over the next table deeply engrossed in the mangled Power Rangers figures there.

"No way! Tell ya' what, since it's a gift, I'll come down a little."

"How little?"

"I guess I could go fifty," he leaned back in.

Dillon figured this might take a minute and turned back to Zach, "So, any good toys? Things that make your inner child sing the theme to SpongeBob?"

"Naw, I thought there was a good Ultraman but it turned out to be a knockoff," Zach replied automatically. Zach was proud of his toy collection, and had a great eye, so if out of the three different vendors selling toys "Still in the box" Zach hadn't seen anything good, Dillon had to assume that what was available was only suitable for the dumpster after they didn't sell today. Zach always complained about these trips, but he always came along, because every once in a while, there was either a comic book or a toy he had to have.

Dillon felt Hannah tap him on the shoulder, when he turned, she thrust the book into his hands, "And here you go, so let's keep walking."

"How much do I owe you," he began to dig out his wallet as they started walking again.

"Nothing, I paid him thirty for it because you're cute when you really want something. Never doubt my Shop-Fu again, it is strong grasshopper, I have spent many hours in the dojo. Now you have money to keep the Beast's gas tank full, which is a good thing because we're going to go to Montgomeryville after this," she replied breezily.

"What's in Montgomeryville?' Zach demanded with suspicion.

"A mall, my gym trainers are shot."

Dillon stifled a groan.

"And there's a big ol' bookstore nearby to you ninny, and thanks to me you have some money to spend there!"

Chuckie breathed a sigh of relief as he watched the girl go. It wasn't often he watched a young piece of ass go and feel good about it, but he did today. Thirty bucks was good drinking money, especially with the cheap crap he drank. But more importantly, he was happy to see that damned book go. Thing had been giving him the creeps ever since he tucked it under his jacket down in Lambertville. He had assumed that the "Not For Sale" card in front of it had meant it was worth big money when he saw it in the back of the bookstore. Those guys knew their books which was why he went in there whenever he bummed a ride down there to do some five-finger discounting. They knew their books and more importantly, they sucked ass at spotting a shoplifter, especially when it was only the younger of the two watching the shop. He thought he'd made a big score this time, but every second since he'd slipped out the door the thing made his skin crawl. He'd tried to read it and that had made it all that much worse. He'd checked the internet and couldn't find a damned thing about the book, so as far as he knew it was all but worthless. Still, even then it was so old, that had to be worth something! Turned out that something was thirty bucks and that was good enough for Chuckie. Thank God almighty the thing was no longer his problem.

Truthfully, putting it on his table today had been a last resort, if it hadn't sold, he was going to throw it the hell out when he packed up to leave.

GG was still not happy, it seemed to be becoming a base state. Unhappy was not a major shock, he was still in hell, and that was supposed to be the point of the place, but that wasn't why he wasn't happy for a change. He was unhappy because he'd had to get his hands dirty on this trip. GG was a man who had eschewed violence most of his human life. Why hit someone with a stick when you can pay someone to hit someone with a bigger stick than you can even lift? Someone who enjoys it more and has more talent at it? That was his motto, well, not really, too long-winded for a motto for one, but it was certainly a point of view. But the point was, GG had made it a point in life to never personally get the blood on his hands. Unfortunately, one does not travel from one level of hell to the next without some really brutal bloodshed, unless you could get that Virgil guy for a guide, and he was booked solid for the next few millennia on the TV interview circuit. Most people would be shocked to find out that hell had television stations, but so many people who worked in TV had ended up here that management had deemed it a unique form of torture to recreate most of the worst shows in Television history so they could be run on loops. So, while there was TV in hell, Cop Rock is playing on one station and Manimal was playing the next station up.

Wait, we still haven't gotten to the point, have we? I mean about the bloodshed and all. We feel we might have gone off on a tangent, let's check back in. GG was mainly using stealth, which is one thing his exile from servitude had definitely taught him. Inevitably, occasionally that didn't work, and that was where the various instruments of murder he had in his pack came in. Even knowing the demon whose skull you caved in would be fine after a few years spent down in the pit, where the most mangled souls and demons were reassembled. Even that absolution didn't make getting their brain matter on yourself any more pleasant or enjoyable. Skulking in the shadows, dodging from hovel to hovel mainly worked, but always having a mace or a sword in your hand was par for the course for those little moments when subtlety failed. A similar course of action is needed to get through life in middle management, except for using a real mace or sword, more metaphorical ones, but who knows, it might be viewed as initiative in some companies if you opened up a few skulls here or there.

Rumor was there was a gate around somewhere on the level he'd gotten to. Oh sure, the company propaganda book "The Inferno" said there was only the one, but that was just name branding and misinformation. Demons higher up had told Dante all of that just to present the correct image that they wanted to the public. In reality, there were gates scattered all through hell. There had to be all kinds of ways just for the demons to do their necessary work of going to earth and fomenting evil by pitching sitcoms in Hollywood, inventing new filing systems, or writing self-help books that made you feel more depressed than you'd ever been by the time you'd finished it. Human souls were not supposed to be able to get out through the gates, they were guarded for one thing. It wouldn't be a good eternal torment if you could just skip out of the place any damned time you felt like it, would it?

GG had asked around, confident that not all gate guards were created equal. In any large corporate structure, there were weak links, it was bound to happen. Slackers who only waited for the moment the boss's back was turned to start playing Candy Crush. They had existed all through time, not Candy Crush, the Slackers, Candy Crush was only roughly a thousand years old. They might not have played Candy Crush all through time, but they did something other than paying attention to their jobs. When archaeologists find inexplicable works of "ancient folk art" that look kind of slapdash, that's because what it really is, is some ancient person, whose boss had just walked away for five minutes, screwing around. The reason these people had been buried with the perfectly preserved little stone dog statue was because they had it in their hands when their overseer clubbed them over the back of the head for slacking off one time too many, and the body had just been buried where it had fallen.

It wouldn't be much further now, he had his way out of here if he got to the right gate, he'd had a way out for years. In reality, GG had never been desperate enough to use it before now since he'd gotten ahold of his golden ticket. Knowing you had it was enough to get you through most days, hope was precious even in hell, especially in hell. That golden ticket consisted of the finger of a Saint. Darkness and evil love nothing better than finding ways to pervert and distort great good. It's in evil's very nature to want to corrupt the most precious and pure. Getting any part of a Saint into hell is a major coup, there's physical resistance to even get it through one of the gates. On earth, a demon wouldn't be able to even be near such a holy artifact, but once it was through the door, all bets were off. You could still use anything holy to kill off a demon in hell, but unlike on earth, it had to be backed by the intent to do it. The artifact still would have power in the hands of the unholy down here, but with its connection to the holy and the righteous path that it had served on earth severed by the overwhelming atmosphere in hell and then tinkered with by demonic forces, it could be harnessed for raw power instead of possible great miracles of goodness.

Saint Baldrick had never been a major saint, or a very good one really. He had been one of those accidental saints. An idiot by all accounts, whose childlike faith in God had somehow imbued him with the power to quell conflicts. Some would argue that Baldrick also had a childlike faith in fairies and pixies too, and he mainly quelled conflicts by tripping and falling in such a hilarious manner that it diffused the tension, but it really was beside the point. When one of the Popes, GG couldn't remember which one, had the man canonized during a two-week bender on really good communion wine when he had loudly declared, "You know what would be funny," the man became a Saint. Even if it had been a joke everything about him became a holy relic imbued with the power of good. Including the pinkie he had lost in a vegetable cutting incident.

GG had already been a servant of Moraspus for some time when he did some things he wasn't very proud of at all to acquire the finger bone he kept in a small pouch under his shirt. He had always assumed that while serving in the court of Moraspus may be the life of luxury in many ways, at some point he was going to want to make a break for it. He had hoped to put it off for some time. Demanding that Danasdius stay had been grandstanding on GG's part to try and protect the boy from himself, he knew what Moraspus was capable of if riled, the boy didn't. Deep down he knew he had stayed in hell after the boy left from some hope the kid would come back before his father found out. Knowing that the Demon Lord had found out about his missing son, and finding himself inexplicably fond of his former charge the way a teacher can sometimes get despite themselves, GG knew now was that time. If not now, when? Because if Moraspus got a hold of GG the things that he would do to him... Knowing one of the High Demons wants to discuss something with you tends to make you want to consider your options, and how many of them involve vacating the immediate area permanently.

GG had done his research, he had his bribe, this was it, time to return to earth. He was frankly terrified as he wandered down the dark and gloomy stone tunnel that led to the gate. Not that they'd turn down his bribe, nor that they'd just try and take it from him, nothing as mundane as that. If they were guarding this forgotten gate, it was because they were not prime guarding material.

He was terrified about the concept of returning to earth. Centuries had passed, he'd be almost lost there. Yes, they got the refuse of the world giving him some idea what it was like up there, but the world itself must have changed so much more than that. Would he even be able to find Danasdius? From what he gathered mankind had spread out a bit, where would he even start? Yes, in theory, a spell he had worked would make the gate he walked out of be the closest one to what he sought, but would it work? Would the ability to speak in all tongues that was part of hell be viable up above? So many questions, so many worries. But one thing was for sure, he needed to go, he needed to at least try. And if he failed to find his former student, he always had the monastery plan to fall back on.

He kept telling himself that as he moved toward the lit area up ahead that the tunnel was leading him towards.

The guards came into view as he got closer to the light. One was a demon of gluttony, the other one of famine, together, they were a classic comedy team. GG had seen enough contraband films in both his master's collection and what he had been able to find in the trash mountain he hid in to have a hard time deciding which one it was. He had narrowed it down to Laurel and Hardy, Abbott and Costello, or Spade and Farley, he'd have to talk to the demons themselves to figure out which one it was.

"Stay back mortal soul!" snapped the thin one.

"Oh hush, I want to see what he wants, nobody ever comes this way," the rotund one replied.

"Greetings great demon guards!" GG hailed them while laying it on thick. He'd never met a demon once who wasn't a sucker for flattery. "I come bearing tribute in exchange for you both having to go to the little demon's room for about ten minutes!"

The thin demon leaned on his spear to peer at GG more closely. Unfortunately, even his frail weight caused the ancient rotted and rusted thing to snap in two pitching him forward to the ground. This caused the other demon to start laughing uproariously. Not the start GG had hoped for, an embarrassed demon was a pissy demon, and would be much harder to deal with.

The thin demon scrambled to his feet, "I'll bloody do you for that one mate! The cost of that spear is gonna' end up comin' out of my wages. Not that they ever pay me my wages, I think they've forgotten we're even here."

"I think what I'm offering you for passage through the gate will more than make up for that," GG replied with a calm he wasn't feeling. Neither of these guards looked like they had been top of their guarding class, they looked like they'd been shuffled here, created for a trend in sin that had died down making them expendable. Sin has trends on earth, what is evil and awful one day, is greeted with a shrug the next, but to supply the sinners with the tempters for the time demons got created. When the sin's popularity died down, well then, the no longer tempting demons often got shuffled off to menial jobs like this and forgotten about if they couldn't adapt with the times. One had probably been created during the whalebone and tapeworm era, and the other during the renaissance when weight was a sign of health and wealth.

"What's to stop us from just takin' it off ya' then," the thin demon's eyes narrowed speculatively.

GG sighed, he was afraid it might come to this, "Well for starters, I have a sword and a bloody great mace." He held the mace up, gore and scales still clinging to it as a visual aid from the last time he'd been discovered.

"Gracilisisis! I didn't sign up for gate guarding to get hit with no bloody great maces!" moaned the fat one, "Find out what he has! When he's on his way, I've got some lovely virgin blood wine I borrowed indefinitely from Slimy Petreo that we can enjoy while we wait!"

"Pingthord! You're costing us negotiating power just givin' in like that!" snarled the thin one. He turned his face towards GG, and now it positively oiled with good nature, sort of like a used car salesman, but not quite as greedy, "So squire, what is it you've brought us that makes you think it would be worth us steppin' down from our duty?"

GG peered around the demons, to where he could see the gate itself hanging from rusted hinges, his sources had been right, nobody had thought about this particular gate in many, many years. He considered for a moment if he should do hell a favor and just bash these two over the head and keep the finger for himself but dismissed it. He had been in hell for centuries, it was true, but he still liked to think that deep down he was an honorable man. Other people might not have said so when he was alive, but it's never too late to build your own self-image. Also, he wasn't sure if a sin committed at the gate counted against your record on earth and he didn't want to chance it.

"I have, the finger of a saint. With that, if you play your cards right, who knows how high you could rise in the legions of hell. You certainly wouldn't be stuck guarding one of the most completely forgotten gates in the abyss for the rest of eternity."

"Done!" said Pingthord happy to see a way to get this over with where he didn't get hit with a mace and he got to drink virgin blood wine.

"Damnit Pingthord! Ya ain't supposed to agree that quick! We's supposed to haggle a bit first," snarled Gracilisisis smacking his rotund companion so hard that his ill-fitting helmet flew off. The bony body took in a deep calming breath that rattled around his throat and his scrawny chest like tuberculosis causing a droplet of slime to drop from his nose, "Well, I cain't rightly get more out of ya than that now, can I? Thanks to fat arse over there. How you propose to make this here exchange? I mean I can't see us letting you through the gate with it, and we ain't gonna wanna' move until we has it."

"Simplicity," replied GG. He reached beneath his shirt and drew out the pouch containing the finger. He undid the drawstring and held the bony desiccated finger up to the demon's wondering eyes. "Seeing it, there is no doubt as to what it is, so, fetch!"

GG tossed the finger violently over his shoulder. The guards gaped for only a moment before both of them began to lumber forward after it. They bounced off each other at least twice before they could make any progress. As they drew level with GG the Alchemist darted forward towards the gates. As he yanked the rusting handle to get the ancient things open, the one called Gracilisisis called back to him from the dark, "When they find ya' and drag ya' back, remember ya' dint come through here! Me and my friend should be higher up the pecking order by then, and we'll be in a position to not take too kindly to squealers!"

"You have my word!" GG called back as he stepped through the gates and began to make the transition towards reality and living again.

His last thought as he left hell, hopefully for good, had been, "Abbott and Costello, definitely Abbot and Costello."

Chapter 5
"I am not lost, I am just temporarily displaced."- Kris
Kolumbus, sea shanty rapper

Insidias Fabrica was enjoying his evenings back on earth, there was so much to relish here. He had missed fresh meals for one thing. Insidias was a vampire demon, which is almost indistinguishable from a normal vampire if you don't know what you're looking for. Normal vampires are just humans who have been infected with that strain of the demonic that comes from vampire demons originally. Nobody knew when the unholy elixir had passed on to humans, so nobody in hell knew exactly who to blame for it. A soul with eternal life is a soul without eternal torment which got up some people's noses. But since demons don't spend all that much time on earth except for TV Sweeps week and elections, and human vampires spend most of their time doing things usually associated with evil, in some circles, it was considered a long-term win anyway.

Vampires almost always end up in hell when some cheeky bugger with a stake gets ahold of them unless it's caught early enough, so he could have been a regular vampire. Old enough vampires eventually end up with some of the extra powers of the demon variety so sometimes it's hard to tell the difference. In his case, he remembered vaguely being a little baby demon in hell and constantly latching onto souls while still in his diapers even if they provided no nourishment. It had been a long time since he'd been on earth, but the reports he'd received from recently vanquished vampires in hell sounded interesting. Insidias hoped to savor this time on earth for a good long time, even if he was technically here to work with the sniffers.

Vampires and sniffers have a natural affinity for one another. Sniffers, because of their dog-like nature, like the vampires because they like their orders firm and commanding, and easy to follow. Vampires liked the sniffers because they did what they were told without asking annoying questions like, "Wouldn't it make more sense to board up all the windows instead of having these easily torn down drapes everywhere?" Over the millennia it had just become natural that the demons began to keep the former humans as hounds and pets. Sometimes the children of the night had been real children once.

Technically, Insidias had a job to do, and just as technically he was doing it. At least, within the parameters of what he could explain away as "doing the job." Nobody had told him he couldn't take over an abandoned warehouse as his base of operations, or that he couldn't infect some new minions to bring him the supplest of human flesh. If asked, he'd say, "Look it takes a while to find someone, you need to set up operations if you're going to be in it for the long haul here, buddy!"

He hadn't been totally shirking his duties since he'd arrived in one of the many sub tunnels associated with the Philadelphia Pennsylvania subway system. The sniffers got their orders from him when he woke, and then he cut them loose to do what they did, sniff. Just because so far, they had not yet caught the scent of the demon stripling was not his fault, or his problem as far as he was concerned. While he was waiting, was it too much to ask that he had some creature comforts to enjoy his time with? Of course not, heck, he was a demon, they had to expect that he'd indulge himself a little bit.

In fact, that was what Insidias was about to do right now. He'd been stalking this female since he'd first spotted her at a bar earlier in the night and the dinner bell in his head had begun to chime. She was bizarre looking, but Insidias looked forward to having years to spend with her where she explained her green hair to him, and why she only had a thin strip of it spiked skyward. She was definitely female though, he was definitely hungry, and she was definitely exotic, so, she was definitely about to become dinner.

Insidias could not believe his luck! She was actually taking a shortcut through an alley! Whatever higher power that looked over vampires was with him tonight, and thanks to that he'd be with his meal shortly! He followed close behind her into the alley, but not too close, he didn't want to spook the succulent doe into bolting for safety.

Just as he caught sight of her again, a shadow detached itself from the wall. "Excuse me," it said.

Insidias' eyes had adapted to the gloom enough to see that standing in front of him was a frail-looking young male. What was especially interesting about him was his clothing, which reminded the demon of nothing so much as the clothing of centuries past with its lace and finery. Maybe it could be a two-for-one sort of a night? They were practically throwing themselves at him! "Yes? What do you want?"

"It's really not nice to eat people you know," the young man said as it pointed something at Insidias.

There was a loud "thwump!" noise before the vampire demon felt a piercing pain in the center of his chest. He looked down to see what had happened only to gape at a stake sticking out from him. The pain erupted immediately after that; he could feel his flesh begin to crumble away in an instant. It had been a trap, this had all been a trap.

The girl had come up beside the male. He turned to her and said, "I'll be damned, it worked perfectly! Air-powered stake gun, who would have thought it!"

"I told you it would. Don't let his looks fool you, Billy is pretty smart ya' know," she replied.

"Well score one for research and development."

The last sight the dying vampire demon saw before his eyes collapsed in on themselves was the retreating footsteps as they left his crumbling body to float away in the breeze.

Moraspus raised his eyes from the soul he was sticking burning needles into to see that Mallocolic was standing there. Worse, Mallocolic was standing there looking apologetic, an unnatural expression on his underling, and one that boded poorly. He jabbed one last needle into the soul's eye and waited for the screams to subside before looking up and demanding, "Yes?"

"Well, we have our.... ummmm first reports on the search."

"You said 'ummm' nobody says umm if the news is good. So, what the ummm happened up there?" he growled, releasing the soul from its torture chair. He suspected he might need to free the chair up for what was coming.

"Well, about the sniffer's handlers...."

"The vampire demons, yes, what of them?"

"Did you know there are still professional vampire hunters up in the mortal realm? Because that was news to me," Mallocolic replied quietly, his eyes downcast.

Moraspus groaned in disbelief. Recovering himself he pointed to the chair the human soul had just vacated, "Take a seat and explain to me, at length, oh such lengths, the steps you are going to take to make sure this doesn't happen again."

GG had been expecting the gateway to lead to a cave, most of them did, but times had changed and the locations on earth had moved to keep them hidden. So, while he had expected a cave when he got through the gate, he hadn't expected the passageway to quickly be reduced to a hands and knees crawlway forcing him to leave his sword and mace behind. He doubted he'd be seeing them again, a shame really, they'd served him well. As far as light, it is here that we should note something, just like there are vampire demons, and just regular old fashion vampires, there is hell magic and just run of the mill using the background magic of the world magic.

For the foreseeable future using anything that came from hell for power, magic-wise was right out. It would be like ringing an alarm bell down below as to where he was, which it should be remembered was something he wished to avoid. If he had avoided that kind of magic in life, he might not have ended up in hell in the first place really. Luckily, in GG's former occupation as an alchemist you picked up things, and an eternity in the pits had allowed him to learn which magic was which, and if he ever did have cause to leave hell, which spells might be useful up above and to hone those. Including a small light spell. So, while he did end up cursing quite often when he hit his head on rocks, it was strictly because of low ceilings, and not because of a lack of light.

He almost cried out with joy when he saw honest to goodness natural light up ahead. He would have been happier if the hole it was coming in from was bigger than the passage he was crawling through, but blessedly, it wasn't any smaller. On a plus note, they wouldn't be able to send a bigger demon after him this way. No way some of the big mean ones would be able to come through that crawl, and at least that gave him a bit of a head start. Of course, a demon would change form to something approaching human by the time they got out, but the bigger they start and all that. Considering he hadn't walked the earth in centuries, GG figured he'd need every moment that might provide him just to get acclimated to the world again.

He was exhausted but couldn't help but feel exhilarated when he finally began to scrabble his way out of the hole onto the good clean surface of the earth. Centuries in hell, and he was finally back! GG ignored the nagging voice that said he could have done this years ago but had been enjoying the luxuries that came with working for Moraspus instead. That was joined by a friend in the nagging voice department that reminded him that Danasdius had offered to take him along when he left and he could have just left then if he hadn't been trying to bully his charge into staying. Nagging voices could go nag elsewhere, his body was telling him to enjoy the actual sun on his face.

He found himself about halfway up a forested hillside, and it was lush and real and it was earth, and that was what mattered. The cave entrance was directly below a tree that almost completely hid the way in. This was a common occurrence, most of the entrances to hell had some kind of obstruction hiding them from curious eyes completely. It was as if nature itself felt the evil that lay beyond and tried to hide it from her creations for their own good by letting the tree and its roots obscure the way. Maybe it had not been completely obliterated and sealed because the entrance was so small and difficult, but it was hidden anyway. It might not be sealed completely because it was so insignificant, just like hell had, nature had forgotten about it.

GG stretched for a long moment before inhaling deep lusty droughts of air. Amazing how he had forgotten how wonderful something as simple as air without any sulfur in it could be. He dismissed his light spell and brought something out from the bag that he had with him. It was a t-shirt with some kind of design proclaiming KISS to be Hotter Than Hell on it that belonged to the human Danasdius had vanished with. There had been a pile of belongings in the secret rooms that had clearly belonged to the boy before GG had devised his plan and decided that he needed them. He wove a small and easy seeking spell, one that would tell him where in the world the former owner of this shirt was now. GG had to be very specific as to which owner since it had probably been plucked from hell's refuse pile in the first place. There was every possibility that someone had discarded it here on earth. The shirt might have been poorly made and tore or something, and when the owner loudly cursed it, well curses carry weight sometimes. Thus, the need for specificity, because if he wasn't exacting in his demands his search might end with some pointless time in a graveyard with a shovel. GG had no way of knowing how long ago the shirt had existed on this plane of existence, so had no way of realizing how recently it had been sent to hell. (in reality, he probably would have ended up talking to a confused grandfather who had completely forgotten he had owned the shirt, but since GG had no idea who KISS was exactly other than the mounds of refuse they produced that ended in hell, he couldn't know)

GG realized his own mode of dress would have been dated before he left, so he had made a point of rummaging around to find things that were at least somewhat plentiful and therefore he hoped timeless. He was dressed in Jordache jeans (which chafed), boots with points on them, and a t-shirt he had found recently that showed the visage of some woman named Britney Spears. Little did he know that for some people where he was going, she had an absolute icon status, and he could not have picked a better t-shirt if he tried. GG was a formal man, and he loathed how he was currently attired. He loathed the uncomfortable jeans, and he loathed the boots his horrid sweaty jeans were tucked into, even if the boots did have paste jewels set in the leather. Well, he didn't loathe everything, he quite liked the t-shirt actually. She looked very pretty and virginal, yet coyly sexual at the same time, it was an appearance that while modern, he could get behind. He wondered who she was.

He began his trek down the hill enjoying things like hearing birds sing, and the occasional breeze through the trees. He had done it! He had managed to break out of hell! How truly glorious this was. It was such a shame that he had something so important to do because otherwise, he would have liked to just experience it a bit. GG had forgotten all the joys of being alive on the good green mother earth and wanted to savor each individual one. Reconnecting with all of this made his time in hell seem more loathsome indeed. Well, it wasn't going to go the same, not this time, this time he'd do things right. If he could stay on earth and manage to die here, before his demise came, he was racking up good deeds by the fistful to make sure he didn't get sent back. Even the relatively comfortable life of a servant in hell was nothing compared to the glory of feeling the grass on your feet in the mortal world! Sure, there were brambles and vines crossing his path, but they were clean and wonderful and nothing was currently burning, especially not him for a change.

Roughly an hour later GG was cursing weeds and vines and nature in general so sulphurously that if he died right then there would be no doubt as to where he would go. The vines had turned to thickets, the brambles had turned to thorns. He was sweating and bleeding from numerous small wounds and had fallen in deep-felt hate with everything around him at the moment. A bird chirped nearby and he told it that he hoped its eggs were all spoiled. He had forgotten about this part of life completely. It's hard to recall the pain of life when the pain of eternity had been so intense.

Finally, when he was discouraged and frankly heading towards feeling disgusting with sweat, he began to see gaps in the trees ahead. That meant either some kind of road or a river where he hoped he might find transport. If not that, maybe a farmer's field, a farmer who might direct him towards salvation, and if he was lucky take pity on a lost traveler with maybe some bread with butter and a nice ale. Maybe a ride in whatever vehicle he used to take GG closer to where Nathaniel must be.

As he got closer to the edge of the woods, he could see through the trees that it was indeed some kind of road. At least that was his best guess. Now that he thought about it, more of these black tar things had been showing up in hell as of late, the tar was close by and handy, it seemed only common sense to use it for the highways and the byways of the abyss. Seemed cruel to seal the workers in, as often happened, but then again, it was hell, what could you expect but to be steamrolled into smoking asphalt anyway? There were a few more modern parts of hell that were almost exclusively covered in the stuff. GG had hoped that it had been some invention of the demons, but it would appear it was more of a case of as above so below.

A road was what he needed, so while he would have been happier with mooching a free meal off of a farmer, he was still pretty pleased to have achieved this much. GG could only hope at this point that this would be the road that took him to wherever Danasdius and his pet human had set up to live. He checked the spell to guide him in the right direction which pointed directly down the road and climbed down to set off. The day was warm, the smell of the asphalt wafted up to assail his nostrils, but on the plus note at least he wasn't at risk of turning his ankle on a stone, or having his feet getting stuck in rutted mud. Not to mention he was finally free of the damnable vines and thorns in the woods. Things were looking up.

As he walked, GG began to realize that he was thirstier and hungrier than he had counted on, it was the kind of thing you forgot about that came with a body. If you were hungry or thirsty in hell, it was because someone wanted you to be, or because you convinced yourself you were, not because you had a body with needs. His only hope was that he would come upon some kind of settlement soon, hopefully, there would be something in his bag that he could trade for nourishment. Frankly, if as much time had passed as he believed, almost everything he was carrying was worth a multitude of times more than a simple meal would be worth. He also knew that at some point beggars would cease to be choosers, he'd need food more than the baubles he had with him.

Better still would be to find some kind of banking establishment, so he could change some of the various currencies that could be found easily around hell that he had brought along into whatever passed for money now. It was one of the supreme cruelties of hell, many of the inhabitants had found their way to hell due to their love of money, and once they got there it was everywhere, it was just completely worthless. Demons amuse themselves by watching new arrivals scooping it up in handfuls, they'll let them spend months and even years at it before they finally break the bad news. Often, they film the whole thing just so they can constantly re-wind the moment when the victim's face betrays their anguish.

GG had just gotten into a bit of rhythm as he walked along when he heard the noise. Something that was behind him, and the sound made him think that whatever it was, must be enormous. Worse than that it was approaching at speed! That was right! There were cars up here now, just like that one level of hell where they were everywhere, and if he stayed where he was, he'd be crushed. His eyes darted everywhere trying to decide what to do. While he was still considering, the thing let loose some braying cry of ravenous hunger as it bore down on him. He leaped for the side of the road...

He was shaking in the bushes as he watched it whip down the road past him.

GG stayed right where he was as four more went by.

He knew what cars were, they were junked all over his level of hell, in one level they were almost in operational status, yet somehow, he hadn't expected them on earth proper. They just seemed so awful that they had to be of hell itself. GG sighed with some exasperation; this was going to take more than a little getting used to here in the real world. If you got hit by a car in hell, you'd heal or be reconstructed, if you got hit by one here, you'd be back down in hell. There was room by the side of the road he supposed, and the cars did seem trapped between the painted lines somehow. If he wanted to find Danasdius any time soon he could see no alternative, he'd have to risk walking next to the road.

As the next car that went flying by it was all GG could do to not go diving for cover again, even though it was on the other side of the road. The first on his side was even worse, he could feel the wind of its passing ruffling his hair and clothes. His mind worked overtime coming up with all the damage one of those could do to a person if it struck them. He hadn't put in that much effort to get out of hell, just to get sent back to the place because he didn't understand the rules of the world now. Seeing how his walk was going, he could only imagine what other terrors the world of today held for him.

But eventually, he reached the point where cars could go flying by, with him doing no more than giving an all-over body shudder in fear at their passing. GG was proud of himself for acclimating so readily to this clearly horrible magic of the modern era. How people could allow themselves to be hurled along through space like that was completely beyond him. The entire concept of moving at such a rate of speed and it not ending terminally amazed him and terrified him. Even in the parts of hell where cars somehow did achieve mobility, they never managed to move like this, the cratered roads wouldn't let them for one thing. There was no getting around the fact that he had to move forward, he just tried to ignore the terrifying monstrosities.

That was until one of them pulled over. There was a space by the side of the road and in a moment, it was occupied by a small green car that he could see said Subaru on the back. Not only that, but he could see an arm waving him forward. What on earth could this person want? Despite his misgivings, GG began to make his way to the aperture where the arm had jutted out from. He just wanted to get this over with, it wasn't like he could flee faster than one of the things could move, so he might as well see what the charioteer, no wait, he'd seen this in a video game, the driver wanted.

As GG approached the contrivance, he could see that the person had short hair so blond it practically glowed, and was wearing a shirt similar to his. He only just caught himself from saying Sir to what he now supposed was a woman at second glance. Instead, he said, "Can I help you, Miss?"

She smiled brightly, her freckled face breaking into a wide grin, "Naw, but I can probably help you. Let me guess, judging by your outfit, you are heading for New Hope." GG inwardly was ecstatic to find that they understood each other perfectly well.

"Am I? I mean, I'm headed that way," GG replied pointing the way the spell was.

"Yep, New Hope. Hop in I'll give you a ride," she flicked her thumb towards the other door.

GG had a decision to make here, he had always avoided cars in hell whenever possible. He had lived a relatively sheltered life there; he'd be the first to admit it. He had just been musing on how frightening it must be to be inside one of these monstrosities to boot. He could have wavered or said no, it was his decision to make. The fact that it was hot, and he was sweaty and tired helped his body make it for him. His mind and senses might have been terrified of the things, but his suddenly fully corporeal being wanted to plant his butt somewhere and to take some time off. "Thank you!" his physical self replied before logic had any chance to get a word in edgewise. His body told his brain that on top of a place to sit, the woman might also have food in her vehicle, and on top of being tired, he was also pretty damned hungry by now so logic could just sit this one the hell out.

The door was relatively easy to figure out, he'd been going in and out of a K Car for years now and GG plopped down gratefully after putting his bag in the back seat. He had barely a nanosecond to even consider his fear of this mode of transportation before his driver was sending a spray of gravel behind them as she sped off and onto the road. As soon as the woman got the vehicle in motion, she turned and glanced at him, "So what's yer name?"

"Girolamo," he replied his eyes a little wide in fear. Seeing the woman's brow crease at the sound of his name he quickly added, "But my friends call me GG."

"Well GG," she smiled, "name's Sheryll. So, where you from originally, that's not a common accent you have there going for yourself."

GG caught himself before he said the region of hell where Moraspus' manor lay, instead he replied, "Italy originally."

"And what brings you to Pennsylvania?"

"I'm looking for a very old friend, I understand he's somewhere in that direction," GG pointed forward.

"Yep, New Hope. I figured as soon as I saw you, know why?"

"Psychic?" GG asked sincerely.

"Nope, that's the gayest outfit I have seen this far north on River Road in a while. Just be thankful I spotted you and not one of the local hicks. They haven't all joined the 21st century yet, the 19th gives them trouble sometimes."

Hannah was over at Dillon's place today. It was more one of those loose, "We're together just to be near each other" than anything serious sort of days. This wasn't a day where they felt the need to do things together. Well, that wasn't entirely true, since Dillon's Mom was at work, they had done something together, but clothing was back on and now they were just hanging out, but with less of them actually out, or hanging for that matter, than earlier.

Hannah was screwing around on her phone, she was tapping a lot, so he figured she must be talking to Amber her best friend from school. Amber was fine, Dillon swore Amber was fine, and he would keep saying it until he believed it. In the deepest parts of himself, the parts that he constantly had to tell to shut up so he wouldn't actually say what those parts were thinking, he thought that Amber was the personification made flesh of all the vapid parts of Hannah's upbringing that Hannah tried so hard to get rid of. In doses, the way he got it from Hannah, it was kind of cute and endearing, in Amber, it was THE ENTIRE PERSONALITY. He had friends growing up that were all the segments of his bad side made flesh, but he made sure Hannah had never met them because he made a point of avoiding them these days himself. Who knew though? Maybe Amber secretly wrote poetry and listened to Lewis Capaldi when nobody was looking. Dillon only knew the Amber he saw the rest of the time who listened to top 40 and wouldn't read a book if you taped her eyeballs to it. Why Dillon wasn't going to say something was simplicity itself, he knew from experience that the last thing you ever wanted to do in a relationship was put yourself between your significant other and a friend. Even if you won the argument, you hurt your significant other. So, in every important way, you still lost.

Dillon had his laptop out yet again trying to decipher the bizarre book he'd bought at the flea market. In theory, he should just view it as a treasure and put it on a shelf, but Dillon liked to know things, and here was a thing to learn. The problem wasn't just that the book was in a foreign language, oh no, nothing as easy and reasonable as that. No, this book was in numerous languages and would change languages constantly, often in the same paragraph. It would bounce between Latin, which seemed to be the base language it used, to Aramaic, to Hebrew, Avastin,

Tamil, Arabic, and at least one other he hadn't been able to identify. Google translate had been a good place to start, but after that he'd actually needed to head to the library, taking out books that sat propped open next to his. With every page he translated, he had to have a bunch of tabs with translators open, and even then, there would be gaps. Not a frustrating project at all! Nope, he was enjoying this!

"God damn it!" Dillon cursed slamming the book shut, only to immediately re-open it.

"Hey hon, I secretly put you on a five curse word limit as to when I arbitrarily decided that you were no longer enjoying yourself trying to decipher that thing. Why don't you close it and come over here and snuggle? After that, I don't know, maybe we can go to see a movie," Hannah interrupted.

Dillon almost growled at her but caught himself. After he got his temper tamped down, he also realized she was completely right. Something like this needed breaks or you'd just drive yourself as mad as whoever had written the thing. So instead of making animal snarling noise he climbed back up onto the bed and cuddled up next to her. "It wouldn't be so bad if it wasn't for those snippets of language, I can't find anywhere that just get thrown in randomly. This time, swear to God, it was mid-sentence, one minute it was, 'to finally break the seal you must' and then the next, gibberish."

"Why don't you call the book guy? He might know something about weird languages."

"Book guy?"

"You know the one that was at that shop at Lambertville talking to the owners. He gave you his card, he said to call if you found anything weird. I think non-existent languages certainly qualifies, don't you?" she explained from where she'd placed her head on his chest.

"Damn, you're a genius!" Dillon replied sliding out from under her.

"Hmph, if I was that much of a genius, I would have known this was going to cost me my pillow. And I was just getting comfy," Hannah replied putting on a little girl pout.

"Just take a sec, promise," he replied, digging out the number where he'd tossed it onto his nightstand.

He grabbed his cell and called the number, after one ring it picked up, "Hello this is Devin Morgan, I'm not in the office right now. If you're calling to ask me to acquire a book, leave the name, your number or email, the edition you would prefer, and top dollar you're willing to pay. If it's about anything else, and it's an emergency, either I'm on my way, or you probably should have called me sooner anyway. Either way, please leave a message and have the best day or night you're capable of."

"Ummm, yeah, hi, my name's Dillon. I met you at a book store in Lambertville New Jersey. You told me to call if I found any interesting books. I found something called ' Lux Abyssum Irent' and it looks pretty rare. I've been trying to translate it, and some of the language is really giving me issues. Anyway, my number is 215 555 1313, thanks."

Dillon clicked off his cell and turned to Hannah, "Superhero movie? There has to be one in the theater, there's *always one* in the theater."

"I suppose, but I wish they made more romantic comedies," Hannah sighed.

"Please don't screw with me like that, it scares me. You won't even watch the Hallmark channel as a joke, so when you say things like that it makes me afraid aliens have replaced my girlfriend."

"Ack ack ack," Hannah replied.

Chapter 6

"None of these meetings are meant to be awkward in the slightest."- Maury Povichski, Polish daytime TV Host

Moraspus surveyed a new group of vampire demons and a new group of sniffers. Many of the last batch were busy being reconstructed in the swamps and pits several levels below this one and would be of no use for years now. As was Mallocolic, who had discovered at length how his master took news like the type from the previous oversight. By the time Moraspus had regained his temper it was all over but the hosing the floor off. Moraspus had no regrets about it, Mallocolic had known the risks when he took the job, more importantly, he had set the search back some time by his incompetence. If you didn't let the imps and demons around here know who the boss was, it would be you down in the pits trying to wait patiently while you grew a new spleen.

His new Majordomo was a green slime dripping demon named Blurglesoth who was currently standing next to the vampire demons. Moraspus did not have high hopes for Blurglesoth, he could be hard to understand, and even for a demon, he was a bit disgusting. Considering his tendency to drip everywhere, it would only be a matter of time before some slight or another caused the demon lord to rend him asunder. But he'd been handy, and he had worked his way dutifully up the ranks to get here, so Blurglesoth would have to do, for now, cleaning bills be damned.

Blurglesoth had the vampire demon handlers lined up smartly in a row in front of Moraspus. The slimy demon gurgled out, "Alright now demons, what is your mission?"

Like little children who had been rehearsed vigorously in a play and are hoping to not get smacked in the ear this time, the vampire demons replied in unison, "To find our Lord Moraspus' son."

"And what won't we do with our time on earth until we do?"

"Act like vampires," the line muttered.

"I can't HEAR you!" Blurglesoth bellowed sending a glob of slime to gloop onto the marble floor.

"We won't act like vampires!" they replied louder, it was still unenthusiastic, but clear that all of them understood.

"Which means?"

"No bloodsucking" the demons pouted.

"Why won't we be drinking mortal blood?" Blurglesoth said a little louder, leaning in to look at their faces.

"Because vampire hunters still exist."

"Very good." Turning his oozing countenance to Moraspus he added, "Any final words for them my Lord?"

Moraspus nodded, not believing any of them wouldn't be fangs deep the first chance they got, "No, that should do it."

He decided that maybe he'd have to keep an eye on Blurglesoth, the demon was smart enough to create plausible deniability for himself if something went wrong.

That kind of forward-thinking cleverness deserved closer scrutiny.

So, this was the modern world, was it? It was fascinating and terrifying to GG as he wandered around the town after Sheryll dropped him off. It was one thing to see the toss-offs and rejects from it as they appeared in hell, it was another to see it in all its glory with things functioning as they should. It had been difficult to tear himself away from the endless bustling people in their modern clothes, the cars everywhere, the stores selling their wares. But he was still here on a mission of vital importance, and who knew how much time he had to work with left to him. He checked the finding spell and saw that it pointed him across the river. Thank goodness there was a bridge nearby, the water didn't look deep, but GG's only other clothes were his normal ones and he was pretty sure they'd be remarked upon. He took a look around as he considered that last thought, alright, maybe they wouldn't be remarked on that much here in this particular town, but he suspected this place wasn't the norm.

The air was pleasant coming off the water far below, he only wished he could enjoy it more. It wasn't just the urgency of what he needed to tell his former pupil; it was how they parted. Even though it was Danasdius that left, in many ways, it was GG who was doing the abandoning by refusing to come along. Frankly, he thought that if he put his foot down Danasdius would abandon his notion of coming to earth without his father's leave. GG had misjudged the moment as well as the amount the student felt he still needed the teacher versus how much he needed his freedom. Coming here now was not only his chance to warn the boy, it was an opportunity to put things right between them.

The spell began to tug strongly as he got closer. By the time he reached the door of the bookstore, there was no doubt as to who would be inside. It was at a moment like this that a few hundred years just drop off of you, and you're a child again standing outside of the house of your best friend since you were little boys, who you had a fight with, and you're going to be the one to apologize because the last week has just been awful. You don't know if he'll accept your apology, in the walk over you've completely convinced yourself that he won't and you're torn between turning around and going home, and just getting it over with. Exactly like that, but with demons and escaped souls from hell involved. And frankly, the book thinks that's way more interesting than anything you see over on Lifetime anyway, which is what the description we used for GG's feelings sort of sounded like.

With no possible reason to hesitate any longer, he pushed the door open. At first, he didn't see anyone in the poorly lit store. That was because the two storekeepers were in the back pulling box after box of books from a storage closet in the rear of the building. When the door clanged shut, one looked up from his task to look to the front of the store.

"GG?" the older of the two men almost whispered in shock.

"Hello Danasdius, I hope I'm not disturbing anything important," GG replied and felt like a complete idiot when he said it. What could be more important in a bookstore on earth than your demon Lord father releasing hounds to hunt you down? That's one of the few things that you could interrupt the sipping a fine scotch, a perfect cheesecake, a beautiful sonata, or even good sex for. No wine tasted as good, no stout tasted as rich, no orgasm as glorious as not being dragged back to hell by the horns. No, not even that beer, you the reader, likes a lot, and tell all your friends about, to the point where the damned company might as well hire you as a spokesman, not even that one. Yes, we have tried it, and still not as good.

Dan dropped the books in his hand and rushed to the front of the store. GG actually cringed, fearing he might be furious with him, and was hoping to show his former tutor how much. Instead, his student, now a fully grown man, engulfed his teacher in a crushing bear hug. Dan's shoulders shook with tears of joy at the sight of GG, who he was sure he'd never see again, since leaving hell is usually only the privilege of full-blown actual demons. Dan just assumed that, because while GG could be a real taskmaster about getting him to pay attention to his studies, the teacher was never evil enough to graduate to full demonhood.

"Come now," GG finally said, his own voice thick with emotion, "there's no call for all that."

"How did you?" Dan waved his hand expansively.

"I might have had a Saints finger bone handy for just such an emergency," GG replied. "But please, we've no time. I have news."

"Wait just a sec," Dan interrupted. He turned towards the back of the store, "Nate come out front, you'll never guess who it is!"

Nathanial came towards the front of the door and froze, so did GG. Here it came, even if Danasdius was too nice to do it, Nathanial didn't have those attachments holding him back from really letting GG have it with both barrels.

"I can't believe it! GG himself! Do you know how happy you've made Dan?"

Or not. That was a possibility that GG hadn't even considered.

Still, relief aside, there were important things to say, "While I'm thrilled to see the pair of you, I have bad news.

Your father has returned home. The word around hell is that he is.... displeased."

"How displeased?"

"Sniffers at least. The fact that you appear to be human might throw them for some time, but if you've been here for any length of time...." GG let the implication hang in the air like the threat it was.

Dan understood immediately, "I have to flee, being a human may confound the sniffers at first, but we've been here for decades now. Even in human form, my aura has saturated this place."

"I'm sorry to be the bringer of bad news Danasdius..."

"Please, call me Dan."

"Dan then, but really, I had to warn you."

Dan smiled wanly, "The important thing is that after everything, you found a way to escape hell to do it. I appreciate it more than I can even really say, but, now that you've warned me, what will you do?"

That brought GG up short, he really had never even considered anything past getting here and warning his former student. That happens a lot, you get this really big goal in mind, you direct all your energies to it, and find yourself standing around afterward with your finger up the orifice of your choice without a clue as to what comes next. This was the position GG found himself in, minus an actual physical finger insertion, more of a metaphorical one, because you know, life would get awkward if people literally did that every single time they found themselves at loose ends as to what to do with their day. Or maybe we'd all just get used to it and be a lot happier for it, you never know. You go first, let us know how it goes.

"Stay with you where you go, I suppose. I mean, if you'll have me of course. To be honest, I fled hell as soon as I discovered your father intended to find you," GG said his face looking flustered.

Dan laughed, "Of course we'd be thrilled. If I remember correctly, you're no slouch at magic. I'm more than a little sure we could use some.

Nate interrupted, "Do we really need to leave everything? Just run off like that? Maybe we could fortify the building? Where would we even go?"

Dan shook his head sadly, "I hate to say it, any chance of us staying put ended when the book vanished. Even if we had sold it to Morgan, he would have let us have it back in a situation like this. For that matter, he's been known to help people in situations like this. Without it.... we best just hope we can run fast enough."

Dillon's phone rang just as they were leaving the theater, he sort of recognized the number, like he knew he'd seen it before, so, not thinking about it he picked up, "Hello?"

"Did you steal it?" a man's voice asked immediately.

"What? Did I steal what?" which is the logical, reasonable response to that question. At least usually, look, we don't know what your life is like.

"The book! Did you steal the book?" the voice asked again. Though now we're wondering how you got this copy of this book.

It dawned on Dillon that this must be the bookseller calling him back, "Is this that guy I saw in the bookstore? No, I didn't steal the book I called you about, I bought it in a flea market a week or so after I met you!"

There was a pause, before Devin Morgan responded, "All right, I'm going to have to take your word for it, but what if I told you that was the book I was in the store that day to buy? Someone stole the thing, Dan and Nate tore the place apart looking for it with no luck. I had to drive back to New York empty-handed. Trust me bud, that book is way too fucking rare for there to be just another copy showing up in any flea market, not even one in hell itself. And you can imagine, a flea market in hell would have some pretty weird stuff."

"No shit? I mean about the book, not the flea market thing. Well, I mean, I guess I have to take it back to them. Is it valuable?"

Devin's voice laughed through the phone, "Kid, let me put it this way. I'll pay them and still slide you a finder's fee for it. At least a couple grand on top of what I pay them for it. Unless of course you just want to cut them out altogether...."

Dillon could not believe what he heard; he was actually going to make a massive profit on this? Once the rest of the sentence got past that surprise, he immediately snorted indignantly, "Are you kidding me? I like those guys; I'm not stealing from friends!"

Devin responded with a light chuckle, "Good, I like that. Most people would already be dickering with me on a number for it, I got a soft spot for you already. So, when and where can we meet to confirm that it is indeed the right book."

Dillon looked at Hannah, whose face looked that combination of questioning and annoyed people get when someone takes a call on what is supposed to be an enjoyable outing. He needed to wrap this up ASAP or there would be consequences, "Hey, I'm with my girlfriend right now on a night out, I don't want to be rude to anybody, but... Was your email on that card, I don't remember."

"Yes, indeed it was."

"Alright I'll email you, but the logical place to meet is the bookstore to get everyone together," Dillon said in a rush hoping to get this over with,

"Alright slugger, you enjoy your out and about time, hope you get lucky. Nice and honest call on meeting at the store. Alright, email me a time. Later gator."

"Umm...yeah, bye." Dillon slid his phone into his pocket to see Hannah's demanding expression boring into him, "Look, you are never going to believe this shit."

"So where are we going?" GG asked as they sped along.

"Lancaster county," Dan replied.

"What on earth is in Lancaster County other than cows?" Nate asked

"Nothing demonic, better yet, there are Hex signs all over the place," Dan replied veering to avoid a car being driven painfully slowly on the highway they were on. Nate and GG both glanced over to see who on earth could possibly be driving that slowly. Judging by his unbelievably old age and general lack of movement as he hunched over the steering wheel, peering ahead with a squint, neither of them could make up their mind if the man behind the wheel hadn't actually died on his way somewhere and was somehow managing to keep the car on the road from beyond the veil.

GG shook himself out of it first, "It will be perfect! No gates anywhere nearby, and the hex signs might blur any of your residual aura, assuming we don't stay too long."

Nate sighed, "It will also be boring, I mean not just a little boring, I mean Amish boring."

"I cannot believe you're going through with this after the guy accused you of stealing," Hannah said from her position in the passenger seat of the Beast.

"Well considering I was in the store that day, the book is hyper rare, and whaddya' know? I call him about that book, it's not the worst assumption anyone has ever made. He did ask me, he didn't outright accuse me," Dillon shrugged.

"True, I mean he didn't know Dillon from Adam, he just knew, missing book, surprise call about the book," Zach agreed from the back seat. Neither of them was sure why Zach had demanded to come along for this. Dillon figured it was because he was bored because his hunky football boyfriend was already in summer football camp making it impossible for them to see each other right now. Hannah suspected that Zach being the bigger guy he was being protective of his smaller friend, which she thought was cute. Dillon was the one who was actually right. Caleb had to work out like crazy to make weight for the upcoming season, so that avenue was closed for the time being and Zach never stuck around the house if he could help it. He loved his mom, but he couldn't say he liked her very much some days, especially if she'd had some afternoon chardonnay while Dad was at work and she was now letting her prejudices do the talking.

"Still, he could have worked up to saying it," Hannah huffed.

"From what I gather from the guy, he doesn't seem to be a real 'work up to it' sort of guy," Dillon replied.

"No excuse for bad manners."

They were crossing the bridge into New Jersey. It was weird, when he walked over, Dillon thought nothing of going over to Lambertville, but every time he drove into New Jersey it felt like he was in wartime sneaking behind enemy lines. Many states in the Union you barely even notice if you pass from one to another, others not only feel like you've entered another state, they often feel like you've entered another dimension. Dillon felt that this would be as good a description for New Jersey as any other. They should put it on license plates. "New Jersey The Normal Rules of Existence Do Not Apply Here."

As they pulled up to the store, all of their eyes fell to the car parked at the curb nearby. How could it not grab their attention? A 50's classic with a flame job and side pipes were enough to catch anyone's eye. Especially if Devin

Morgan was sitting on the hood of it smoking a cigarette. He was wearing a leather jacket, black jeans, and engineer boots, along with wraparound shades. His only concessions to formality were the black dress shirt he had on, but the collar was turned up and it still had his purple hair falling inside the collar.

Dillon pried his eyes away to look for a spot. "Is that guy for real?" Zach demanded from the back.

"He'd have to be, a ride like that isn't cheap. I guess if you have enough money, you can dress how you please," Dillon shrugged as he began to parallel park the Beast. This quickly reminded him why it had taken him three tries to get his license. Of course, he'd have to get used to this kind of thing once he and Hannah had a place closer to the city, so he might as well get the practice in.

"Funny, he'd accuse you of stealing, he's the one who looks like a hooligan," Hannah sneered, not letting up on her instant dislike of the book dealer.

"He's obviously rich Hun', rich people can't be thieves, rich people conduct leveraged buyouts," Dillon replied.

"What's the difference?" Zach asked.

"According to my dad, a lot more money," Hannah answered.

"Come on, let's get this over with," Dillon said putting the Beast in park and digging through the center console for change for the meter.

As they got out on the street, Morgan slid off his car and started walking towards them, the cigarette vanishing as he walked. "You're early, I like that!" he called out.

"But you were still waiting for us," Dillon replied when they got close.

"You got the book?" he asked ignoring the implied question.

"Of course, I do! It'd be stupid to come here to give it to you without the book."

Morgan's eyebrow shot up, "All right, you have no idea what you have. That's cool, I won't rip you off. It also makes me trust you, if you'd stolen it, you'd be thinking little thief thoughts. Thieves would have wanted to see the color of my green before they let me anywhere near the book."

"Do you know you talk like a movie?" Hannah interjected.

"I'll make a note of it. So, you gonna let me see the book?" Devin brushed her comment off.

"What? Out here? Why don't we just go in the store?" Dillon demanded.

"Ah, we got a problem there. They ain't in. Sign in the window says they were called away on family business. Which is weird, I didn't think either of them had any family they'd want to have any business with," Devin explained.

"Sounds like mine," Zach muttered.

"Possibly worse," Devin replied. Devin knew about Dan and Nate's background, but you could never tell with some people's families, and he didn't want to assume here.

"So, what are we gonna do?" Dillon decided they needed to cut to the chase here.

Devin's face changed, he wasn't looking at them, but over their shoulder.

Hannah spotted it as well, and turned, "Who's that? Just some guy walking his dog."

Dillon turned to see what they were talking about, but that wasn't what he saw at all. What he saw was something out of a horror movie, one of those weird ones that view like someone else's nightmare. On the ground on all fours was something that mostly looked like a naked human, except for its disfigured face, that sort of looked dog-like. What was holding its leash did not look human at all, it looked like the monster in either the original or the remake of Nosferatu, or maybe Salem's Lot instead, Dillon wasn't going to nitpick at this point. It was dressed in archaic clothing, human, just old-fashioned, but that wasn't what made the distinction between just a guy and a monster. It was the long fingers that ended in claws, the bald pale white head with the huge wolf-like ears, and finally, the rodent-looking fangs sticking out and almost completely obscuring the lower lip entirely.

"I don't think that's just a guy walking his dog, at least not any kind I've ever seen before. It isn't even Halloween yet," Dillon disagreed. He was confused by their response, what he was seeing, and from the look on his face what Devin was seeing as well, looked like a vampire walking his slave at an S&M club. Like one of the really out there ones that you need a special invite and they ask you your blood type and next of kin for. The other two were acting like this was totally normal.

"No, that is absolutely not just a guy walking his dog," Devin added before turning to Dillon, "you're seeing this too?"

"Yeah, it looks like the guy William Dafoe played in the vampire film doing bondage with a guy dog thing."

Devin paused for just a second, "Actually, not a bad description."

Devin pushed past the others and went up to the freakshow which was now standing directly in front of the bookstore, "Excuse me, can I help you with something?"

The thing's eyes turned from the plate glass it had been staring at and took Devin in, its expression was that of someone viewing a bug. Like not even a cool interesting bug, like a disgusting nuisance bug like a stink bug. It hissed through its pointed teeth, "No, no I don't think so. I need something from inside of this building." It paused a moment with its head cocked as if in thought, then it smiled, "Actually, I think you can help me!"

The monstrosity lunged forward and grabbed Devin by his jacket's lapels. In a powerful motion that belied its stick-figure arms, it easily picked the bookseller up. Almost casually it held him up to its hideous face and said, "You can open the way for me!"

There was a loud crash as Devin went sailing through the plate glass. The monster stepped in through the open window after him.

"Holy Shit!" Zach exclaimed.

On instinct Dillon rushed towards the open window, calling back to Zach and Hannah, "Don't go anywhere near that thing!"

He couldn't help but note as he rushed to the window that the dog/man thing had sat down where it was before, as if obediently waiting for something. Dillon reached the window just in time to see the horror movie ghoul trodding on the broken glass inside as it moved in the direction of Devin Morgan. Devin looked helpless as he lay there cursing and groaning where he had crashed through the window display and down to the floor.

Dillon heard the hissing voice say, "And now you can do something else for me magician! You can feed me!"

Chapter 7

"Gah! I am so sick of god damned vampires!" - A.
Rice, not that one, someone who is definitely not an
author of any kind

Dillon didn't think, he didn't have time, he just moved. He might have done something completely different if he had thought it through, like run like hell in the opposite direction for instance. He may not have known exactly what was happening here, but the words "feed me" in this context did not involve a nice sit-down meal at one of the fine local restaurants that were in such abundance in the area. It most definitely didn't mean that coming from the freak that was now stalking towards the fallen bookseller. Dillon grabbed the remains of a shelf as he rushed in. He had no idea what effect this would have, but it was the only weapon available. The creature completely ignored him, it was far more intent on doing something horrible to Devin, who at least was conscious and trying to scramble backward away from it.

At least, the thing had been ignoring Dillon, but only until he snapped the hunk of bookshelf over the creature's back.

The monster whirled on him, grabbing him by the throat. With almost no effort at all, it lifted him off his feet until he was staring directly into its blood-red eyes. "So," it hissed, "you've decided to offer yourself up as an hors d'ouevre? I need to watch what I eat so I don't get fat. But when am I likely to be in this neighborhood again to savor the local cuisine, I ask you?"

"Oh, Christ! I'm about to get killed by a vampire who spits one-liners," Dillon thought madly as he saw the creature's mouth open and felt himself being drawn forward. He could smell the thing's putrid breath as he drew ever nearer to the teeth. Dillon closed his eyes in anticipation of his own demise! Which is why he didn't see its eyes go wide right before the monster dropped him.

Looking up from the ground, he could see Morgan standing behind the creature holding a blade of some kind, a blade that was coated in a very dark liquid. Dillon could only guess it was the creature's blood, either that or motor oil, but considering the odds of used 10W30 suddenly interjecting itself into this situation, he was guessing blood. The monster hissed in rage as it turned back at Devin, forgetting all about Dillon, dropping him negligently as it stalked its original objective who was backing up as carefully as he could.

The thing should have kept some attention to what was happening behind its back. If it had, it would have noticed Hannah and Zach climbing through the window themselves and helping themselves to the ample lumber that had been created when Devin had been thrown through the window and had helpfully broken the bookshelf with his body. The thing might have been able to have prevented the two crashing blows the pair of them landed on the creature's head and legs if it had. Paying attention to details, it's what separates winners from losers in life kids.

As it turned to take stock of this new threat, Devin dove forward with his blade outstretched stabbing the thing in the leg. Dillon couldn't help but notice that there was a sizzle as the blade sunk into the monster's thigh. It was the kind of thing that caught one's attention, most stab wounds don't sound like bacon in a pan. The creature's distraction gave Dillon the chance he needed to scramble back to his feet and hopefully back in the fight. He wasn't sure what in the hell the thing was, but he was absolutely positive it was evil. Even the worst shopper misunderstandings in this town didn't involve sizzling flesh and fangs.... ok, well maybe fangs, but not ones that were THAT big.

It growled at all of them, "Alright you got some licks in, but I can ignore mere beatings, the magician dies first!"

Dillon spotted the way it favored the leg that had been stabbed but not any of the other places he'd been struck when it turned back towards Devin. He was taking a chance getting near the thing, but he had an idea. Stepping within range he drove his foot into the back of the creature's knee on the wounded leg with everything he could behind it. Just as he'd hoped, with the thigh wounded it wasn't able to support its own weight and went crashing down to its knees on the floor letting out another snarl.

Devin saw his own chance and moved like lightning to take advantage of it. He quickly drove the blade into the thing's shoulder as the monster tried to recover from the kick. As the thrust went home Dillon heard the same sizzle. He could also see that the thing had lost considerable power in its arm immediately, which it could only feebly raise to ward off any more blows. When it did, Morgan dove in again and stabbed the other shoulder. That caused a tense moment when one hand moved with surprising reserve of speed, snatched at Devin, and for a brief moment held him in place. There was still considerable strength in the creature's hands and it held him firm beginning to exert pressure on his wrist.

When Dillon rushed forward to try and help Devin, the monster's other hand flashed out and caught him by the throat. A second later Dillon heard another telltale sizzle and the creature thrust Dillon away, sending him skidding to a stop near Hannah and Zach. It dawned on him why he was hearing the cheeseburger on a grill sound effects. Devin's blade had to be silver, and the thing had just been burned by the silver necklace Hannah had bought him!

While the vampire was distracted, Devin snatched the blade out of the trapped hand. Wincing in pain as the creature ground at his wrist bones of one hand he brought the blade around in a powerful sweep. There was sickening thunk mixed with another sizzle before the hand that held him fell away entirely from the monster's arm.

Hannah let out a small scream. Zach released a "Holy fuck!"

"Quick! Grab him and hold him down!" Devin gasped out.

Dillon was the only one who moved to do anything, grabbing the thing by the arm that was weirdly only oozing blood from its stump. He turned back to see that neither Zach nor Hannah had budged. "Guys, trust me on this, please! This is not just 'some guy' who went psycho."

Zach looked at his best friend, Hannah looked at her boyfriend. Almost in a mirror image of one another, both of their faces said, "Only for you," before they moved to grab the other limbs to hold down what to them just looked like a very wounded man.

"What now?" Dillon asked Devin who was shaking his hand trying to get some life back into it, "do we put a stake through his heart?"

"In a minute," Devin replied, straddling the weakly struggling fiend.

"What are you waiting for?"

"Hey what did you mean stake through his heart?" Zach demanded.

"Yeah, go back a bit," Hannah agreed.

"He's a vampire, I don't know why I can see it and you can't but that's what he is," Dillon replied with exasperation.

"Nope," Devin added causing all three of their heads to turn.

"No? Then what the hell is he?" Dillon demanded.

"Vampires are only a symptom. People who catch the plague of vampirism. Bad, sure, but they were still people once but they wouldn't be out in the daytime like this. This, this is what infects them in the first place," Devin replied calmly using one hand to clench the back of the thing's jaws forcing them open. "Hey kid, see how I'm grabbing right here on his jaw? Take my place?"

"No way! He might bite me!" Dillon protested.

"Naw, he's too weak to do that now. Well maybe he might, but I doubt it. Alright, if you don't want to do that, reach in and grab his tongue."

"You said to hold his mouth open just like you had your hand on his jaw?" Dillon quickly replied, because there was no way he was reaching into that thing's mouth.

"Yeah, just like that," Devin replied. He reached into his jacket and pulled out one glove which he placed on his left hand carefully. Before anyone could question it, his hand thrust forward into the open maw and grabbed at the creature's tongue. He yanked backward so it protruded far from beyond the teeth, further than anyone would have guessed, further than even Gene Simmons. His other hand came down with the blade and sliced at it deeply.

The creature thrashed in agony at this new pain, managing to buck both Hannah and Zach off itself as they gawked at what was happening. It tried gamely to get back to its feet but the previously wounded leg went out from under it even as it started. Before anyone had a chance to react, Morgan swung again removing the other hand.

"What in the hell are you doing Mister Crazy Person?" Hannah demanded in horror at seeing what she thought was a creepy man getting dismembered by the psychobilly fan in front of her whom it would seem had decided to live up to the genre name.

Devin casually picked up both hands and the tongue grabbing a bag from behind the counter and thrusting them inside, "Don't want it being able to report back. Hey, stand back a bit from the thing will ya?"

Hannah, Zach, and Dillon needed no encouragement, all three of them went scrabbling away from the vampire demon. As soon as they were clear the thing tried to find the strength to rise. It was in the middle of trying to figure out how to use stumps to sit up when Devin lunged forward and plunged his blade directly into the thing's sternum. It let out a gasping hiss as it fell the rest of the way back onto the floor. There was a whumph as the thing ignited.

"Holy shit!" Hannah said.

"Urk!" Zach agreed.

Dillon noticed the bookseller seemed intensely calm for a moment as he looked around the bookstore. It was remarkable that he seemed so calm because the books directly around the vampire demon were already beginning to catch fire. In three quick steps, he was behind the counter where he reached down and pulled out a book, a small leather looking thing which he slid into the pocket of his jacket. From there he walked right past the three of them, scooping up his bloody vampire bits baggy, and filling his free hand with a few more books before turning back, "Umm, you guys might want to move. In case you haven't noticed your standing in the middle of a burning bookstore, and the thing that caused the fire, i.e., the evidence of self-defense and no wrongdoing on our part is also vanishing."

Dillon grabbed his friends and hurried after Morgan. When they got outside, they could see Devin was already hurrying towards his own car. Dillon rushed forward and grabbed at the older man's jacket, "What in the flying fuck is going on here?"

Devin stopped dead in his tracks, he turned and looked Dillon over, "Oh yeah, you still got the book, huh?"

"What? I mean, yeah, of course, I do!"

"Any chance of you just selling it to me right now without any explanation? It would make my life a fuck of a lot easier if you did? Yours too."

"No way he fucking sells you that book until you explain this!" Hannah said before Dillon could even think of a reply.

Devin sighed gustily, "All right, we'll take my car. I think I'm going to need a hotel locally for the night, at any rate, maybe you can point out one."

Dillon squalled at that, "But my car! I didn't put nearly enough cash in the meter!"

"Kid, if this works out, I'll buy you a better car. Now hurry the fuck up before someone calls the cops!"

They were sitting in a room that Devin had rented at some chain hotel. All chain hotels are roughly the same, this was of the slightly nicer variety in that it had a small kitchenette which allowed the bookseller to nuke a burrito he had gotten on their way here after disposing of the body parts in the river. The other three looked completely shell-shocked by all that had happened. The fact that the guy they thought of as some high-end hoity-toity book guy was completely unfazed by any of it only made it worse. It's like having your whole family escape a blazing inferno and your grandmother just shrugs and says, "Yep, conflagrations, you'll get them some times. Is the cat OK or are we going to have to stop by the pound for another one?"

At least they could finally talk, which was more than could be said for the car ride over here. None of them wished to comment on the quality of the "music" Devin had blasted the whole way, something called Los Carniceros del Norte. When asked him to turn it down some, Morgan had only responded, "Less talk, more escaping." On the next occasion, he responded by turning it up, which more less inspired the rest of them to just give up on the idea. His musical choices and occasional demands for directions over the din had done nothing to ease any of their worries.

With Devin finally settled down to wait for his convenience store burrito to cool, Hannah got to finally say what was on all of their minds, "So, other than mangling a guy who attacked you, before of course killing him, which was totally fine. Other than that. WTF was that about?"

"Yeah, and how come Dillon could see stuff we couldn't?" Zach added.

Devin took a mouth full of burrito and stared at all of them as he chewed, finally he swallowed, "Succo daemonium, and one homines venandi canis."

Dillon who had been dealing with a lot of Latin lately trying to figure out the book translated in his head, "Vampire demon and a human hunting.....dog?"

"Yep on both counts, though the dog thing is usually called a sniffer. Bad news regardless," Morgan nodded.

The room was silent for a moment before Hannah exclaimed, "Oh bullshit! I just saw some guy walk up with his dog and throw you through a window!"

"I didn't, "Dillon said quietly.

"What did you see?" Zach demanded looking at him still in shock from what had happened.

"Ever see that film with John Malkovich? The one about the making of Nosferatu? Something of the Vampire or something?" Just like that. The dog wasn't a dog either, it was more of a person than a dog," Dillon responded, his voice still not rising any as he spoke in almost a flat monotone. It was one of those things, it sounded so crazy you almost didn't want to say it, so you said it quietly in the weird subconscious hope that no one would hear.

"That is correct," Devin added, "interesting that you could see it at all. Most people never see stuff like that, they have filters to shut out things they can't accept for sanity's sake."

"So how come you do?" Hannah demanded.

Devin actually laughed at that, "Young lady, first off I deal books. Expensive and rare books, not kinda rare, but the ones that change hands for seven or eight figures without anybody knowing they even exist. Many of the books that really justify that kind of money are about...things like this. Since I read things out of curiosity while I'm waiting for a sale to go through....well I've picked up a thing or two. To make matters worse, or better, occasionally I've been known to help people deal with the problems that books like that can cause for innocent bystanders."

"Why should we believe any of this? We just met you?" Zach demanded. "I mean you're talking about absolutely crazy shit here dude!"

Nobody spoke until Dillon turned to his best friend, "But do you believe me? I mean I saw those things as plain as day."

Zach didn't reply, he just shrugged. Dillon turned to Morgan, "So, why in the hell were they there at all? And where the hell is Dan and Nate?"

Devin sighed, "Well now we get to the really crazy part." He ignored the snort from Hannah before continuing, "I've known Dan and Nate for a long time now. They are, not exactly from around here. By which I mean, our plane of existence, that particular here. They've just lived here for quite a while now. My guess is someone finally noticed they were missing back home and sent someone to look for them."

"Home being where? Hell?" Hannah demanded with a sneer.

Devin smiled, "You're good! Got it in one."

There was a stunned silence for a moment. This was the kind of silence like after your grandfather announces he left the family money to Scientology, or Mom has left your Dad for a Hell's Angel named Scar. The kind of silence where everyone's brain has just locked up in a scream of clashing, smoking gears, and now even if you do actually get your own brain to finally function again, you know everyone is so keyed up that your afraid that if you speak first everyone is going to lash out at you just for something to distract themselves.

"You gotta be shitting me," Zach breathed at last. His face blanched, thinking back to how he was raised and where his Mom had said over and over people like him were going.

Devin held up a hand, "Look, I don't know if I mean in any biblical sense. Who knows who even wrote the bible, right? There are spirits, there is a hell, that's all I know for sure. What the creator's plan is, which religion is even right, if any of them are even right...well... I really think it's a matter of whether or not you think you deserve to go. So if anything, the leading recruiter for hell is religion."

"You're sure of all that?" Dillon asked.

"Well, I deal with people who think the answers lie in that direction, and books that teach you how to ask the questions. In the course of that and my sideline, helping people avoid the wreckage left after people play with the books, that's about as close as I've gotten down for sure," Devin responded his face still holding its lingering smile, at least until he took another bite of his burrito, it's hard to look beatific and knowing when eating a burrito.

"So what now?" Hannah asked.

"Well, while there may have been a mysterious fire at the bookstore that works to our benefit. Fewer belongings of our fugitive friend's lingering for someone to acquire to try and track them with. Also, the body will burn to ash, so no murder ever occurred there. The dog thing will just wander off, maybe someone gets a really, really smart dog from a pound down the road, maybe they'll put him in shows, but screwed if I know under what breed. Clearly, they haven't found Dan and Nate's house yet, and we don't have time to worry about it. Also, I don't want to burn down their house on purpose or by accident. But what really happens next is, I write out an enormous check to your friend, he gives me the book, and then I go hunt down Dan and Nate myself to try and defend them from any more of those damned things, or worse, whoever sent them."

"One problem," Dillon said quietly.

It's difficult for three heads to turn at once in one direction, even when it happens in movies they have to re-shoot it repeatedly to get it right. So, we aren't going to say three heads turned towards Dillon in unison, but it was a near run thing regardless. Three voices did say in unison, "What?" which was actually pretty weird if you think about the timing required.

"Dan and Nate are my friends too, I want to help, and I haven't agreed to sell you the book yet. I just said I'd meet you, and now that I have, I want to see what happens next," Dillon replied. Turning to his friends he said, "Look you two can just go home, but I've figured out enough of the book already that I....well I need to know that my friends are all right."

"Kid, I appreciate the loyalty and all that, but let me just drop you off at home with more money than you can spend, huh? I mean I can transfer the funds to your account right now! I'm looking out for your best interests here, you know I am."

Hannah grabbed Dillon's arm, "Hun, I usually agree with you about stuff, but really don't you think the crazy guy who does this for a living might be better equipped to deal with this?"

"You mean the one that almost got taken out by a vampire demon today?" Dillon asked with a slight smile.

"OK, point, but do you really think you should be doing this?" Hannah pressed.

"Well, there isn't a crowd of people queuing up."

Devin cleared his throat and they all turned towards him. "I was going to try and talk Dillon here out of it, really I was, but he makes a good point. Having someone along who has a head start on translating the book would probably save my ass if hell is actually looking hard for Dan and Nate. I mean nobody else has to come, but I've been doing this a while and on a plus note I have yet to get someone killed."

Zach made a mental note that he specifically said killed. Zach could easily imagine a whole litany of things in his line of work that could have happened to an innocent bystander in the maiming department. Zach had seen enough movies to know that. Sure, maybe the guy who got turned into a vampire hadn't technically been "killed"

killed, hard to argue he had been if he was still walking around and all, but still...... Despite knowing this, he found himself saying, "Dillon's my best friend, and I'm bigger than him. I'd also point out the pair of you had been pretty boned before I came in. I'm going too."

Hannah sighed gustily, "Alright then if we're doing this we're stopping by my house."

"Why?" Dillon asked in surprise.

"Because, his ultra-cool classic car was recently seen near an arson, if anything like this comes up again it's easily recognizable, and if you think I'm sitting in that cramped back seat for however long it takes to get the book to Dan and Nate you are all out of your minds. I have an SUV, everybody on earth has an SUV, it's practically like suburban camouflage."

Nate was bored, on so so many different levels. First off was the conversation that he felt weirdly excluded from. Weirdly so because one of the conversants was Dan and he never felt excluded from anything involving Dan like that before, not in all these years on earth. Dan and GG had a lot of catching up to do, he understood that, but knowing that didn't exactly change his feelings about things. The only time he seemed to be included was when GG took a moment to ridicule something he'd found while living in the tunnels Dan had carved that Nate had in hell back when he had been trapped there as a perpetual teenager.

The other reason he was bored being that they were in a revoltingly quaint bed and breakfast outside of Lancaster Pennsylvania in a little town called humorously enough Bird In Hand. They had traveled for hours, driven he didn't know how many miles, and here they were in a tourist trap after they had fled an even bigger tourist trap back home. It was a completely different type of tourist trap though, this oozed wholesome family money removal, whereas

New Hope and Lambertville was more of the interesting artsy type with a hint of sin here and there. Nate had come to enjoy his artsy little world, their interesting artsy friends, and the overall acceptance they enjoyed there. This felt way more god-fearing than he was comfortable with. They had seen a horse-drawn buggy on the way here, these people thought gasoline was sinful, what they thought about sex would probably boggle the mind. But they certainly kept the tourists busy, there were plenty of them about taking pictures of the folksy locals, while said locals tried to ignore them in a folksy and most importantly photogenic manner.

He was taking a walk, not out of any real desire to see the lay of the land or to get any exercise in, but more to let them get on with catching up. Nate refused to admit he was jealous, even if he knew damned well he was. He was also disconcerted, Dan hadn't mentioned their own relationship once to his former teacher. Like in all the gushing descriptions of their life on earth together, not a single mention of the fact that they shared the same bedroom for all these years! Was he ashamed in the face of the adult role model human in his life? Worse, had he had thoughts towards the father figure in his life? Time had aged Dan, like time on earth will do to anyone, now in appearance and physique, there were no longer those uncomfortable age differences there had been in hell. Was GG their savior or was he the source of homewrecking marital strife on the horizon? Also, was Nate just being ridiculous?

Of course, all of it could mean nothing at all, and he was just being uptight because dear god he felt out of place here. Nate could understand the logic of going to the godliest place they could think of in a hurry to maybe fuzz the remaining demonic parts of Dan from easy detection, but... Nate also suspected none of this would work. There was also the added feeling that maybe this place had been making money on its local curious Amish religious sect so long that it might have lost all of that holy background noise that would hide Dan. Maybe that much commerce happening had cheapened the whole thing? If this didn't work, where next? Certainly not the Vatican, WAY too many entrances to hell around that place.

He'd suggest when he got back that maybe this place had lost its holy hidey-hole bonafides and they should keep moving. But the question still presented itself, where? Nate definitely wanted to ponder hard on that one before making a suggestion. Really, if he was being honest with himself, something he had no intention of doing because he already realized jealousy wasn't an attractive look, he wanted to think of anything but what a horrible terrible homewrecking snake in the grass their new addition was. Doing it in private meant he'd be better prepared to put on a happy face when he got back. He could keep telling his conscience that.

He tried to think of something positive to say about their current location so he wouldn't seem that he was just being cranky when he mentioned moving on. The best Nate had come up with was that the ice cream was pretty good, and the traffic wasn't terrible. Somehow he thought he'd have to come up with better than that if he was going to make a convincing case that they needed to put more distance between themselves and home. And for the life of him he couldn't think of a nice way of suggesting that when they left this place, they also leave Dan's former tutor tied up in the closet of the Bed and Breakfast.

"There is news?" Moraspus demanded as his second in command oozed his way into the Demon Lord's throne room.

"Indeed, and I find it heartening," Blurglesoth, ummm, gurgled. Look, we saw the rhyme coming there, but it couldn't be helped, since that's exactly what he did.

"Heartening? How could anything short of conclusive be heartening," the lord snarled leaning in towards his majordomo, hoping against hope that Blurglesoth would finally give him the excuse he needed to rend him limb from....to rend him.....to...maybe explode him over the walls?

"We have only lost two of the new demons," Blurglesoth reported. Seeing the look of consternation cross his master's face he added quickly, "but only one of them was in the normal 'thinking with their stomach' sort of demise. That one was lurking around a remote village in the Andes and ended up staked out to ground at Machu Picchu after three women of marriage age vanished from the tribe."

"The other?"

"The other was mangled, my lord. Mangled very specifically so it would be years before he could tell us what he'd found while up above."

"Mangled how?"

"His tongue and hands were removed before he was killed, they didn't end up here with the rest of him," Blurglesoth informed him.

"I fail to see how the mutilation of one of my minions counts as good news," Moraspus said disdainfully, while at the same time wondering how hard it was to get slime off the walls after an explosion.

Blurglesoth bit off the exasperated sigh that almost escaped his opening where lips might be under the slime, "But Master, someone knew to do it! While it might be understandable, especially if they were feeding, to want to, and to know how to kill a vampire, whoever did this knew to make sure that he couldn't report back to us any time soon! How many humans would even know a vampire demon and a sniffer as more than a vampire and his hound? Let alone recognize them as hunters? Whoever did this knew them for what they were and why they had been sent! We might very well have a lead to your son's whereabouts now!"

Moraspus tapped a claw against his goatee in thought, "Very well, send a succubi to ask around. They say you get more flys with honey and all. I don't agree with that by the way, I think you get more with rotting corpses myself. But regardless, we might get the information we require, and possibly a few souls pledged to us in the bargain that way."

Chapter 8
"Wrinkles are SEXY"- J. Hall, H. Mills, P. Holm, A.N. Smith, J. Conroy, Empress Theodora

It was half-past noon before they finally got on to 78 heading for central Pennsylvania. Dillon had the road map out, which was stupid since Hannah's ridiculously expensive BMW had onboard GPS, but it enabled him to feel like he was contributing in some way. Actually, the thing had enough bells and whistles that it barely counted as a vehicle as much as a mobile office. For all he knew there was a fax machine and a blender hidden in there somewhere. Dillon had been afraid to touch anything inside since her Dad had gotten it for her as an early graduation gift. He was used to a car that had an air conditioner and a stereo on good days, and even then barely, and only when whatever voodoo it took to make them function was working. This was like being in a Star Trek episode, and he was stuck playing Sulu to her Kirk, except his Sulu had never gone to Starfleet Academy.

They knew that they were at least heading for Lancaster, finding that out when Devin had finally been able to get a terse and very brief text back from Dan telling him where they were hiding out. The text brevity wasn't off-putting since every text Devin had ever received from Dan was terse, Dan hated technology. Devin kept joking with him that he should learn it in case he ever went back to hell. With everything people did to themselves with all this new tech in the form of life-wrecking tweets, drunken Facebook rants, overreactions to innocuous posts, etc., hell would be able to do some amazing stuff with it. For that matter, many people would be surprised that it wasn't hell behind all of that already. Not only might Dan be forgiven for leaving, he'd probably be in for some kind of promotion. Just because the guy was a demon didn't mean you didn't try to make helpful suggestions to a friend.

It had taken so long to get on the road for numerous reasons. First, sleeping had been crowded and uncomfortable, even with Devin renting another room nobody woke up bright-eyed and bushy of tail. Then there was getting breakfast and getting everyone to agree to the diner Dillon had suggested in the first place after numerous other places were suggested and discarded. Then they had to go by Hannah's house and pick up her car, then they had to find a place to park Devin's car. In the end, they put it in Amber's parent's garage since they were on vacation anyway. This led to Hannah having to tell Amber she was going to be gone, so more time was wasted while Amber gave Hannah shit for not being in town while Amber's parents were away as well. Amber was planning on partying the entire time, so the shit was only being given for appearance's sake, plenty of other people would be happy to come to her house and drink her folk's booze. After all of that, everybody piled in the Beemer, and they headed for Easton to get the highway. By then it was around lunch so that needed to be taken care of, and *finally,* with no other distractions available, at last, they were on the road. It almost felt anti-climactic at this point considering this was supposed to be a rescue mission and they made worse time out the door than the average family vacation.

Finally, Hannah had time to demand the answer most of them wanted, "Why in the hell Lancaster?"

"Well, if I was to guess, the Amish. All those hex barns and pious people all around, it creates a fuzz that makes it difficult for demons to see through if they're tracking," Devin said looking up from his phone. He wasn't doing anything useful on it, he was playing a game, but from the expression on his face, everyone had been loathed to interrupt, thinking he was engaged in some vital research about demons or something.

"They don't get out much, do they? Because I wouldn't go there for that," Zach replied.

"How do you figure?" Devin's eyebrow rose.

"Kutztown isn't far off, it's where I'm going to college, it's one of the top 20 party colleges in the state. That part of the state has lost some of its holy from what I've seen. Most of the Amish stuff in Lancaster is mainly for tourists these days," Zach explained.

"Hmmm, that might be problematic. I better text Dan," Devin nodded.

That text was not answered. By the time it was sent it was pretty superfluous anyway.

That probably needs an explanation, we're getting to it, stop being so damned impatient, you'll enjoy things more.

Nate was having another walk after the breakfast that had been served at the B&B. This one was not so much a byproduct of his discontent with what people called "Amish country" as it was an attempt to walk off the *stunning* amount of cholesterol the morning's porcine heavy breakfast had contained. He assumed that the pancakes were only added to the meal to sop up all the grease from all the sausage and bacon that came along with it. He knew at his age he probably should have begged off and just eaten a couple of the flapjacks, but they rarely bought meat at home and it was *sooooooo* good!

Now, as penance for his early morning meal-time sins, he was taking another lap around Bird In The Hand and hoping it would suddenly be more interesting than last time. He had his doubts that they had the time to install a Ferris wheel while he was making his loop or anything else that might be exciting in any way, but you had to believe for miracles to happen. Nate had just reached one of the quaint stores in the area when he froze in his tracks. What he saw going into what he guessed was an antique store had no business in this town, or on this earth for that matter. What it left tethered to the porch was also no dog. The dog thing turned just as the door closed on the gaunt figure that had gone inside and began to sniff the air vigorously.

Nate turned and ran.

It wasn't a huge distance between the store and their B&B, it just wasn't that big of a town, but ask any middle-aged man about how he feels after being suddenly called on to run and he'll tell you it's awful, assuming he doesn't die of a heart attack right there and then. Nate had a gym membership, considered himself to be in good shape for his age, but sudden acceleration was still not his forte, and he was panting like a racehorse on the last leg by the time he stumbled up onto the porch. One of those gasps was of relief when he turned and looked back in the direction of where he had fled and saw there wasn't any pursuit yet. But there was still a sniffer out there, if the hunter figured out it was them that had caught the thing's interest, there would be pursuit soon enough. They needed to go now!

He rushed upstairs and burst into their room, GG and Dan were talking, both sitting on the bed. Dan got up immediately his face shocked at Nate's appearance, "Nate what on earth?"

"We have to go, and we have to go at exactly this moment!" Nate managed to gasp out.

"Why?" asked GG

"Sniffer and vampire demon in town!"

That ended any possible argument before it began. They packed quickly and settled up with their hosts before rushing out to the car. They were in such a hurry that they hadn't noticed that the phone, hidden under the covers that morning. After they were already on the road speeding away, its muffled pings signifying an incoming message could just be heard in the empty room.

"Was there a reason I was ignored when I said we should take the Turnpike?" Devin asked, finally getting something off his chest that had been bothering him for some time.

"Yep," Hannah replied.

After being silent for a moment, thinking she had paused, and realizing she hadn't, Devin asked, "And that was?"

"Oh, yeah, simple, I absolutely hate driving on the turnpike. I hate paying tolls, and it wasn't so much faster that you could make me do it," she replied.

"Ah"

A little while later he asked, "So, where in the hell are we?"

"Macungie," Zach answered, "you can tell by the brewery."

"OK that explains the smell, thanks," Devin nodded.

A few minutes later Devin added, "Jesus Christ!"

"What?" Zach and Dillon said in unison.

"The giant children of the corn shit reaching towards the highway!" Devin replied his breathing coming under control.

"You mean the Amish statues? That's just what they look like!" Hannah laughed.

Morgan was quiet for a moment, "Alright, I can see that being Amish too, but I think my Children of the Corn description fits just as well."

"Hmmph! Yeah, I suppose it does, never thought about it," Dillon agreed.

"Yeah, we won't get heavy Amish yet, that's just tourist shit, as much Mennonite as it is Amish. Really where we're going isn't as hardcore Amish as some places. Mifflin County you get some serious Amish," Zach added.

"How do you know so much about Amish?" Dillon asked his friend.

"didamissionasakid," Zach mumbled.

"What?" Dillon demanded.

"I did a mission with my folks as a kid to preach to them," Zach's face turned red.

Devin started laughing, "Wait, you tried to preach the bible to people so all fired holy that they don't even have lightbulbs?"

Everybody else, including Zach, laughed, before he added, "Yeah, there are reasons I won't be attending church much after I leave home."

Rebecca Aldefer didn't want much out of life, just peace, and quiet, and wads of cash out of tourists who wanted to experience "Amish country." That was why she convinced her husband, Timothy, that after a lifetime together, and with the kids gone to college, what they really, really needed to do was buy this place. He had made plenty in upper management at an investment firm, and frankly, she wasn't subtle about what they should do with it. She also told him that she knew about the secretary and the business trips, and if he didn't want to lose a very sizable portion of the rather large nest egg they had built up he might wish to consider country life with her. Timothy, having had time to think about it, and after having discussed it with his lawyer, realized that at his age his libido wasn't what it used to be so maybe he could live with country life. On top of that, he rationalized that there had to be gullible younger women out there in the sticks, and was it worth a lifetime's labor to continue how he was going? His lawyer hadn't thought so, and he had charts and figures to back him up. So, he eventually agreed as long as she agreed to let bygones be bygones in their daily life. Rebecca hadn't, but to her credit she was relatively good about it, only mentioning it when she was REALLY pissed off at him about something. So, all things considered, he concluded he had gotten off light. His lawyer had agreed on that point, she had video.

Right now she was fretting. It had been a slow week in terms of guests, and the ones they had had only lasted one night. While they swore it wasn't that there was anything wrong with the place, or anything the couple had done making them feel welcome, well you couldn't help but wonder, could you? She was so upset about it she hadn't even gone up to make the bed and tidy up the rooms that they'd used for possible new arrivals. Not that it mattered, there were two more rooms, and they were just as empty. If a miracle occurred and someone needed a room, it wasn't like they would be found wanting. So with Tim out in his workshop puttering around with something or other, Rebecca found that what she personally was wanting was this glass of wine and to catch up with one of her shows on Netflix.

She almost spilled her wine when there was a knock on the door. It felt like she'd been caught day drinking. One-ish was not prime renting time in any case, people usually made reservations, that's why they had the website. Having two walkups in the same week when there wasn't a festival of some kind in or around town was unprecedented. (This is a dirty secret of quaint towns everywhere, the more festivals they have, the more likely they are to also have a flourishing bed and breakfast industry in town. So while that wine tasting festival might be sold as original and quaint, it really only exists because Donna and Laurie on Maple street's kids both went to college around the same time and they thought of a way to make some money from their empty rooms) She quickly downed the wine, and discreetly hid the glass before making her way to the front door. A breath mint was quickly ground down on the way, leaving her with minty fresh alcohol vapors by the time she got to the door.

Standing there was a tall man with his dog. She couldn't quite remember later exactly what he looked like, she just remembered him being "tall." Same with the dog, she would always remember it being a mid to large-sized dog, but if anyone had ever pressed her, she would have said, "I don't know like a shepherd or a lab or something like that." The man was smiling pleasantly, which oddly made her feel slightly ill at ease.

"Yes, can I help you?"

"Yes, I believe you can, I am to understand you have room to let?" his voice, just like the rest of him, struck her in being absolutely neutral and non-descript.

Rebecca blinked for a second before saying something she was sure she'd regret, "Oh but I don't know, we usually have a no pets policy. Not for me, you understand, but poor Timothy he does get allergies something fierce."

The man chuckled, again it was somehow as bland as weak vanilla, "Oh no, the room is not for me. I'm just passing through on business, but I have a niece that is going to be in the area tonight. I was wondering if I could just reserve a room for her in advance of her getting here. I will of course make payment on the room as well. Frankly, I think that's why she asked me, to see if she'd get me to pay for her. Even when they grow up you find yourself spoiling them, don't you?"

BINGO! Cash on the hoof! "Of course Mister....."

"Alucard"

"My what an interesting name. Yes, I still send care packages to mine in college, but what are kids for? If you wouldn't mind leaving your puppy outside, I can get everything written up for her, and we can see about making payment," Rebecca smiled with the warmth of someone who had one more booking for tonight than she had five minutes ago.

Why in the name of the devil couldn't he just have good news and good news? He had good news, potentially very good news, but of course, it had to be tempered with bad news. Why couldn't eternal everlasting hellfire and torment just run on a nice even keel for one lousy century? Blurglesoth decided there was nothing for it, if he could just baffle the ancient psychopath with the good news he was delivering, maybe the bad news would never even have to be delivered. Hey, if the old monster didn't ask, it wasn't like he lied about anything right?

"You have something to tell me?" Moraspus demanded from his throne as stopped playing with the remains of a lesser demon he had been peeling the skin off of with a jagged and rusted-looking butter knife.

"Yes your vileness, I think it's good news indeed. One of our sniffer units is positive that it caught the smell of something demonic in an area where we have no operatives at all. More importantly, not far at all from where we lost the vampire that's being rebuilt down in the vats," Blurglesoth oozed with something that he hoped appeared to look obsequious despite being pleased with himself at the same time.

"Were any personal effects located to help with the tracking?" the demon lord asked casually as he wiped his claws with a nun's whimple.

"I've dispatched a succubus to get access to the building where the scent was detected. But the vampire handler was sure the sniffer had caught a smell of something that led to that building," Blurglesoth replied in what he hoped was a firm and in control tone of voice. Which is actually something very difficult to do when your face is constantly oozing into your mouth.

Moraspus almost showed the hint of a smile as he considered it. Whatever passed for a heart in the shambling demonic mess that made Blurgleshoth's chest soared for a moment, his master was actually pleased! "What of the other succubus we dispatched to the first scene?"

DAMN IT!

Blurglesoth groaned internally, this was the part he had been absolutely dreading. "Ummm we've had some difficulties retrieving her my lord."

"Difficulties?"

Blurglesoth would have looked as if he was shuffling his feet in discomfort if he had proper feet instead of blobs. He replied quietly, "Apparently the area has a history of... shall we say...ummm activities that would appeal to a succubus? She has found little difficulties finding ummm...very willing partners."

"Well tell her to return to hell at once!"

"We did send such an order, we uhh did my lord. She told us to umm piss off, and before I could stop her she had already filed for some vacation time on earth that she had accrued. It was approved before I had even been told about it."

There was silence in the throne room, except for the dripping of ichor from the demon that Moraspus had hung from a hook when Blurglesoth had come into the room. Finally, Moraspus spoke, "Blurglesoth, I am of two minds at the moment, would you care to guess what they are?"

"I wouldn't dare to assume the knowledge of your great wisdom lord," the underling gurgled.

"Very wise of you. One is, I should throw you in a pot and see how hot I would have to get it before the ooze you're made of began to boil. You have lost a sniffer team, and a succubus, well I admit, the succubus isn't lost, we'll get her back. While she thinks she's gamed the system, she'll think quite differently when I transfer her to the chastity ward for a century," the demon replied. Then he leaned forward and stared pointedly at his underling, "Now, would you like to know why you are not currently coming to a rapid boil and having noodles tossed in with you?"

"Why sir?" Blurglesoth practically whispered.

"Because so far, you seem to actually be getting results. I would see that it continues. More importantly, I would see that it continues with fewer losses, because I have ever so many pots to choose from. After you've been turned into a hearty nourishing soup, we can always serve you out in bowls."

Rebecca was out shopping, which meant Tim was at peace. He loved his wife, lord knows he kept telling himself that. It was far better at his age to love his wife than it was to pay the alimony only to find out that he had already aged past "hot in a distinguished sort of way." At best he'd find himself dating women who...well, looked like his wife but weren't used to his bullshit. Tim was pretty sure he had gotten too old to start over anyway. Funny how it happened, five or six years difference between being a silver fox and where he was now. The point was, he was beginning to feel like he was actually getting old. Of course, a Beemer and an expense account certainly added some hotness back in the day, no doubt about that. Alas, those had been lost to the marriage-saving move out here. These days he drove an Explorer which allowed him some small amount of masculinity, in that it purported to be an SUV, but he knew it for what it was deep down, a glorified minivan.

Back on point, in theory, and enforced practice, Tim loved his wife and he really wanted to believe that. But having her around the house meant sudden and inescapable chores that always seemed to be needing to be done when he was right in the middle of something out in his garage/workshop. His main project was a 1967 Cougar that he would probably never actually finish all the way. Timothy had done the most absolutely masculine thing he could have thought to do soon after he got it, strip it all the way down. A lot of parts break in the hands of a home mechanic like that. So between finding the new parts, and finding the time to slowly build the thing back up from the frame, Timothy doubted he'd ever drive the poor car again. He was fine with that, it gave him the excuse he needed to be out here, and away from mindless busywork chores.

He was startled when there was a knock at the side door to the garage. Rebecca said they had rented out another one of the rooms, but he hadn't really been expecting the person until this evening, and certainly not out here. At least he thought Rebecca said this evening, to be honest, he hadn't been paying that much attention. Sighing he put down the other reason the Cougar would probably never run again, one of the poorly written spy novels he read out here, and got up.

When he opened the door standing there were most of his teenage and young adult fantasies come true. The girl standing there couldn't actually be Christina Applegate, but she did a wonderous impression of her circa early "Married...With Children." He had the hots for her character on that show in an absolutely major way, and standing in the doorway was her spitting image.

"Can I....can I help you?" Timothy managed to sputter out.

The girl smiled coyly, "I'm pretty sure you can. My uncle said he rented me a room here?"

Timothy recovered himself, "Oh, yeah sure. Sorry my wife normally handles those, but I suppose I can help you."

She smiled again, her teeth flashing white behind her bright red lips, "Yes, I'm sure you can. Can you show me to my room then?"

"Umm yeah, just a sec, I gotta wash my hands," Timothy replied. He went over to the sink that he'd put in the garage when Rebecca kept complaining about him washing off grease and grime in the indoor sinks.

He could hear the girl's footsteps behind him as he went over to the sink, "Cool project. What is it? A 67?"

Timothy's breath caught in his throat, this goddess actualy knew cars? "Yeah, yeah it's a 67, I'm rebuilding it from the ground up."

He wasn't even looking at her, but he could swear he could tell she licked her lips before she replied, "Man, I'd love to take a ride on that."

Timothy grabbed a towel and dried his hands with exaggerated care before turning around, "Why don't I show you to your room then."

"I'd like that, maybe you can show me some of the other rooms before I settle in?"

"Well all but two, we had guests last night and Rebecca hasn't had a chance to tidy them," he replied stepping past her out of the garage and onto the concrete sidewalk that ran between the garage and the huge white house that he had to remember he technically owned.

He lead her upstairs and opened the door to the room Rebecca had set aside for her. He couldn't help but gape at her ass as she swished by him in her tight mini-skirt. Suddenly she stopped and whirled back at him, "It'll do for now. You can give me a tour of ALL the rooms in a little bit."

"Umm, except for the two rooms Miss...."

She silenced him by grabbing the front of his dockers and stroking at the erection he'd been trying to hide since he had first seen her. "But first things first. First, I think you should fuck the ever-living hell out of me. Don't you?"

By an amazing coincidence, he did indeed think that.

Chapter 9

"Get thee behind me Sata-...oh, actually you're kind of
cute."- Jerry Christ to Mary Magdalene

After what seemed like an eternity to Devin, a fact he had informed the others of repeatedly, they pulled up to the bed and breakfast Dan had told them that he and Nate were staying at. There were two vehicles in the small driveway that led up to it. The door to the smaller one was open, as was the door to the large white house with the sign out in front of it declaring that it was indeed a far more pretentious version of a hotel, and therefore far more expensive, but with less privacy. In other words, this was a bed and breakfast and the little tile hanging out front said it was the right one.

"Well, now what?" Hannah asked.

"I guess we go and see if anyone's around," Devin responded, his eyes narrowing with concern, "and umm, Dillon, do me a favor, make sure you bring the book."

"I'm sure someone just stepped in the house from picking something up, I don't know why everyone looks so worried," Zach said, opening his own door to get out.

"Yeah, sure, that'd be cool," Dillon said as he got out as well.

All of them moved slowly and with trepidation towards the house, no matter what Zach had said. Other than the open door there was nothing to say there was anything wrong, but some extra sense had kicked in telling all of them that there damned well was. The entire place just looked abandoned. Like everything had been normal not that long ago at all, but then the people just vanished. It was not a good feeling at all to be climbing the steps.

"Hello?" Hannah called out only to be greeted by silence.

"So, yeah, we called to see if anyone's around, now what?" Zach said as they stood there.

"Now, we go in," Devin said pushing past them into the house.

"Aren't we trespassing?" Zach pressed.

"We are entering a place of business where our friends told us they were, also, we are nosy and nosy people do what they want," Hannah replied with conviction.

Once inside Devin heard a creak of wood ever so faintly. Such as might be caused by someone moving about upstairs while trying to be quiet. Not looking to see if the others were following him Devin made for the stairs. Out on the porch Dillon shrugged at the others and headed after him. Zach looked at Hannah for support and seeing none sighed and following them into the dim light of the hallway.

On the landing upstairs there were two doors, both of them open. Devin went towards the one furthest away from the landing. Dillon followed fast on his heels, but Zach and Hannah paused at the first door deciding to check on the room the one closest to the stairs and therefore the one they could run outside from the fastest. They gasped at what they saw. Lying on top of the bed was an older couple, both naked. They were unconscious as if sleeping, but both of their pale bodies were covered with a sheen of sweat that glistened in the daylight coming through the window. Whatever they had been doing, they had only gotten done with it very recently. Deciding that they didn't need to gape at an older couple sleeping off sexual escapades they hurried after Devin and Dillon.

They didn't have far to go, the two of them were frozen in the doorway of the room they'd picked. Peering around them, they both looked to see what had stopped the other two.

"Oh my," said Zach.

"Oh, my, my," agreed Hannah putting her hand over Zach's eyes. She actually felt relief when he did the same to her. Also, she felt very, very warm. Which was probably the correct response to who she saw standing in the room looking through the drawers. Incidentally, Zach also felt very similarly about who he saw, which was coincidentally, also Jason Mamoa stark naked.

That might have been what they saw, but it wasn't what Devin and Dillon were seeing. What they were seeing was still attractive enough to get the pulse throbbing, but only if you were into red women who were built like something off a sailor tattoo artist's wall of flash art. The devil woman turned to look at the both of them and smiled, "Well hello! It would appear this IS my lucky day. Always room for more has always been my motto."

"Dillon?" Devin said quietly.

"Yeah?"

"The backpack you are currently carrying."

"Yeah?"

"Does it have a certain book in it at this time?" Devin practically hissed.

"Yeah, yeah it does."

"Could I umm borrow it for just a mome?"

The demon in front of them spread her legs wide standing in front of them like a challenge while Dillon hurriedly fumbled open his backpack and thrust the book at Devin. "Come on boys. You know you want to, and I know I want you to. Let's get real nasty. Or do I have to lead you over to this perfectly good bed by your cocks? There's plenty of room at this inn"

With a flourish, she threw back the covers off of the bed. Sitting on it was Dan's cellphone. Her smile got even wider, "Well now, that is the bonus round. I was looking for something like this." She leaned down and inhaled deeply and held the breath inside her before setting the phone on the nightstand, "Exactly what I was looking for in fact, so why don't I move this and we can play a bit before I've got to go? Mind you, four of you is gonna take a little time."

"Dsiwa Buzrana!" Devin said in a loud voice, reading from the open book.

The demon girl stumbled back a step across the room towards the window, "Hey if you guys don't want to party there's no reason to be nasty about it!"

"Baraya a snagara sulita!"

"Screw this, I got what I really need anyway, for mortals you people are no fun at all," she snarled. In a single fluid motion, the demon girl dove through the window with a crash of glass that made both Zach and Hannah jump.

"Is he gone yet?" Hannah asked quietly, Zach's hand still over her eyes.

"Is who gone yet?" Devin demanded.

"Naked Jason Mamoa," Zach replied.

Devin actually laughed at that, "No, Aquaman was not standing in the room. What was here was a succubus, they can appear as whatever turns you on. They drain your life force through sex regardless of gender, but they also steal semen from men to go create more demons."

Hannah turned to Zach, "You saw Jason Mamoa too, right?"

"Yeah."

"Oh, we need to send pictures privately on Instagram honey."

"If you have one, I haven't seen, I would be impressed," Zach replied.

Dillon didn't know what to say as he took the book back from Devin and put it back in his backpack. Again, he was able to see the demons when they couldn't. How many of the damned things (quite literally) were there running around anyway? Also, he'd have to have Devin show him the passage that freaked out the succubus, he didn't know if it only worked on oversexed living tattoos and record cover art, but if he was going to be able to see the things it would be comforting to know he could do something about them other than giving in to their wiles. Because if he was being completely honest, he had considered her offer for at least a moment, maybe two.... or three.

Devin took his phone out after handing the book over. A moment later the phone the demoness had abandoned on the nightstand in her flight to escape began to ring. He turned to the others, "Well, that explains why they haven't been getting back to me, now doesn't it?"

"Why in the hell are we going to North Carolina?" Nate demanded as their car flew through the mountains of Virginia.

"A few reasons," Dan said in a reasonable, but distracted tone of voice. "First off, the Amish thing didn't work out. We hadn't taken into account the tourist gawker factor. But we tried Amish, why not try old-timey southern religion? They go on about it the most, maybe they are the holiest? We are going to North Carolina specifically because it has the Billy Graham Museum, and I cannot stress this enough, almost no caves. The vast majority of caves aren't portals to hell, but they make convenient places to stash them. That's why we didn't go deeper into Amish country away from the tourists, lots of caves."

"But North Carolina is so......"

"We'll get three rooms just to keep our head down."

"Depressing. We've got to figure out how to get out of this all together if the alternative is living amongst Bible thumpers in the South," Nate sulked.

"What's wrong with this 'South'?" GG asked from the back seat where he had been drowsing.

"It has a reputation for being a bit backward, we've never been. But that's the reputation."

"Ahh, well that's to be expected from the particularly religious, always has been. Hopefully, they don't still burn people."

Dan gave Nate a hard silencing look.

Nate's phone rang.

Elthiath's hips shook as she walked behind Blurglesoth her head held high and proudly. Out of all the demons on earth, she was the one who would be delivering on her assignment and she wanted to flaunt it. She had some other things to do now that she was back, and with human semen stored away, but the boss took priority. Well, Moraspus certainly took priority if you wanted to keep all of your important bits attached. She was hoping to turn this success into a bit of off-the-leash time on earth as well, so, best to keep him happy. Her brief stay had been enjoyable, but it had only served to remind her how much fun she could be having. Not to mention she'd already heard a rumor that that bitch Mishthala had blown off the assignment entirely, and from what Elthiath had heard in the short time she'd been back in hell, that wasn't all that Mish was blowing up there.

Moraspus looked up from something that he was in the middle of doing to a struggling creature that looked like a cross between a Care Bear and a squid, something which appeared to be sexual in nature. "If you are interrupting me, I should hope you have news," he growled

Blurglesoth was about to speak but Elthiath stepped around him, "If it's that kind of entertainment you need my lord, you know, you only have to ask."

Moraspus leered, "I may take you up on that the next time I want to make someone scream. Blurglesoth, you have something for me, or were you just bringing me harlots in the hope of distracting me."

"She has the very thing we need my lord," his majordomo gurgled.

"My son?"

"Not yet my lord, but she has brought us his scent, the way he smells on earth, the thing we need to seek him out wherever he goes," the demon beamed as much as was possible with what he had to work with.

To the relief of the plush toy thing that had tentacles where arms should be, Moraspus withdrew himself and without bothering to cover his erect member turned to face them. "Bring a jar to capture the scent at once!"

"I anticipated your wish Lord, and I have one with me," Blurglesoth replied.

He held out what appeared to be a glass jar, with a cork stopper holding it closed. Inside, a wire curled and twisted, glowing as if an electrical charge was being put through it like a light filament. The demon removed the stopper and held it under the mouth of the succubus next to him. She looked at it for only a moment before her chest started to constrict. Elthiath made a series of motions and sounds not unlike a cat bringing up a hairball. Considering her upper endowments, at least Moraspus appreciated this part of the show. At last, a cloud of yellowish gas began to flow out of her mouth. It was drawn into the jar immediately like there was a fan pulling it inside. As soon as the jar was filled with the cloud, Blurglesoth slapped the cork back into place.

"Wonderful!" Moraspus clapped his hands together with glee. "Blurglesoth reproduce it immediately and get back with me to discuss how we should proceed."

"Right away my Lord, is there anything else?"

"Give something to the little lady for her troubles," the demon Lord replied. Then he put his hand up as he leered at the succubus, "But, maybe a little later huh? I want to give her a reward of my own right now."

"All right, I just got off the phone with Nate. I guess I'm going to North Carolina, which, is nowhere near New York, and nowhere in the Northeast, so I'm just about fucking thrilled," Devin said as he hung up his cell phone and put it on the table of the diner they were eating at. They had been considering if they needed to get a room for the night, and the soon-to-be confused and possibly distressed owners of the bed and breakfast they had just left were probably not the people to ask right now. Anyway, everyone was hungry.

"You said just you. I'm coming too," Dillon replied.

Devin nodded his head, and looked at each of them, "Well, now we're into the big decision time, ain't we kids? This is no longer a little jaunt out into the hinterlands of dull dreary Pennsylvania, this is now becoming a major road trip. I think this would be the time when it would be decent and right to give everyone a chance to bail out who wants to. They still have car rentals, and dealerships for that matter even out here, you won't be leaving me hanging if you decide this is too much."

There was silence for a moment, but finally, Hannah broke it, "Look, I am not so naive that I don't know that the odds of Jason Mamoa being in this room and then jumping out a window because you said a few words at him are astronomically against it. I also realize that I have gone this far in my life without anything this weird ever happening before, and will probably go the rest of it without it happening again. All I'm being asked to do is drive, so, yeah I want to see it through."

"How about you Zach? We can rent you a car if you want," Devin turned to the final member of the group.

"Hey bud, if you want to split out, that's totally cool. This has been a really screwed up couple of days and I can't say I blame you," Dillon added.

Zach chuckled, "Yeah, this has not been normal." He looked around the room and smiled, "But really, I'm digging this. I know that may seem weird, but when I realized who I was deep down, I kind of lost my faith altogether. I couldn't believe there could be a god who could create me and then hate me at the same time for just being who I was. This all gives me back a little of what I lost then. Even if it's just the bad stuff, it's nice to know there is something more to it all."

Devin smiled, "Hey, just because it might not be in the books you've read so far, doesn't mean there isn't a good side too. I mean, how else can we contain demons and send them away, it has to be by the power of something right?"

"And maybe one day, I'd like to figure out what that something is, but for now thwarting evil with you guys will have to do," Zach agreed.

"All right then, we'll have some food, and then get our thwart on. We'll see how much we can close in on our wayward friends before we pack it in for the night."

Moraspus had his cloven hooves slung over the side of his throne. He was wearing an incredibly tacky smoking jacket from the Hugh Hefner collection that barely covered any important bits. This wasn't some knockoff; it was straight from the man himself. Since he'd been here Hugh had been allowed to create an exclusive line of the tacky things in hell in exchange for doling out some sex advice to one of the major demons. Nobody knew exactly which one it was, but Moraspus' bet was on Asmodeus. Who else goes around killing guys just as they're about to consummate their marriages but a guy with major hang-ups he needed to work through?

Blurglesoth entered without knocking, something Moraspus noted with annoyance, "I came to discuss our methods going forward as soon as I knew you were no longer occupied. I saw the succubus in one of the hallways."

"Fine piece of tail on that girl, she could suck the gold plating off a communion chalice," mused Moraspus with a stupid grin on his face that let his fangs show over his lower lip. He shook his head, "Anyway, get some hitter demons. You know, guys that could hold their own in a holy war. Send them with some sniffers, as many as they think they need. I don't want them hurting the boy too much, but I blessedly well want him back. He is my son though, so if he doesn't want to come, he'll get ugly about it quick. Vampire demons won't cut it for muscle, but maybe a mouthpiece, he'd squish them in a hurry. Call back as many of them as we can too, stupid jackasses can't keep their fangs to themselves if they're topside too long, and who knows when I might need them for something."

The four of them were just finishing up their early dinner and were getting up to pay and leave when Dillon froze. He grabbed at Devin's sleeve frantically. When the older man turned Dillon hissed, "Look over by the door!"

"Well, shit!" Devin said as soon as he looked where Dillon indicated.

"What? What's...oh," Hannah said.

"You can see that?" Dillon demanded.

"Ummm so can I," Zach said since he could see the enormous vampire demon loitering outside near the door.

Dillon whirled on Devin, "Any answers on how they're seeing this shit Mister Magic Expert?"

Devin shrugged, "Repeated exposure. Note, I could see them even before I looked at the book you picked it up from. Once someone points it out to you, you start to become able to see not only what's there, but what's REALLY there. I guess it was bound to happen."

"All right, what do we do about it? There are people in here!" Hannah demanded, gesturing towards the five or six people in the booths and at the counter.

"We don't KNOW he's even here for us, "Devin said calmly.

At that moment they all heard a sound like fingernails on a chalkboard. They turned and looked towards the window in the direction of the vampire, who was standing right next to the door. When the creature knew they were looking he held up one finger and indicated with it that he wanted them to come over.

"All right, scratch that, he knows we're here," Devin shrugged.

"Well, what do we DO about it?" Zach implored.

"Anybody got a wooden stake handy?" Dillon suggested.

All of their heads turned towards him, everyone treated him to that look. The "How fucking stupid are you?" facial expression. The look you get after you actually shut down all conversation by asking aloud if anyone else wondered if dogs have porn that they watch and they just hide it really well, that look.

"OK, how about good suggestions?" Hannah said refusing to look at Dillon again, even if she did love him.

"Well, I do still have a silver blade on me. I've got more in my bag in the SUV," Devin supplied.

"We can't just kill what looks like a guy to everyone else right there in the parking lot!" Dillon exclaimed.

Their train of thought was interrupted by the thing tapping on the glass. They turned to look at it. When the vampire saw they were looking he gave them a wide grin. Which, considering the fangs was particularly gruesome to witness.

"All right, I don't like it either, but knife it is. If I slide it up my leather, maybe nobody notices me stab him. You three run for the damned SUV," Devin said.

"We're not leaving you!" Hannah exclaimed with shock.

"You're damned right you're not. No way I get a heart shot in; nobody is that lucky. So, I need somebody to start the SUV and drive it up so I can get in and we can get the f out of here! If it follows us, at least we can get it the hell away from population, and getting in the SUV gets us back in the vicinity of more weapons," Devin decreed.

All of them just looked at Devin dumbfounded as he calmly paid the check. Finally, Dillon asked, "Why don't we just use the book?"

Devin nodded as he accepted his change before he turned back towards Dillon and headed towards the door, "You know what has actually lessened the powers of evil in this world? Lack of belief. People don't believe in them as much as they used to, they aren't as easily manipulated by them like back in the old days. Demon offers a guy riches, well most people think they're one good idea away from being Bill Gates anyway and besides they don't believe in demons in the first place. So yeah, they think, fuck this weirdo and they hit the bricks before the demon even gets to show them a trick. Now what happens if we make that guy vanish in front of all these people?"

"Oh."

"Yeah, even if we win the day, we have just done evil a major solid. Trust me, this will work fine, they aren't that bright, and if I get killed, well I'll be giving you a hell of a head start."

"That is not encouraging," Hannah sighed as Devin pulled the door open.

As soon as they were outside, Devin whirled on the vampire demon who had stood there patiently waiting for them with a sniffer by a leash, "Do you want something?"

"Why yes, there is indeed something I want. You prevented an associate of mine from procuring something. I understand she got part of what she needed, but the thing itself would be ever so helpful," the vampire smiled as he spoke, they were all pretty sure it was doing it on purpose so they could see his fangs.

"No can do, it belongs to a friend and I'm taking it to them. I like to be helpful, but it's not yours, it wasn't hers, and at least I'm actually friends with the guy it belongs to," Devin replied casually, but they notice that his hand behind his back was frantically waving them to get going already.

When the vampire noticed the others moving off to the SUV he snorted, "Do they really think I'm not going to kill them too? My pet has their scent, I'll find them."

"Hey you can't blame them for trying, can you? I mean what would you do in their situation?"

The vampire nodded, the sun gleaming off its bald head before he replied, "You know, I might just be merciful and let you carry a little part of my power in you if you just give me what I want. Think of what you could do with eternity! Some men have committed amazing atrocities to acquire such a gift, and that will save me time when you devour your own companions later. It starts you off with a full belly in your life as one of the undead, and I get to go back to hell a bit sooner, how about it? You won't get a fairer deal anywhere."

Devin smiled his most charming grin and replied, "Huh? Now that is a tempting offer, I got to admit. You are right, a lot of people would kill for that never get old, never die shit. It is something for a man to consider. I just don't know if I want to take the dark gift from someone who leaves his shoes untied."

The second the vampire looked down; Devin punched him. Except Devin was packing more than just a punch. While they had been talking, he'd been working his silver knife down into his hand. So, from the vampire's perspective, it was less a punch to the gut and more of a stab wound. The monster doubled over, and it sunk to its knees in pain. Devin didn't see what it did next, he was too busy running like hell for the SUV. He did hear it gasp as he ran, "You...dick!"

Devin didn't even look back, the door to the SUV flew open and he dove for it. "Drive!" he shouted as he pulled his legs in and slammed the door behind him. "I cannot believe he fucking fell for that," he added chuckling as he settled into his seat.

They were already on the road and accelerating when Hannah said, "OK, quick but important question, where the fuck am I driving?"

"You see all of those fields on the way out here?"

"Yes."

"Find the most deserted ass country ass road next to one of those fields and pull over," Devin replied. He turned and reached into his bag, coming up with two more silver knives, "This was all I brought, I did not expect this much action or I would have brought more. I mean how often do you even leave a knife in someone? Who wants one?"

"How many of those things do you own?" Dillon demanded in shock. Shock that did not preclude reaching for one of the knives for himself, but shock nonetheless.

"As many as I need to keep me alive and still residing on this plane of existence. I don't know why evil hates silver, maybe because it has curative properties, I don't know, but why argue with success is my motto. Who else, Zach? Hannah?"

"I'm the biggest, you might need me to tackle him, I don't know if it's a good idea to try that with a knife in my hand," Zach said.

"Good thinking. Hannah, you cool with me giving you one when we pull over?" Devin asked.

"How do you even know he'll follow us?" Dillon asked.

"Well first off, I just really pissed him off," Devin said. He looked back in the rearview, "Second off I'd say he's already stolen a ride judging by that black Silverado I can see weaving through traffic back there. Hannah, you might want to pep it up a bit so we can get a bit further out of town by the way."

"I might also not want to pep it up too much, can you imagine getting a ticket now?"

"Point."

The town began to drop away from them, fields got larger, and houses became less frequent. They were all checking behind them hoping they'd lose the vampire demon. Every time they looked, that hope was dashed by the enormous, gigantic monstrosity of a vehicle that the original owner bought for reasons that one hoped were something other than major league compensation, still weaving around back there. Dillon couldn't help but wonder if the vampire had killed the man he'd gotten it from, and considering the enormous tires it rode on and all of the girth-increasing accessories it was laden with, if that hadn't actually been a mercy.

"There! Up ahead!" Devin pointed, "Where that little road goes off into the woods like that! It's perfect."

"For what? You still haven't told us the plan," Zach pointed out what he thought was a pretty major flaw in the plan that he had yet to hear.

"Just get out of the vehicle when we park and hide the knives. Trust me, I've got something in mind, but I don't want to stress your acting skills," Devin grinned.

"Oh, that just fills me with faith," Zach muttered.

"Hey we're all still alive and on this plane of existence, I must know something."

Chapter 10

"You ain't ever catching me! I am the wind!"- John
Dillinger

Everyone piled out of the vehicle once Devin told
Hannah to pull over. They had reached a spot where
the road had turned to dirt and gravel, and the trees
encroached over it, making the whole area dark and
gloomy. At least it felt dark and gloomy now, if they
weren't being pursued by a vampire demon intent on
slaughtering all of them it would probably have been a
pleasant spot to rest during a walk on a hot summer day,
but being as the vampire demon chasing them WAS the
situation they were dealing with, dark and gloomy it was.
Which in turn was not helping anyone's nerves any at all.
To make matters worse, they could already hear the big
monster truck approaching from the rocks being crushed
by its enormously masculine, completely studly, and virile
tires. The growling, barely mufflered at all, motor they
could hear in the distance was also probably perfectly
necessary for the proper operation of the vehicle as well.

"Hey, I've got a question," Dillon asked as they stood there waiting in trepidation.

"Shoot," Devin replied as he scanned the road for the oncoming truck.

"If it's a vampire, well, it is daylight."

"It's a vampire demon, the source, but not actually a vampire. It doesn't matter worth a shit to it what time of day it is. I don't know, something about the transmission to humans makes daylight an issue," Devin shrugged.

Whatever the response was going to be was lost as the truck roared around a corner and slammed on the brakes. The door flew open and the vampire demon flowed down from the cab and towards them, its limbs barely touching the completely not compensating step ladder needed to get into the truck as it moved. Even as he came into view his finger was pointing directly at Devin.

"You are such a dick! What the hell was that about?" the creature snarled at him.

Devin threw up his hands and his face was one of shock, "Buddy! I am positive I did you a massive favor!"

"How in the love of heaven do you figure stabbing me with God blessed silver was any kind of favor at all, let alone a massive one?" the monster growled his face incredulous.

"Got you away from population, didn't I?"

"Like I give a blessing about what humans see," the vampire spat.

"Ooooo boy, you been under for a while, haven't you?" Devin grinned almost mockingly.

"What is that supposed to mean?"

Devin started walking over to the creature. Before the thing could stop him, he had his arm around the bottom of the creature's shoulders, it was far too tall to get it over the top, "Things have changed Bro-sef! How'd people get rid of you guys in the old days?"

"Mobs usually," the vampire had a lost expression on his face. This is the same expression people get when they walked onto a used car lot specifically to buy a cheap little clunker for their sixteen-year-old daughter, and from just talking to the salesman for only a little while, have somehow found themselves just moments away from buying a low mileage, high payments, only driven on Sundays by a little old lady, Escalade.

"Not like that anymore at all, Sahib. There are whole organizations out there dedicated to quietly eradicating you guys in ways the populace never even sees. You do something like that in public, word gets around, next thing you know you got more stakes coming out of you than a party bus coming out of an Outback during a salmonella outbreak," Devin assured him.

"They mentioned something like that in the briefing, Wait, what is an... Outback...?"

"Never mind, trust me that analogy worked perfectly. What I'm saying is, you do something really public, you are going to get wasted for it. I pretty much just saved your ass. So, whaddya say we let bygones be bygones here and go our separate ways, huh?" Devin oiled.

The vampire demon actually looked like he was considering it before he said, "Only problem is, I still need the thing you took from that room, I can smell it on you."

Devin looked forlorn, "See the thing is, I need that. What the hell do you need it for anyway? I mean you said she got whatever you really needed, so why bother? Why not just enjoy your release back into reality? I mean look at those kids there, there are tons of them everywhere just ripe for the drinking and enslaving, and here you are worried about a stupid phone."

The vampire demon looked with uncomfortable intensity at Hannah, Zach, and Dillon who were all frozen in shock at what Devin had just suggested. After too long a moment he sighed, "Sorry, there's some new policy memorandum or something. I don't know, the last guy put it in place, and even though he got dismembered horribly the new guy hasn't rescinded it yet. We can't leave any loose ends, and that object is definitely a loose end. I'm afraid I'll have to insist."

Devin sighed gustily, "I was afraid you'd see it that way. Well, you can't say I didn't try to find the easiest way for everybody."

"Hey!" Hannah protested.

She would have said more, but her voice caught when she saw the vampire stiffen abruptly. The gray shirt it wore suddenly bloomed a darkening stain. The creature made gurgling noises as it fell to its knees clutching at the small speck of sliver that poked through its shirt at the epicenter of the growing splotch of black. Devin dove away from the monster quickly. He just managed to get out of range right before it ignited into a ghastly ball of yellow fire.

Picking himself up, he brushed himself off and said, "Chump don' want no help, chump don't GET da help! Jive-ass dude don't got no brains anyhow!"

"You suggested he eat us!" Hannah accused.

"Only to distract him, I swear!" Devin protested.

"Distract him from what?" Zach demanded.

"Damned knife got stuck in my sleeve," Devin shrugged. After the fire started to die down, he grabbed his blade and came walking towards them.

"Maybe you need a better system," Dillon suggested going back towards his own seat.

"I swear to god, it's never happened before," Devin at least had the decency to look embarrassed. "All right boys and girl, despite how wondrous the wilds of Pennsylvania are, we got lost time to make up for. Doubt we make North Carolina at this rate before bedtime, but we can at least knock off some miles before we get some hotel rooms, my treat."

At least it wasn't Nate doing the pouting as they drove through the Virginia night. They were on some back road, thanks to the GPS deciding that it knew a quicker way, which, in point of fact did not seem to be quicker at all, more of an anti-quick route. Dan had no way of knowing that the closer to Appalachia one got the more of a sense of humor map systems developed. Instead, he had dutifully pulled off 81 when it said so, woven through Roanoke, and now had them hopefully pointed in the direction of Charlotte North Carolina. Hopefully. They weren't seeing signs, or much of anything else out here to know one way or the other. The conversation that set GG on his own pout started soon after they got off the interstate.

"Hun, I think GPS sold you a bill of goods," Nate said as he looked at Google maps on his phone.

"Well dearest boy, we're on the road now, we'll just have to see it to the end. As long as we don't make any wrong turns, we should be fine," Dan winked, his eyes on the road.

GG sniffed audibly in the back seat, "I'm sure we'll get there when we get there, I don't approve of these larger highways. Man wasn't meant to go that fast."

"That's not all you don't approve of," Nate said under his breath.

"What?" GG sounded offended.

Dan sighed, "My dear tutor, we might as well have it out in the open. You don't approve of Nathaniel and my's relationship. The look of irritation on your face every time we hug has been more than apparent. Like it or not my friend, we have been a couple for over thirty years now, so you'll just have to learn to live with that."

"Well, I never!" GG let his voice carry his indignation.

"Not with that attitude you haven't," Nate muttered.

Dan couldn't help the snort of laughter that escaped him. GG glowered so intently from the back seat they could palpably feel it where they were sitting. The car lapsed into a gloomy silence.

Finally, Dan said, "Come on GG, I don't want you to be mad. These things happen. Here on earth, it doesn't matter anymore, times have changed and nobody really cares."

"Things haven't changed everywhere Danasdius. Could you pull over near these trees coming off, I had been hoping for some facilities or something for some time now. Since that hasn't been forthcoming, there looks to be ample area to pull off, and needs must and all," GG replied.

Dan sighed and pulled over letting the tires run into the wide grassy side of the road. GG didn't say a thing, he just got out and sprinted for the trees. So, there they were, GG was in a huff and in the woods, leaving Dan and Nate alone in the car and not in a huff.

"I wish he'd calm down about us," Dan sighed.

"Look, he'll get over it. He's old and the world has changed, he's out of his element, out of what he's used to. He obviously cares about you to have even come here to warn you, he'll want you to be happy," Nate replied rubbing Dan's shoulders like he always did when he was tense. It might not do much physically on the tension but the emotional support seemed to help.

"I hope your right, it's been so long and we've been so settled, I just don't feel prepared for any of this," Dan replied, "but thank you for trying to be understanding of him."

"C'mon, the guy was holding on to what he needed to escape hell for years and he used it to help you. He's like a dad to you...oh, sorry," Nathaniel cut himself off.

Dan smiled slightly, "No you're exactly right. My sire wasn't interested in parenting and considered it a job, so like any job, he delegated it."

Nate laughed, "And what Dad ever likes their kid's significant other?"

They were both laughing when GG came up to the door, "Well at least the mood has lightened in here," he smiled himself, "in more ways than one, I really needed that tree."

"Being on earth again certainly takes some getting used to," Dan grinned as he started the vehicle back up.

"In more ways than one," GG agreed.

Dan had just put the vehicle back in gear and was about to pull forward when the front of the car exploded in a shower of glass and metal! They were all thrown back into their seat by the impact, belts snapping tight from the shock, it was only a miracle the airbags didn't deploy. In front of them, an enormous gray fist sat surrounded by twisted metal where it had smashed completely through to their engine which was emitting a cloud of steam and the sounds of tortured steel.

Dan recovered almost instantly. "Stay here!" he snarled at both of them before forcing his door open.

As their brains recovered from the shock, their eyes adjusted enough to see the enormous demon that was connected to the fist. The creature was a normal warrior demon, like something out of Fantasia or Lord of the Rings done in colors of gray instead of black and red which were the normal demonic favorites. It was grinning wickedly at the damage it had done to their vehicle. Which was no surprise, the things were built for war and destruction, crushing a car fit in with its overall self-image. It probably hadn't gotten to do anything like this in eons, hell kept them on a tight leash for obvious reasons.

"Hello Princeling, glad we finally caught up with you. Daddy misses you," it hissed when it saw Dan. The creature's grin widened even further as it saw the look on Dan's face.

At least he was grinning until Dan leaped through the air and punched the monster directly in the face. After that, it was hard to tell what the thing's expression was as it rocketed off its feet and sailed into the woods with a massive crashing of tree limbs.

"And he can just keep missing me," Dan snarled.

"Ah, ah, ah," said a voice behind him.

Dan whirled. The voice was loud enough that it had caught Nathaniel and GG's attention as well. Standing next to the car was another of the enormous demons.

A vampire demon with a sniffer on a lead stepped out. "I was surprised at how quickly we got your scent so we could finish this," it said showing its fangs. "I'm sure you could give my two helpers quite the tussle Danasdius," it continued seeing he had Dan's undivided attention, "you could probably even best them. That's not really in question considering your impressive lineage. What is in question is whether or not you could do it before my friend Tiny here brings his fist down on the remains of your conveyance, where I do believe you currently have two companions lodged. All I ask is that you come along quietly. And before you consider any shenanigans, keep in mind, a scent can be retrieved from the nose of a dead sniffer, and mine clearly has their scents. Even if you escape today, I promise you they will be dead in days. Even if you abandon them, we can kill them as we track you."

Dan's shoulders slumped, he turned from the vampire to look at the remains of the vehicle and GG and Nate trapped inside with the monster's fist above them like the Sword of Damocles. Dan sighed, "All right I'll come along peacefully."

"Do you hear that, Oscar? He's coming along peacefully," the vampire demon called to where the other demon had landed after Dan had hit him.

A muffled voice carried across the distance, "That was fucking peacefully?"

"What? Jesus Christ! Alright, I'm sorry for blaspheming Nate. Where are you now?" Devin said into his phone as he looked at the onscreen navigation system. "OK, let me think.... we're about an hour out... No! Do not call the police they'll lock you the fuck up as a nutjob. Alright, find somewhere where there's woods, I'm doing this on the fly. Go into the woods, but not so far you lose signal, I'll call you when we're fifteen minutes away from you, I'm pretty sure I've been through that area before. Nathaniel, don't cry buddy, we'll work something out, but I need you to hold it together for a bit."

As soon as he clicked his phone off, he was greeted with three, "What happened"'s from all around him. He shook his head, "They got Dan, we've got to go get Nate, and do it now. Hold on with the rest of the grilling, I need to text somebody."

The SUV was shrouded in stunned silence except for Devin's fingers tapping away on his phone. At last, he looked up after hitting send to see both Dillon and Zack staring at him. "Look best I can figure is that the succubus got his scent off his phone. Once demons have a good whiff of you, well there's nowhere that you can hide they can't smell you out eventually. Maybe North Carolina would have worked for a little while, but they never made it. You have to keep moving and even then, if they can stay in any kind of range, it's just a matter of time really. I'm sure the guys stopped for food, stopped for gas, any one of those spots would have been a place where the sniffers picked up their trail and started following them."

"So, what are we going to do?" Dillon demanded; his face almost close to tears. This was supposed to be some grand adventure to save their friends, and here it was crashing down around them before they'd even so much as seen the people they were supposed to be rescuing.

"Let me think of something. Believe it or not, this is something I'm good at, I'm sure I mentioned it. But first thing we have to do is get Nate and this other guy, and I need to cover up what the fuck happened to their car. Good luck getting your insurance payments for 'a demon smashed my front end' trust me, insurance agents don't want to hear that shit, I've tried," Devin replied.

"But what then?" Zach asked.

"Burn that bridge when we get to it. If I am going to make heads or asses of this mess, I have to think point by point and try not to get too far ahead of myself. Right now, we still have Nate, so we gotta take care of him first and foremost."

Nobody had much to say after that, the SUV fell into what would have been a gloomy silence if the stereo hadn't been playing happily away. A gloomy silence is different than a stunned one, trust me, you can feel it when it happens. The stereo could have been easily turned off at that point, nobody was paying it the slightest attention at all.

They pulled over onto the side of the road shrouded by the Virginia night and waited. Devin punched in a text. A moment later he got one back saying, "Look for us." Coming out of the woods was Nathaniel and GG looking ghostly white in the darkness, which considering how their night had gone was only understandable. Devin and Dillon got out as they approached cautiously.

"Hey guys, glad we finally caught up to you, wish it could be under better circumstances," Devin called out.

"Oh, thank God it's you!" Nate gasped.

"Well, I did just text you."

"Considering what we've been dealing with...."

Devin nodded, "Alright I'll grant you. Let's get the third-row seat up and let's get moving, we still have stuff to do before we get any sleep tonight."

Once that was achieved, they sat there for a minute contemplating what came next.

"What could we even begin to do?" Nate asked in a shaken voice.

"First and foremost, we are going to get you checked in, in a room in Roanoke. I've already arranged for an associate to say you were down here on business visiting him. Then, you're going to call in your car as stolen. They'll find it, they'll tell you what happened to it, and you will be oh so angry about it, you shouldn't have to fake that at all," Devin explained. "It'll take me about five minutes to make it look hotwired before we get out of here."

A few minutes later he swung back into the vehicle and sat down, "Drive my good woman, let us be clear of this mess!"

"And now we go home?" Nate asked.

"Oooooo about that, yeah the car isn't the only insurance claim you'll be making," Devin's face tightened as he replied.

"Our house or our store?"

"Vampire demon went up like a firecracker right in the historical fiction section," Dillon supplied.

Nathaniel's face was a riot of emotions for a second before he replied, "Well at least you got one of them."

The other person in the vehicle spoke at last, "Nathaniel, who are these people? I mean I'm grateful but...."

"Oh yeah, sorry should have introduced you as we were getting in. Everyone this is Girolamo Gentili, he was Dan's tutor.... where.... well, where he comes from. Dan always called him GG. GG this is Devin Morgan, he deals in books...."

"Among other things," Devin supplied.

"Among other things," Nate agreed, "in the front seat is Dillon, he's a regular patron to our store."

"Who found 'Lux Abyssum Irent'," Dillon supplied.

"Oh, it was you who found it? Where was it?" Nate asked.

"Would you believe a flea market?"

"Oh, dear God, that poor book. And your friends are?"

"Well, this Zach, he's my best friend," Dillon said.

"And I'm his girlfriend and the owner of our ride, Hannah," Hannah finished for him.

"Sorry Hannah, I couldn't see that it was you up front in the dark. GG, she's in our store quite a bit as well," Nate informed the alchemist.

"Charmed to meet you all I'm sure," GG replied formally. "Did I understand correctly that we have 'Lux Abyssum Irent?' I mean I've never seen the book personally, but its reputation precedes it."

"Me and Devin can read it to a degree, so that has to help," Dillon replied.

"You really do think of everything don't you Devin," Nate smiled wearily as he slumped back in his seat.

"Not yet I haven't. We still have to get Dan back," Devin grunted, his eyes looking out the window intently at the dark passing trees.

"You know these seats all the way back here are incredibly uncomfortable," GG groused.

"We'll rent another car tomorrow, but it beats walking, right?" Nate replied.

"If it makes you feel any better, this is not exactly how I would have handled this," Blurglesoth said as Dan was thrown into the demon's office in chains.

"Oh, well that's all right then," Dan sneered. "Hey, wait, you're new, what happened to the other guy, Malla something or other."

"The risk that working for your father is fraught with I'm afraid. Mallocolic forgot to warn the vampire demons we first sent to look for you to keep their activities to strictly what they were there for. A few blew their cover and were subsequently staked for it. Your father was displeased."

"Tore him limb from limb?"

"There was some unpleasantness related to his dismissal, yes."

"So, what happens next?"

The demon put some slimy appendages that may have been legs, or pseudopods, it was hard to tell for certain, upon its desk, "Next? Next, you stay on the grounds under lock and key until your father is able to make time to speak to you, I suppose. My duty was to ensure that you were returned to the palace and that you weren't to leave until his return. I've more or less discharged my duties at this point."

"Until he returns? This wasn't even important enough to him to wait to see if it was completed?"

"He had the utmost faith in me once we had your current scent. He just wanted it done, he wants the souls of those who have displeased him tortured too, he doesn't hang around the dungeons for each and every one of them. My understanding is there was some sort of African rebellion and tribal conflict he had hopes of inspiring to greater feats of butchery and depravity. He's on earth right now suggesting things to some apt pupils in the CIA as we speak," Blurglesoth shrugged, or at least moved some slime below his mouth and above his middle up and down.

"So, what do I do? What now?"

"What now, what now? Go to your rooms and get settled in. Amuse yourself on the grounds, there are some first-rate sinners loose at the moment for sport, and a fine selection of toys to use on them. Of course, we'll also send you some personal ones for playing with, we aren't savages. As long as you don't interfere with the operation of the household it frankly it's of no concern of mine. At the moment the grounds are sealed and your father left no provisions that you were to be punished in any way. What do you wish me to do, scold you thoroughly and send you to your room to think about what you've done?" the slime demon practically sneered, which is not that easy to achieve when you have those kinds of deficiencies ``in the face department.

Dan rose to his feet, "Well then, I suppose if you need me, I will be in my rooms."

"Be my guest, can't think of a thing I need from a rebellious stripling of a Prince before your father gets home, and when he does, I'd just be in the way anyway."

Dan got up from his seat, Blurglesoth snapped his ooze (again, neat trick if you can do it) and the chains fell off of Dan before he walked out of the office. As soon as the door shut the illusion that hovered over the house made the door fit back in with the rest of the Italian villa styling of the palace. He ignored the various demons that were on the grounds, he especially ignored the souls that were here for the entertainment of those demons. This was not his world anymore; he wanted no part of it. His feet operated mostly on auto-pilot while his mind swirled with upset and confusion at being dragged back here to his father's house.

When the door slammed behind him after he'd entered his rooms Dan just stood there looking around his former living quarters. It hadn't changed at all; it was just as he left it. He knew even looking at it all that he had changed, he no longer belonged here. Which left one important question.

What on earth could he do about it?

Chapter 11

"The preparations for a long campaign are the most important"- N. Bonaparte somewhere near Smolensk

"So, what now?" Hannah started off as she sat on the bed in one of their motel rooms. They were ensconced for sleeping across three rooms at a mid-range motel outside of Roanoke. The police had already come and gone after taking Nate's well-crafted and heavily coached statement about his car. With that out of the way, they had gathered again in one of the rooms to have a palaver as to their options.

"Well, now we drive back to Pennsylvania first off. Nate has to make a claim on his store, so somewhere to stay there will have to be arranged," Devin said.

"I still have our farmhouse," Nate said. "We only stayed at the shop if we didn't want to drive."

"I'll need somewhere as well I suppose," GG said.

"I thought I'd find you a place in the house," Nathaniel said.

"I wouldn't want to impose," GG said coldly.

"Hey, what in the hell is your problem with each other?" Hannah just blurted out. Dillon was actually grateful; it had been bugging him the entire car ride and finally someone had flat out asked it.

"HE, doesn't approve of Dan and I's relationship," Nate supplied with a roll of his eyes.

"You're right, I don't," GG replied his voice getting much hotter with withheld emotions.

Silence reigned for a long moment as everyone in the room realized what they had thought was a smoldering snit fit between people was actually a full-blown fight that any moment could break out in to a full-blown domestic dispute with cops and statements and everything. Now, everybody was searching for the exact right thing to say to move this to a resolution while at the same time trying to make sure that resolution didn't involve gunfire in any way. Homicide IS a resolution after all.

"You're upset that they're homosexual?" Zach timidly asked the one question that was on most of their minds.

GG looked stunned. He actually sputtered before he finally spat out, "No! It has nothing to do with that at all, what kind of bumpkin do you take me for?"

"Well, if it's not that, then what in the hell is it?" Hannah pressed.

"Danasdius is a demon prince! His destiny is to rule legions in hell, not to run off with a mere.... human soul!" GG declared with all of the pompous air a statement like that deserved.

Nate actually started chuckling ruefully, "You still don't get it do you? Part of all of this was because Dan wanted to try and just be human! Getting old, living, trying to be a good person the whole nine yards! I'm just part of that. I like to think I was an important part, but this wasn't just him running off on some love tryst!"

"But why?" GG's face changed suddenly at that, he was actually shocked by what he'd heard and it showed.

"What's the big deal? So, he didn't want to be a demon, most decent people wouldn't?" Dillon asked.

Devin interjected to explain, "First off, demons view themselves to be far superior to humans. Most of what they see of human souls in hell are at best people trying to work their way in to lower level demonhood. Just being an evil prick in life isn't a golden ticket there. You've got to be vicious to your fellow souls in hell, you've got to back stab them, sell them out to actual demons when they try to hide, the whole enchilada, even in the midst of the flames. From what I understand, Hitler still hasn't made it yet."

GG sneered, "That one-balled sketch artist? Him and his buddy Himmler keep getting beaten up. Even Napoleon beat the hell out of them, both. Keith Moon made them cry."

"On a plus note, at least they're suffering," Hannah shrugged.

"Immensely," GG confirmed.

"What's secondly?" Dillon asked.

"It's never really been done. I've talked with Dan about this. He really wants to have the full experience, live to a ripe old age, die relatively free of sin, and see if he can't escape hell all together," Devin explained.

"But again, why?" GG breathed, still not comprehending and letting the shock he was feeling have room to grow and breathe a bit.

"You've dealt with his father for how many years and you really need to ask?' Nathaniel said hotly. "His Dad will never stop micro managing his existence as long as he exists in the abyss, and since his father's immortal, you could say Dan has committed no sins on earth, but he's already damned in hell."

GG was quiet for a long moment before he sighed. It was a great gusting thing, "Maybe I've been in hell too long myself. I just assumed your life with him was one of those larks children sometimes have. I never even considered the broader implications, dear lord, as you say, the boy is in a damnation all its own really. One of the great joys of growing up is finally leaving an overbearing parent and that's denied him for eternity." There was another long pause before GG added, "I know it doesn't excuse my behavior any, but I am sorry for it."

Dillon turned to look intently at GG, "So, if you didn't know that, why did you come here?"

GG's face went blank for a second, then his eyes clouded over with thought. Finally, he said, "Well, it was the only right thing to do! He's my pupil and more importantly my friend. I practically raised the boy! I had no idea what he was up to up here, but I couldn't let his father catch him totally unawares. His father is ruthless when upset. I only regret that I was used to trap him at the end."

"We can go in to hell to get him," Devin said quietly, "at least some of us can go."

He waited until the tumult settled a bit, "Look, with the book we should actually be able to escape from anywhere in hell. Even places that could hold him, or spells for that matter, some of these spells seem to bypass any magic perpetrated by demons. We might even be able to fight some of the things there off with the right spell. Load up on some gear here as well, relics and such, go in and break him out."

"Well of course I'll come," GG said offhandedly, "I know my way around, and I can get us through at least one gate."

"I'm coming too," Dillon said quietly.

It took a moment for the next, much louder tumult to settle before Dillon raised his hand, "Look, I'm not exactly chomping at the bit here but.... I'm the other person that can read some of that book, I've spent time with it translating. What if something happens to Devin? We've already faced some things up here, and some of us need to stay here to protect Nathaniel in case something comes for him too. But we're also going to have to do better than just hoping nothing happens to Devin down there. That's a recipe for failure and disaster."

"But Hun! We're talking about h-e-double hockey sticks hell here," Hannah practically pleaded.

"Bud, I'm your best friend, so don't take this wrong, but I never thought of you as the hero type," Zach added.

"Dillon, I appreciate all you've done for me and Dan but I can't ask you to do this," Nathaniel said.

"You didn't Nate, I offered. I don't know what I would have said if you'd asked, if that makes sense. Look, I'm sure Devin is going to want to get some things together before we go, we haven't even gotten back home yet, so we have time to talk yet. Still, me going along gives us the best chance to pull this off," Dillon replied.

Hannah looked at Devin almost pleading for him to say something to talk Dillon out of this. Instead, he just nodded, "I didn't expect you to offer but you made a solid point kid. Why don't we all table the discussion here tonight, hit the hay, load up early and regroup back in PA?"

Everyone took that for the cue it was meant to be and headed off to their prospective rooms. Devin was rooming with GG, Zach with Nathaniel and Hannah and Dillon were in the last room. Hannah was quiet the entire time they got undressed and got in to bed, which worried Dillon. Mainly because he wasn't a total idiot. You volunteer to do something dangerous and your significant other isn't talking to you, she's going to start at some point and odds are heavily against you being happy about it.

As they lay there watching the TV play quietly in front of them, Dillon was just about to pick up his phone to check his messages when Hannah said, "You're not actually going through with this, are you?"

Dillon sighed, well at least that shoe was finally dropping. He didn't have to just sit there on eggshells waiting for it. "Yeah, that's kind of why I offered."

She rolled over and looked at him, her eyes looked something they rarely sincerely looked, pleading. He'd seen similar expressions on her face, but that was usually when she was working her dad over for something, this looked actually heartfelt. So much so that it was having the effect of making him feel like a total heel. "But why you? I mean why, out of all the people on earth, do you have to go to hell? They own a bookstore you like, it's not like their family or something!"

Dillon sighed again, it wasn't like this was something he really wanted to do in the first place, and yet he now had to explain it. It was like arguing for broccoli, you knew it was good for you but you didn't like it enough to actually want to come rushing to its defense either. "Look, the best I can explain is, how would you feel if the roles were reversed. Say they'd accidentally taken me somehow, and say Devin could help get me out. He doesn't know me from Adam, let alone consider me a friend, he'd be well within his rights to bail on it, right? But how would you feel about him knowing he did that?"

She didn't say anything, she just stared at him making him feel terrible.

Dillon soldiered on, "Well, that's how Nathaniel would look at me if I didn't go. He'd be right, and I don't want to be the kind of person someone has a right to look at like that. I don't think you'd love me if you thought I was the kind of person who would be fine with it."

They were both silent for a long while before Hannah pouted and said, "You suck, you know that?"

"But, you love me anyway."

"Which is why you are going to at least be extra special careful and come home safe," her expression changed from petulant to pleading again so fast that Dillon was afraid she might have strained her face muscles.

"That is the plan, at least I hope it's the plan. I mean frankly we haven't really worked out a full plan yet, but I know I'll argue hard for the careful and safe one."

She looked at him for a long time before finally chuckling a little, "All right, I suppose you can kiss me now. Maybe other things if you do a good job with that, I don't get to spend time in a hotel with you nearly often enough and I want to really concentrate on creating a lasting impression that will make you want to come home."

The next morning, immediately after getting breakfast at a local restaurant, they rented Nathaniel a new car. Zach offered to ride with him to keep him company. GG and Nathaniel had worked out their major differences last night but it was agreed upon without a word being said that that fragile truce might be helped along considerably if they weren't stuck in a car together for hours. There was a white Jeep Wrangler in the lot that both Zach and Nate agreed upon almost immediately which put their little wagon train on the road by ten that morning.

In Hannah's SUV the mood was subdued. Why wouldn't it be, really? Three of the people in the vehicle were scheduled to go to hell and the driver was dating one of future brimstone sniffers. Those are the kind of thoughts that can make anyone morose and not particularly conversational. There aren't a lot of positive avenues for discussions when in the back of your mind you keep thinking, "Wow, I'm really going to be in the actual hell soon." Hannah wasn't actually going, GG had just gotten out and knew his way around, Devin had experience with things from there, but none of them could say they were any happier about it than Dillon was. It's just hard to get enthusiastic for something like that. Well, some people manage to get enthusiastic for anything, and whole cults are enthusiastic for hell, but we generally think of them as weird.

"Look, it could be worse," Dillon said to lighten the mood.

"How? I would love to hear how it could be worse," Hannah looked genuinely shocked by that statement. Devin and GG both raised an eyebrow as well.

"Well, I mean we're going in willingly and prepared. What if one of those things from earlier had just snapped us up? That'd be worse," Dillon replied.

"You aren't making a really compelling case there chief," Devin chuckled. He nodded as if to himself before saying, "But he is right, I've got practically a warehouse full of demon fighting crap sitting tight in Queens right now. I always wondered when I'd have a chance to use half of it. Frankly, kind of hoped it would come up eventually just not like this. We can kit ourselves out pretty well, and make sure you three have some stuff to work with here in case anything comes hunting for Nathaniel. So, while I can't promise you everything is going to be honky and or dory, we at least should have a reasonable plan of action."

"You kind of hoped it came up?" Hannah demanded.

"Well, you know, you get a new toy..." Devin responded almost demurely.

"A new toy..." Hannah replied flatly, showing that while this train of thought might have made total sense to her boyfriend who had nodded his head at Devin's response, she was having problems with the concept.

In the other car, they were having an entirely different sort of conversation. Conversation was probably easier to start and lighter in general since nobody in that car was going to hell any time soon, well, hopefully not at any rate.

"It must have been great to get back to earth," Zach said by way of a conversation starter, one that you don't hear every day.

"It presented its own set of challenges," Nate replied evenly.

"How so? I mean you had a demon boyfriend; he could have magicked anything for your guys."

Nathaniel shook his head, "But he didn't you see, well very little at any rate. He wanted to experience what it was like to be human, with all the hardships and foibles still involved in the undertaking. He made sure we had the paperwork we needed to get started, like High School transcripts, birth certificates, what have you. After that he wanted us on our own."

"But without a family...."

"Well, we had a knack for books. Dan especially, especially the sort of books Devin deals with. We started out doing garbage jobs, things that you only do because nobody else would hire you. It was still back when you could do that and survive. We'd flea market with books on the weekend. One of us went to college when the other worked, then we started doing more or less what Devin does until we moved into the New Hope area. Moving there was such a relief," Nate described as he swirled through traffic trying to keep pace with Hannah's SUV.

"It does seem that New Hope is pretty nice," Zach conceded.

"It wasn't only that, we finally had acceptance there. We went from Hell where our relationship wasn't accepted because let's face it, it's basically a caste system there, to Pennsylvania where we weren't accepted because we were gay. It was like we couldn't win no matter where we were," Nate explained. Zach couldn't help but notice the exasperation in his tone. He couldn't say that he could blame the older man for the frustration at having to work twice as hard just to have your life.

"I can understand wanting to be accepted. I haven't told my parents, they wouldn't understand," Zach said quietly.

The Jeep refilled with the noise of the road for a long while before Nate broke the silence with a sigh. He turned his head slightly towards Zach so he could keep one eye on the road, "You know you have to tell them, right? I mean it isn't like it's going to go away all on its own. Well maybe the physical act part, but only in your fifties at the earliest, and even then, only without Viagra, but you get the gist of what I mean right?"

"Yeah, I just...."

"Hope they'd get an acceptance transplant or you'd finally get an interest in swimsuit models?"

Zach chuckled, "Yeah, something like that."

Nate nodded, "Well, here's my advice, for what it's worth. Don't try to make yourself someone you're not. A lot of unhappy women and men found out that their spouse was only playing a role at some point, and you don't want to do that to anybody. I know this may hurt to hear, but at some point you may just have to cut your parents out of your life. Because it IS your life, nobody else can live it for you, or be with you in the quiet moments in your own head. That's what Dan had to do to come here, what we're trying to help him go back to doing now. Or, alternatively, and this may surprise you, it may turn out that they just get over it. After the shock dies down, of course. You are their son, and while I don't know them, I have to assume they love you more than they love hate."

Now it was Zach's turn to sigh, "I really hope so."

At lunch they all got back together at a burger joint in Font Royal Virginia. The place was a mom-and-Pop shop that was working hard towards quaint and kitschy with solid road food. The topic of the discussion was what next. Between the right at that exact moment part and the going to hell part. The hell part was the ultimate next, well even then getting Dan was the ultimate, ultimate next, but there were a lot of fiddly bits in between those ultimates and the mundane act of sitting in a burger joint in Font Royal Virginia in the here and now. There was where everyone was going to stay and rendezvous for starters. Nate having to deal with "finding out" that his business was just so much smoking ash was a big one as well, with Dan missing, that became complicated. For now, they were going to go with a bit about Dan searching for a specific book in Montana and being off the grid. This part was where Zach came in damned handy, he was going to school for computers but most likely would be teaching his teachers when he got there. He'd just send a bunch of emails to Nate, that Nate would dictate to him to sound like Dan. They'd show up in Nate's inbox with a timestamp from the last week, with the last one arriving from Dan's phone number before the fire saying he was leaving for a part of the state where there wasn't any kind of decent service. It bought time, but really, only if they succeeded in getting Dan back after which it would fall apart quickly under examination.

They needed to rescue the Beast as well, which meant Nate seeing what had happened to his beloved store unfortunately. Nobody was particularly looking forward to that, it really wasn't the kind of thing a sane person looked forward to. After that, Devin would make for New York with just GG for now, and call if he needed anybody else to help him. Dillon and Hannah would head to their prospective homes. In a surprise move Zach asked to stay with Nate. Zach explained that the whole reason Zach and Hannah were even staying on earth was to protect Nate, so it seemed kind of stupid to leave him alone now so soon after the last attack.

"You know, when you put it like that. If it's OK with you Nate I'll come over too, we'll, I don't know, order pizza and watch some flicks at your place," Hannah said.

"OK, after I check in with my mom to remind her she can't sublet my room, I'll be over as well," Dillon added.

"Are you guys sure? I don't want to be a bother," Nathaniel replied with an almost embarrassed look.

"Like Hannah said, that's why we're staying anyway right? I'll ride over with you, that way when those two get lost later I can give them directions," Zach replied smiling.

"Hey!" protested Dillon and Hannah together.

"If neither of you text me from the road for directions, I will buy you a beer," Zach smirked.

Getting the Beast back was indeed a solemn occasion, because there was another reunion to be had at the same time. Nobody knew what to say to Nate as he looked at the gutted building that used to be his business. What do you even say in that situation? Hallmark doesn't sell "Sorry A Battle With A Vampire Demon Burned Your Business Down" cards. You might be able to get them on Etsy but they didn't have time for waiting for it in the mail. They all stood there, a little back from Nathaniel, as he looked at the ruins of his livelihood. Dillon was holding a small stack of parking tickets and quietly inside his head thanking all that was holy they hadn't towed the Beast, he doubted if the poor thing could have survived the experience. Watching Nate standing there, he felt he'd gotten off lucky.

Finally, Devin broke the silence, "I know insurance will cover more than the value and all, but I also know that doesn't matter right now. You can rebuild, but you won't be able to replace those individual books. I'll help as much as I can when I get back, I just want you to know that I'm truly sorry for what happened."

And he was, to a man who made his living trading in, and tracking down books what had occurred was an undeniable tragedy of epic proportions. Nathaniel looked at his friend and nodded, he knew he meant every word of it, books were Devin's life. Books were a major part of Nate's but they weren't the most important part. The most important part had already been taken from him, and damn it, he wanted Dan back.

He sighed, "I know my friend, but as awful as this is, it will be even worse if we don't get Dan home. So, I suppose we'd all best get on that."

"So why did you insist on staying with me right away?" Nathaniel asked as they drove out of town to his house.

"Well, I mean the whole point of us staying behind is that you'd have somebody with you right? My folks aren't expecting me back, they think I'm staying at Dillon's, so I'm the obvious choice. I think I can forgo the pleasure of driving around in the Beast, so I just figured I'd head out with you now," Zach shrugged.

"The, Beast?" Nate's eyebrow shot up.

Zach chuckled, "That's just Dillon's nickname for his car. He started calling it that when the power steering went out and he had to manhandle it around corners. He kept calling it that because as often as it breaks, he's positive it's possessed or the Antichrist."

"I drove a car like that not long after I came back, I think everyone does at some point. Some weird rite of passage to make you better at cursing," Nate laughed.

"So, what was it like? I mean... hell?" Zach suddenly changed the subject, to ask the question that had been gnawing at him since he had found out about Nate and Dan's situation.

Nathaniel contemplated the question for a while, before replying, "Well it depends on why you're there, I suppose. Not everybody gets a personal hell, but some people get more of one than others. I was not one of those. In reality I hadn't done all that much to deserve it, but when I had been alive the first time it didn't take much. Back then just about everything sent you to hell. But the thing was, in my mind I had done wrong, and that's really what it takes to go to hell, to do wrong and to know you did wrong. Missionaries and hellfire preachers should probably be discouraged, they teach more people about reasons they're going to hell than anyone, and most of the time the preachers are just making it up as they go along."

Zach nodded, he would never say it to his parents, but that more or less jibed with what he believed. He didn't think God sent people to hell for every little thing, or even worse, just for who they loved. If there was a god, that seemed stupid on its face, especially since people had the ability to change so much over time. With that question answered there was more he wanted to know, and who could blame him? This was a once in a lifetime experience, most likely the next time the opportunity presented itself, it wouldn't matter because he'd be in the midst of it. At least if his parents were to be believed, which he was beginning to have serious doubts about. "So, what was your part of hell like?"

Nate chuckled, "Well the plane of hell I was on was almost like a city, a lot like a garbage heap. I think a lot of hell is like that, but again, I didn't exactly get to go on walking tours. My level of hell was for thieves of something, so we get tortured with want. It was made up of anything that anyone wanted dearly before it came out, that turned out to be not worth having mostly. Trash, on the pile. K Cars, AMCs, Chevettes, Peugeots are all very popular motor vehicles in hell. Things that were fads end up there as well, as soon as nobody could possibly want one. Things that become antiquated without having any charm or soul. I suppose, since then a lot of a lot of Yugos have shown up, but we left before the benighted little turds came to America. There are buildings in the midst of it all, I used to think that they were made out of trash, but if you can clear away enough debris you can find ancient stone walls. There aren't set torments on that level, it's not that organized, it operates on the idea of set a bunch of demons loose among a lot of souls and see what happens. A lot of torture mainly, demons enjoy it, and the souls are there for it."

Zach's eyes were wide at the description, he had pictured fire and brimstone, and while Nate hadn't said specifically that there wasn't.... it more sounded like he was describing hell as a landfill with whips. It wasn't what he expected to hear. "How on earth did you meet Dan in all of that?" Zach asked when he realized that the silence had gone a little long and he didn't want it to get uncomfortable.

"Well, I don't really like being tortured, so I was hiding. A lot of souls try and hide, the demons don't discourage it. Eternity is a long time, I guess hunting for us gives them something to do when things get slow. Between demons trying to sell me Amway or worse, I was digging a place of my own out of one of the trash mountains. That's how Dan found me. At first, I thought the worst, I'd lost my hiding place, and now I was going to be tortured. I couldn't have been more wrong, it turned out, Dan wanted to hide too."

"So, was it love at first sight?" Zach enthused becoming fully engrossed in the tale.

Nate chuckled ruefully, "No, quite the opposite really. He was a DEMON. I was terrified of him for years. But little by little he would come by and help me dig the place out some more, so it was an actual home. Then he started furnishing it with the better objects that had become obsolete and awful and ended up there. Bringing me food, because hunger is a constant in hell, and one day, I just started seeing him as Dan instead of as a demon. I suppose at some point he must have started seeing me as more than a plaything or a curiosity. And then one day.... well, that's where love came in. So, how about you? Is there someone special?"

Zach shrugged, "After hearing all of that, I don't know if dating a football player counts as that. I mean we're going to the same college to be together, which I THOUGHT was romantic until I heard your story."

Nate smiled, "It's not the trials the torch goes through, it's how bright it burns."

Chapter 12

"I thought we would have a longer calm before this happened!"- Galveston resident 1900

Dan sat on a couch in his rooms trying to read, which was really trying to ignore the people in the room with him. Three souls had been brought in for him to torture at his leisure a few minutes ago because as Blurglesoth had put it, "It isn't our job to punish you, just to keep you here. You should have souls of your own to torment to alleviate your boredom of course, like any demon should expect. We aren't barbarians here."

Dan had tried to protest that that was the last thing he wanted, but for a slime demon Blurglesoth could pull off a fast dramatic exit with the best of them. Which left him in his rooms with three souls huddled near the door that led out into the hallway with worried expressions on their faces, and a trail of slime leading out of it. So, for now, he tried to ignore them. Which proved easier said than done, you just can't do it in these circumstances. If there's someone in the room with you, focusing all their attention on you, you just feel it, like an annoying itch just dying to be scratched. Married couples use this tactic when they're spoiling for a fight all the time, letting the latent waves of hostility build and build until one of them finally breaks and asks what's wrong, even though they know THEY are what's wrong and if they ask, they are going to find out at length WHY they are what's wrong. It doesn't matter, that kind of eyeballing will break even the strongest willed.

Dan's will was not feeling that strong today, He put down his book and turned to glower at the unwanted souls, two men, and a woman. The first man looked old and feeble to him, like he had lived a long, hard life and hell had only resigned him to more abuse. The other, while younger, looked rabbit scared, like he still thought flight had possibilities of success despite hell being more or less the end of the road for last-second escapes. The woman had died at the height of her beauty and was nothing but curves to go along with a surprisingly cute and petite face that was darkened with worry. All of their eyes dropped to the floor as soon as Dan looked at them; as if it might work out somehow that if they couldn't look at him, he might not be able to see them.

Dan sighed, "Look, I have no intention of torturing any of you, so could you all stop trembling with fear? I'm trying to read a rather boring book and I'm having enough problems concentrating as is."

He could see that they felt that they might want to shore up this arrangement some. The woman decided to take the lead, she stepped forward, her eyes only slightly raised, just enough to see Dan but not nearly enough to look him directly in the eyes, "Ummm....while I'm thrilled to hear that.... cause you know....no offense.... but most demons are perverts and I can use the break.... but what should we do if you don't want to torture us?"

Dan actually smiled, "Look, there are a lot of rooms here. There're books, I have a TV, a computer, sorry my email is blocked so no contacting loved ones or descendants, video games, what have you. Just leave me alone so I can read and I'll be thrilled. Well not really thrilled, it's a boring book, but I'll be happier at least."

While they still weren't looking at him, he was pleased to see all three of their faces brighten a bit. The woman still did their talking though. The old man had probably learned that silence was useful long before he'd died for when you were frail and couldn't defend yourself and it turned out what you said wasn't liked. The younger of the two had probably learned similar lessons from life, he looked like he'd spent a lot of his running away from things. The woman's voice sounded slightly less timid when she said, "So we should just go wander around for a bit? Just like that?"

Dan nodded, but allowed some of his old demonic appearance to slide over his face for emphasis, "Yes, now if all three of you would please FUCK OFF!"

Dan was impressed, he didn't think an old codger like that could run that fast. When he heard their footsteps recede in the distance, he turned back to an ancient tome of magic hoping to find some spell that would get him out of here.

GG and Devin were not hitting it off. They weren't openly arguing or anything like that, it hadn't reached that point. It turned out that they were not nearly as similar as they would appear at first glance. They were both studious and interested in all things occult, so one would have expected that it would almost be a given that they'd be fast friends. It turned out that a modern-day tattooed psychobilly book dealer from New York and a long-dead alchemist... Put bluntly, Devin wondered if GG had changed the stick up his ass since he'd been on earth, and GG wondered if he was working with someone who was already possessed.

"Must you play that.... music I suppose it's called, so loud?" GG demanded as they made their way into the Holland Tunnel.

Devin reached over and turned it down all of one bar. He had been tempted to crank it to vent his annoyance at all of the little comments along those lines GG had made, but he was generally employed by rich old men, and he knew that the gesture would be completely lost here. Instead, he said, "Aww, c'mon this is just early Meteors, I could be subjecting you to Demented Are Go."

GG's eyes got wide for a second, then he huffed, "It's funny, I'm positive all of those words are in English. I'm quite fluent in it, during the period of their empire we got quite a few British speakers in hell you know. Yet, I find that I understood almost none of that."

"Just sit back and enjoy the ride, I've got to slide by my office, and then we can go to my warehouse," Devin replied, his mind racing to find something, anything that might loosen his companion up a bit. He had no idea how long he'd be stuck with the ancient alchemist, and getting in an argument now helped nobody, it would only make him FEEL SO MUCH better.

The office wasn't much better, though GG at least showed some interest in the computer. Devin was an adult, he had been one for some time, and GG in appearance at least wasn't THAT much older than him, but it didn't stop him from feeling like he was hanging out with a friend's dad. That same "well it's not my place to disapprove because I'm not your parent, but I want you to feel that I absolutely do not approve of you or anything about you" vibe exuded from the guy. This is a very specific vibe, but you've definitely felt it at least once, maybe more than once, no matter how good a kid you were. If you were anything like the author of this book it would feel weirder to not be feeling it.

It wasn't until they reached Devin's warehouse of goodies in Queens before he felt that the ice might finally be cracking. Once they were in the sealed inner rooms, the man's whole demeanor changed. If GG didn't approve of Devin, he definitely approved of Devin's private collection of books and various bits of magical paraphernalia. At least Devin was pretty sure that was what all of those "ooh"s and "oh my"s were about. Either that or the ancient alchemist had returned to earth only to have a stroke. Devin hoped not, they kind of needed the guy to get into hell.

"So, I take it you like?" Devin said as he stood in the doorway holding some duffle bags he had gotten from the backroom to load up gear.

"It's...I mean...how did you ever acquire such a vast collection," GG replied as his fingers danced over the spines of ancient books of magic.

"Clients give me gifts, they pay me well, I pay spotters to be on the lookout for things. Sometimes something catches my own fancy, a little here, a little there, it all adds up," Devin shrugged.

GG looked at him with something approaching awe, "I had no idea dealing in books was so lucrative, you must be extremely wealthy."

Devin started loading various pieces of religious paraphernalia into one of the bags, "On paper for the government I'm very, very comfortable. But that's as far as stated wealth. Many of these books are not listed. If they were, I'd have to pay for extra security just to keep an insurance company happy. Other people want them very badly, and not everyone deals with the niceties of hiring a guy like me when they want a specific book. I don't need anyone knowing I have them or entering that information into a computer." Devin grinned for a second, "Hey, do me a favor, look up one shelf and to the right-hand side. There's a slim volume I might want to take along."

Devin heard the other man gasp. A moment later GG said in a quavering voice, "You have my book?"

Devin walked over to him and pulled a slim leather-bound book with intricate tooled patterns still visible down off the shelf, "Quod Ex Igne Tenebris, one of fifty that were printed, one of three that still exists. I knew I recognized your name when we met. Thankfully you've already signed it. Signing it now would do me no good, the inks would never match up right."

GG took the book from Devin with shaking hands, his face glowing at the recognition of who he was for just a moment as he opened it and viewed the long-lost tome for the first time in centuries. At last, he smiled softly, "I'm afraid that you might as well put it back. I've learned from very personal experience since then, that quite a bit of it is rubbish I'm afraid."

Devin chuckled as he took the book back carefully putting it back in its place, "Hey, in the quest for knowledge you can only work with what you have to hypothesize from. At least you were searching."

"Thank you for that, it means quite more than you realize," GG said smiling.

Devin smiled back, things would probably be better now, at least they had found some common ground at last.

Dillon was worried. Hannah had seemed to be taking all of this really well. She didn't seem mad or upset at all. He felt like this clearly meant that a trap was being laid for him. She had every reason to be upset, she had been upset before, and now she didn't seem nearly so upset all of the sudden. His spidey senses were rattling their cages in 3/4 time, nothing this major goes that well in a relationship. Finally, as they were driving over to Nate and Dan's house outside of New Hope, after having dropped her SUV off at her house the need to poke at it had gotten the best of him. Against every survival instinct he had, which all told him that this would be the PERFECT time to shut the hell up and enjoy it, he needed to ask.

"Are you OK? I mean with everything.....and...."

"No...wait don't say anything yet. No, but. No I'm not OK, but I know why you have to do this, and I can actually understand. So, instead of talking about it and risk having a stupid argument where I'll be wrong no matter how many good reasons I have, I've elected to enjoy the time we have together where you're right next to me all safe and sound, and not....well, where you're going," she said as she reached over and grabbed his leg.

"You know, we don't have to go right over to Nate's. I mean, Zach is with him and all, and he expects us to get lost on the way anyway," Dillon said with a grin.

"I love that idea."

"Want to stop for pizza when we actually are heading to Nate's? I can't imagine they have pizza in hell, maybe Godfather's but....yech."

"You went from romantic to pizza?"

"Well, when we're especially romantic, and I hope to be REALLY extra special romantic, I get hungry afterwords," Dillon shrugged.

Hannah was quiet for a moment before replying, "You know, now that I think about it, I get hungry too. Pizza it is, that good place that does the New York thin crust is in Doylestown, right on the way."

A week later they were all meeting at Nate's house. It was a lovely, small, old farmhouse on an equally small plot of land outside of New Hope. Dillon and Hannah had been by before, but it had generally been only briefly to check in. Nate had said he'd understood about them wanting to be alone and sent them on their way with his blessing. Zach had been pulling almost all of the guard duties happily. He didn't say he was avoiding home, and no one had brought it up but Dillon knew him well enough to guess.

Zach's eyes got large taking in the neighborhood the first time he'd come out here. This was a high-end part of the state. Nate explained it away, "When we first bought the place nobody was that excited about living that close to New Hope, and since we didn't want to actually farm we didn't need a lot of land, we got it pretty cheap. It needed a lot of work, but, no kids, we had time. Now though, the taxes alone...I can only imagine what it would sell for. But who wants to sell the place they've built a life in?"

Since then Zach had been spending a lot of his time there. It was not only what he considered his job, but it was also glorious to be around an adult adult, not a peer adult who didn't care about who he was and who he didn't have to hide from. That was rare for him, with the possible exception of Dillon's mom, who barely batted an eye when he confessed his sexuality to her one night when he'd been staying over and she'd found him crying on the couch. She had just hugged him and said, "I already knew honey, I just didn't care. Your my son's best friend and that's the most important part to me." Zach didn't get to just be very often, not hiding from the world. There were so few people he felt he could trust, anyone who knew his parents, and that counted as most of the adults he knew, could not know about him, any friend he had his own age from church, the same. In theory, Zach was guarding a middle-aged man against the forces of darkness, but instead of apprehension, he felt lighter and freer than he ever had before.

Dillon had ridden over with Hannah. He had no idea when he was going to be back, so if his Mom had car troubles she could use the Beast. More likely she'd rent something first, she thought that the Beast should be condemned as a health hazard, but it was the thought that counts in life so he'd left the keys on the hook. When they arrived, Dillon was kind of glad they had gotten here before Devin and GG. That wasn't anything against them, nothing like that, hell, he was going to actual hell with them he clearly was OK with them. More, he just wanted to spend a bit of time with his friends before they left and. Devin and GG were barely above acquaintances at the moment. Dillon was desperately hoping that being around those closest to him might calm him down some.

Zach was waiting for them out front with Nate. As soon as they parked Zack rushed over, "Hannah, come with me now!"

Concern lit up both their faces but Hannah asked first, "Um why, what's wrong?"

Zach grinned, "Nothing, but you HAVE to see the barn, they have antique tack in there!"

Dillon didn't know what that meant exactly. He had to assume it was something to do with horses because it had Zach's desired effect, Hannah's face lit up immediately. She leaned over and kissed Dillon on the cheek, "I'll be back in just a minute honey." They vanished in the direction of the ancient-looking structure near the house to go gawk at something that was truly beyond his ken.

Nate walked up to Dillon smiling lightly, "The house used to be part of a bigger horse farm. We refurbished and all, but decided to leave the barn as intact as possible when we had it repaired instead of converting it to more living space. Not that we want animals or anything, but, a farm should have a barn. I think they're excited about the old saddles and suchlike that we made sure stayed in place."

"Ah, yes, that would explain it," Dillon nodded. Hannah had been raised as a little rich girl growing up, and all little rich girls want, and get, a pony at some point in this part of Pennsylvania. Zach's family had relatives further out in Berks that had a full farm, including horses. It was something his best friend and girlfriend shared, along with something to do with Aquaman apparently as he had just recently learned. Dillon didn't think much of horses one way or the other. The few times he'd gone riding with Hannah he'd asked for the most docile beast they had, and strictly tried to stay on the thing and keep it pointed in the desired direction for the length of the experience. They'd ride for a while, go home, have sex, and after she fell asleep he'd take a lengthy shower to get the horse smell off of him. Other than horses equating evening fun with Hannah for some reason, he had never bothered to form an opinion on them, it wasn't the kind of thing he expected to own in life. That wasn't to say he minded her lingering fascination with them, how could he? Hannah had changed a lot in the time they had been dating, she was more earthy and grounded, but it would be mean-spirited that they spent all their time together doing broke kid stuff just to keep him on his own comfortable turf. If she wanted horses sometimes, he'd learned to not fall off a saddle.

They stood together in silence for a long moment before Nate said, "You know, if you back out now and want to stay I wouldn't think any less of you. Nobody can rightfully get angry about someone not wanting to go to hell."

Dillon shrugged, "I'd think less of me. And I have to live with me the most.

Nate smiled, "Well, I want you to know you have an out."

"And leave poor Devin with GG, I am too good a man for that," Dillon grinned.

"No doubt in my mind."

Devin and GG arrived about an hour later. As they were getting out Devin called out, "Sorry about that, there was an accident on 78. I tried to text."

"Well, you're not leaving until tomorrow anyway, so no harm," Nate replied as he went out to greet them. He surprised everybody by giving GG a hug as he got out, "Thank you both so much for doing this."

GG smiled wanly, "If this works, I'll probably need your help in staying in this reality and living here. I don't think Moraspus will be particularly forgiving if he finds out, or even suspects my involvement this time. I was already in hiding what with Dan's disappearance."

"Of course, I'm sure Dan would agree that you could stay with us until you get your feet under you," Nate replied warmly.

That night was nice. It was a forced nice, three of the people were nervous about what they had to do, and the other three were nervous for them. Nobody wanted to say or do anything unpleasant just in case it turned out the first three had every good reason to be nervous. Nobody even really wanted to consider what that just in case was, because that would just make the nerves all the worse for it. You don't want the last thing you say to somebody you care about to be snapping at them in irritation.

The next day they got up early and had a hearty breakfast that Nate cooked before they drove split up in Hannah and Zach's vehicles to the spot where GG promised that there would be a way through to hell. The food was aimed for filling and the kind of thing people were used to. There was no point in being fancy only to find out one of the adventurers got gas from cilantro after the fact.

At first, GG had gone on at length and difficulties of the journey to the cave, and none of them were looking forward to the trip at all. That was until Zach had brought up Google Earth and found that a small dirt road took them almost directly to the cave's entrance and GG had just gone the wrong way down to the road and totally missed it. GG had spent more than a little time after that cursing technological "witchcraft" until he had finally been convinced that it could have happened to anyone by the others.

As they hefted the duffle bags each of them carried with supplies and books Devin said to Nate, "Run my car at least once a week if you have to, but hopefully we aren't gone long and you never have to even turn it over. But still... And hang tight here for about an hour, huh? We don't know if there's going to be anything unexpected right inside the gate and we might need to take a quick powder. I don't feel like walking anywhere if we need you. Or running out of there needing a ride with something hot on our heels only to find we ain't got no ride."

"No problems, we can amuse ourselves for a while," Nate assured them.

Hannah and Zach hugged Dillon. Hannah leaned in and held him for a long moment, "If they let anything bad happen to you....."

Dillon kissed her forehead lightly, "I don't plan on letting ANYTHING happen to me. I plan on us getting in, reading the spell that will let us pull Dan out, and getting while the getting is good."

"You've shown a recent upsetting trend towards heroism you know, it worries me," Hannah frowned.

"Look, once we're out of this, I swear, nothing more adventurous than a waterslide at Dorney Park," Dillon raised his hand like a boy scout.

"OK, maybe you can have a little more adventure than that when you're back, maybe we can go to Six Flags too," she smiled.

With their goodbyes said it was time to go. Dillon didn't want to, he was going to, he just absolutely did not want to in even the slightest little bit. Sort of like church in that....actually scratch that, pretty much the opposite of church really, even if the feeling of dread reminded him of Sundays when Mom used to want to go to Czestochowa. He let Hannah go and turned to the others.

"Guess it's time, huh?"

"Yeah kid, let's get a move on," Dillon replied as he shouldered his bag. "C'mon GG, you know the way, it's time for us to get our hell on."

They all turned on the headlamps they'd bought for this and trudged up the small hill to where the cave awaited them. There should have been ominous music playing or something, along with some dark and foreboding clouds instead of clear sunny skies. Life has no real sense of drama sometimes, imagine some of that stuff in your head instead.

"For the love of Pete, Thomas! Duck! It's the B button, it was the B button last time I told you!" Dan barked as he twisted around with his controller as if his own body english would somehow affect the game they were playing in any way.

"I'm sorry, oh dark demonic lord!" the frail old man replied, his body twisted for a different reason, he was trying to lean out of Dan's reach.

"I told you before, don't call me that! All right, I am a demon prince, I grant you, but c'mon nobody can help how they were born right?

They were playing Mall of the Dead on PS3, he had both of the game system and the game because it turned out that he still had the clout to make demands of the servants in the house. During a fit of throwing a book of magic down in disgust, he had called out and said bluntly that if he was to be locked up in this house he would be damned for all eternity if he did it without a game system and a good TV. The servants didn't giggle at him saying "damned" in that context, and that kind of depressed Dan, it had been a good play on words.

Both the PS3 and the disc had been easy finds in the rubbish heaps of this plain of hell. The system because it had been obsolete for years, and the game because in the wave of zombie games it had just gotten lost in the shuffle and hadn't been very popular. So, here Dan was trying to get souls who were all easily a hundred years dead at a minimum to understand the concept of "multi-player." It was at least providing some amusement to him in his captivity, just not the kind they'd been sent here for.

Thomas, Patrick, and Adrianna were offering some service in that they provided a distraction from tedium at least. Trying to teach them which button worked the gun had whiled away many an hour already. Of course, Adrianna had spent much of her time trying to throw herself at him sexually, which he didn't want. He could see the logic, it would secure her safety at least for a little while in her mind, but that was a no-go as far as he was concerned. Dan was keeping himself sane by convincing himself that he could still figure out a way to get out of here, which meant he still had a husband to be faithful to. Adrianna had been in hell quite a while, and based on her afterlife experience, she just wasn't seeing that at all.

Dan was also worried that he'd get used to being here again, to being a demon again. He'd caught his feet changing back to hooves more than once when he was involved in something that really had his attention. It was like hell was trying to reassert its dominance over who he was. Dan was bound and determined that it was absolutely not going to happen. He'd left here to be human, and Dan fully intended to leave here still thinking and feeling like he was human.

"Thomas, if you aren't going to use the lazer cannon right, give the controller to Patrick!" he snarled. Yep, thank goodness for these three souls, they were definitely providing a welcome distraction. "Adrianna, even if I did need a massage to loosen up my muscles, that particular one works the opposite, so please stop trying to touch it."

Chapter 13

"The revolution will not be organized!" Dewey P
Newton

"I did not expect to be crawling into hell," Devin said.

"Well, every entrance is different in some way, but it's the one I know that was easiest, as it were," GG replied from up ahead.

"Are we in hell yet? Because this hurts like hell," Dillon grumbled as he banged his knee on a rock on the cave floor.

"No, we won't actually officially be in hell until we pass through the gates," GG replied completely missing the bitter sarcasm in that statement.

"You said there were guards, do we have a plan in place for that?" Dillon pressed. Really, he didn't care about the plan at this exact moment, what he was doing was distracting himself from the crawl. He assumed that Devin and GG had already worked out something in advance, but it was this or constantly whining, "Are we there yet?" and he didn't think he'd sunk that low yet.

Devin replied from behind him, "Don't worry about it kid, I'm on it."

To Dillon's disappointment, that statement shut that window of conversation relatively effectively. Not that it mattered, he could see that a little in front of him GG was able to stand with a stoop at last. GG halted (or stopped as he stooped, ha, ha...we're sorry, that was lame) and turned back to the others, "We should probably stop talking here, the guards are relatively incurious about much of anything except bribes from potential escapees, and even then, not even that curious about that. Still, I don't suppose it would do us much good at all if we were to alert them to our presence too much."

The cave increased in size quickly after they got up until it had finally changed into a full tunnel. Dillon kept expecting it to get hotter as they went, something that continued not to happen if anything the air was a bit chilly. Here they were on this adventure of Netflix series proportions (hint hint), and his expectations were absolutely not being catered to at all, what would the special effects department even be able to do with this? Then again, he was in a creepy tunnel, moving by headlamp, deep underground, with the spirit of a long-dead alchemist returned to the flesh and a psychobilly book dealer/magician, maybe he could call that adventure enough for the time being. (And it would be PERFECT as a SHUDDER original)

He almost walked directly into GG's back when the man stopped suddenly. Dillon saw why as soon as he looked ahead. There it was, their goal, the gateway to hell. An actual gate leading to the actual hell. For a brief moment as he stood gaping at it Dillon wanted to whip around and bolt for the surface, which was entirely sensible all things considered. Once he went through, there would be no turning back, he would actually be in actual hell. His terror lasted only for a brief moment, thankfully, his backbone reasserted itself quickly.

Once they had regrouped GG started forward, Dillon made to follow until Devin reached out and put a hand on his chest. Dillon looked at him in surprise. He was even more surprised when Devin made the stop sign with his hand and hurried off to join GG up by the door. GG had his hand on the enormous crusted metal ring set in the door, Devin stood off to the side of him holding something in his hand that Dillon couldn't see in the gloom from where he was.

Suddenly GG pulled on the door with all of his might, falling back and out of view from anything in the darkness that loomed from the other side. Dillon was shocked when suddenly Devin yelled, "Kid get out of here, this looks bad, and you look way too tasty to be in a place like this!"

An enormously fat green, Dillon was going with Demon, since no normal person looked like that, loomed out of the darkness at him. He grinned, showing rows of teeth. The thing was so fat Dillon almost didn't see the bone-thin wraith that peered around his enormous girth with deep sunken eyes set in a face that was almost a skeleton. The thin one jabbed a spear in Dillon's direction weakly.

"Looks like some damned fine eating on this one," the throaty voice of the fat demon snarled.

"Oh, and I suppose I'm supposed to watch the gate while you make a pig out of yourself?" the wheedling voice of the other demon complained.

"Tell ya' what, help me catch him, and I'll give ya his hands."

"DEAL!"

Dillon was already backing away even before his hands got bartered off. He had no idea what had just happened here, but he had every reason to believe that if he didn't get out of here right now, he was going to end his days as demon poop. He hadn't suffered through twelve years of public school for that! The demons came the rest of the way out from the doorway and started to rush towards him. Dillon was just about to turn and run back towards the surface when he heard two popping noises from near where Devin stood.

A look of confusion fell over the faces of both demons. The skinny one managed a few uneasy steps before collapsing in a heap at Dillon's feet. His compatriot flopped on top of him with a sigh covering the thin demon so completely, that if it hadn't been for the hand sticking out, you'd have never known he was under there.

"What the hell just happened here?" Dillon demanded.

"Tranq gun," Devin grinned, "fifty percent holy water, fifty percent high-grade heroin. Those two will be out for days!"

"You used me as bait!" Dillon accused angrily.

"C'mon, you were never in any danger," Devin protested.

"You didn't even tell me you were using me as bait," Dillon huffed.

"It had to be believable or they wouldn't have fallen for it."

"You could have trusted my acting ability."

"Better to go for the sure thing with something like that, trust me on this kid," Devin smiled with so much winning confidence that Dillon kind of wanted to punch him.

GG interrupted their brewing argument, "Even so, we should do something with them. We don't want them to wake up here and be right outside the gate, angry at us if we have to come back this way for some reason. Not to mention, if they aren't at the gate, people will think they just wandered off, demons do that, but if they're here in a lump like this...."

Dillon interrupted, "Umm guys? What's happening to them?"

They all turned to look at the two unconscious demons. Before their eyes, the demons were changing. As they watched they became more human in appearance by the second. Scales vanished, their tails shrank rapidly to be replaced by pink skin and....well nothing, because only in special cases do humans have tails and this was not that case. What had fallen onto the rock floor might have been a pair of demons, but already, what lay there were two mismatched humans who would have a great career in Hollywood as a comedy duo if they chose to pursue it. They still couldn't see much of the skinny one.

"They're outside of hell," GG said, "I suppose since they guard the gate, they have a natural camouflage that they fully turn into, built-in in case they have to step out into the real world after someone. I wouldn't count on these two to think of a suitable disguise on their own."

Devin grinned widely, "And now I know what to do with them now. Grab one of 'em"

"Grab 'em why?" Dillon asked.

"We got two cars waiting out there. Have our people just dump these two as far away from the entrance as they can get in an hour or two. I'm betting they haven't been on assignment in our world in centuries, no way they find their way back," Dillon explained still grinning as he rolled the fat one off the thinner demon.

"Seems kind of cruel," Dillon said grabbing the leg of the thin one and hauling it towards the cave passage.

"Never take pity on demons or lawyers kid, they see it as weakness, now let's get 'em topside."

It was a struggle getting the two demons through the crawl, although it got a lot easier when Devin admonished Dillon and told him to, "not worry so much about bouncing them off of stuff, they won't break, and if they do then we don't have to haul 'em the whole way." Still, all three of them were sweating heavily by the time they made it past the crawlway to where it opened up a little.

Devin was up ahead, he immediately let out an exclamation on reaching the open air, "Thank god, they're still here!"

As soon as they saw him, Zach, Nate, and Hannah were out of the cars. "What's wrong?" Zach demanded.

"Nothing wrong exactly," Devin replied, "just need a little favor."

As he was saying it Dillon and GG lugged the heavier of the two now fully human demons up to the mouth of the cave. "Holy shit what did you do to those guys?" Zach exclaimed.

Devin shrugged, "To be fair, they aren't exactly guys. These are the demons that were guarding the gate. As soon as they came out of hell a disguise morph kicked in."

Hannah had joined them at the cave mouth by now, "OK, so what exactly did you do to those demons who look a lot like a fat guy and a skinny guy?"

"Heroin and holy water in a tranquilizer dart. They'll be out for mucho hours. Which leads to the favor I want to ask. Please dump these two in opposite ends of wherever. Just as far away as you can get them in say two hours, and leave 'em there. In case we need to come back out this way, I don't want to run into them guarding the gate and pissed off at us."

"Ummm......" Hannah began.

"Sure," said Nate stepping up to join them. "Hannah, help me with one, Zach, I suppose you can pretty easily handle the thin one by yourself."

"Oh, oh ok," Zach said walking over to grab his demon.

"One thing, before you take them," said GG. He quickly patted down the fatter of the two before his hand came out of a pocket with a finger bone which he put back in its pouch, "They were still on gate guard duty even with this. Totally wasted on them."

"So, I guess this is goodbye again," Dillon said.

"Yep, good luck," Zach grunted as he picked up the fallen skinny demon, who was even nattily attired in a nice suit as the disguise spell took further hold.

Hannah quickly ran over to Dillon and kissed him quickly, "Love you babe, but if we hang around someone's going to ask something. We'll try and get back and check on you before we all go back to Nate's"

"Oh, yeah, right," Dillon replied before turning to follow GG and Devin back into the cave.

In less time than their first pass, they were once again standing at the gate to hell. Well one of the gates to hell, GG had explained that there were quite a few of them and that this was a minor one that wasn't even on many of the incredibly inaccurate maps of hell. Which explained why it had been left to those two chunderheads to guard. In all honesty, GG further supposed, hell's administration, such as it was, had most likely completely forgotten about this one.

GG went through first, followed closely by Devin. Dillon took a deep breath as he peered into the darkness on the other side. This was it; this was the Alice Cooper record coming to life, he was about to go to hell. He couldn't help himself; he closed his eyes as he stepped over the threshold. Despite watching Devin and GG pass through with no ill effects, some small part of him expected it to hurt for some reason. He opened his eyes to discover that GG and Devin were already striding up to another door in the distance. He gaped at what clearly looked like a standard office door in the distance. "Why is this here if we've already gone through the gate?" he managed.

"They put it in years later, they needed something to fit the general atmosphere of this level of hell," GG explained.

"Which is?"

"Bookkeeping kid, this level is hell's bookkeeping department," Devin grinned back at him.

"Quite," GG sniffed. "Demons learn from you, you know. Humans come up with all kinds of things that the demons themselves aren't nearly clever enough to. One of them is the mind-numbing tedium that's involved in office work. The shuffling papers with no real need or meaning from one place to another over and over again, the team-building exercises, the just.... all of it. When what you people were up to was discovered centuries ago, hell decided it needed a proper bookkeeping department. Souls who were perpetual layabouts, artists, musicians, playwrights, anyone who had managed some freedom from the mechanisms of industry in life are consigned here for eternity."

"So, they really have records on every soul in hell, huh?" Devin asked.

"In theory. I mean there's paperwork, and I suppose now there are computer files as well, but good luck finding anything. After all, it is staffed with musicians, artists, and playwrights," GG shrugged.

"But you've been to this level before, right?" asked Dillon.

"Well, I came out this way, but even before that, my master would send me up here on occasion to see if I could find something out he wanted to know. I don't know why, they'd say they would have the file waiting for me, then I'd get here and they'd say they lost it." GG was quiet for a long moment before saying, "Actually come to think of it, even if Moraspus protected me from the worst torments hell had to offer while I tutored Dan....it is still hell. I think he sent me up here out of sheer mischief on his part."

"Now that that's settled, let's get it over with," Devin said striding across the empty chamber towards the door.

"We need to try and get our hands on some papers when we get inside," GG said as he scampered after him. "Nobody will even notice us after that hopefully."

"You think?" Dillon asked as he caught up.

"Yes, everyone carries paperwork around in this level of hell, they're all hoping nobody notices them. Paper denotes busy, and you need to look busy in case somebody thinks you're enjoying yourself."

Devin pulled the door open, neon light flooded through. Somehow it managed to be dim and lifeless instead of the crisp and bright they expected. Dillon looked over their shoulders towards what lay beyond and put a knuckle in his mouth to suppress a cry of terror. Even Devin, a man who seemed phased by nothing, developed a notable slump to his shoulders.

"Horrible, isn't it?" GG said quietly.

They came out at a short set of steps leading down to hell proper. Stretching out in front of them was an endless sea of cubicles. All covered by the same carpeted material, something that wasn't quite brown, nor quite steel gray, which somehow managed to subdue the neon lights that came from the air itself, turning the whole expanse into a depressing uniform morass. People could be seen shuffling down the aisles back and forth to the various workstations. Their shoulders were slumped, they all wore what had been white dress shirts that were now stained to almost blend into their surroundings. Almost all of them carried stacks of paper as they went. A few unfortunates were forced to push carts, all of the wheels managed to squeak and rattle in an irritating manner. Phones rang making a muted noise that seemed to come from every direction at once, giving the appearance that no one was answering any of them, probably because nobody knew which phone, if any, was actually ringing.

"This is the most modern section of this plane, there are older sections with actual steno pools somewhere, even some with legitimate scribes," GG explained as they stood there taking it all in.

"If this is the modern section, why don't they use computers? Why all the paper?" Dillon asked.

"All of the computers are Packard Bell; I am to understand that's bad?"

Dillon made a retching sound.

"Anyway," GG continued, "let's make for the files and records department where they keep the hard copies. We're most likely to find some unattended paper there. If we try to take any from someone the souls will attack. Punishment for losing a scrap of paper is severe, something called an Annual Personal Assessment."

Dillon and Devin shuddered.

"Why didn't you tell us to bring some with us?" Devin asked.

"It has to look official if we're stopped. If we just had a blank stack of papers, it would draw attention to us immediately. Don't worry, that department isn't too terribly far from the entrance, closer than the way down to the next level, that's for certain," GG reassured them.

"Won't anyone try and stop us?" Dillon asked.

"The souls will ignore us for the most part, nobody except the worst bootlick among them wants to attract the attention of one of the supervising demons. They don't want to risk being swept off for something called a 'virtual meeting.' As long as we don't run into any actual demons, we should be fine. Once we get the papers, barring bad luck, we should be able to move freely."

They began their way cautiously down the hallway, GG in front. He had been correct, the souls that moved from station to station treated them like objects instead of other people, carefully stepping out of their way to avoid them. Dillon couldn't help but notice that some of the souls here did look at them, but every time all their group got by way of recognition was a tight rictus of a smile and a nod of the head. There was no real acknowledgment of them as actual individual fellow souls at all in those expressions, just a vacant-headed nod like it was something they had been instructed to do whether they wanted to or not. Each set of eyes were haunting, gleaming brightly with either terror or misery possibly gone to madness. It was hard to tell for sure if those were the fake grins of an average office or a manifestation of lunacy.

GG took a series of twists and turns as he went. Thankfully, he seemed to know exactly where he was headed, and both Devin and Dillon were glad for it, because if they had been asked both of them would have admitted to being a little lost already. It was just the endless sameness of the place, row after row, aisle after aisle of boring cubicles filled with boring people doing boring things. Nothing could be used as a landmark in a place like this, not even the occasional conference rooms, since they all looked identical to the last one as well.

They were just passing another of the conference rooms when suddenly the door burst open. Before they could even really react, hands grabbed each of them by the arm and dragged them inside. Devin got out, "What in the hell?" without any intentional irony whatsoever when the doors slammed shut.

What awaited them were five rather grubby-looking souls. One of them had the sleeves torn off of his dress shirt for starters. One of them had his tie wrapped around his head. Before he could stop himself, Dillon said to the one with the tie, "Did you hurt your head?"

The man ignored the question instead responded with one of his own, "Did the Revolution send you?"

"Revolution?" Devin said carefully moving slightly towards the door.

There was silence for a moment.

"Look you're testing me, OK, I get why you would, but we spotted you easy. And if we did, trust me, the demons will soon enough. If you don't want to be doing roundtables and number analysis for the rest of eternity, you'll need to trust us to help with your mission!" said head-tie.

"And you are?" Dillon asked, joining Devin in imperceptibly moving back towards the door.

"We're the SLA!" said one of them who was wearing a trench coat, and a heated, overexcited expression blazing out from under his long dark bangs.

"The Symbionese Liberation Army?" Devin asked, his eyebrows shooting up, "I mean I figured you guys for hell but...."

"I told you SLA had been used before Don!" growled one of the revolutionaries who had a green mohawk that clashed with his dress shirt, even if the sleeves had been torn off.

"Puke, it doesn't matter now," head-tie replied, cutting off the argument between bangs and mohawk. "The important thing is, these guys have to be with the rebellion! We're finally going to get a mission!"

Dillon was about to say something, but Devin stilled him by putting his hand on his arm. He looked at the spokes-tie-around-his-head-guy and said, "Look, who the hell are you guys? More importantly, how do we know you're good enough."

That set the mouthpiece alight, he almost bounced up and down with repressed glee, turning to his four compatriots, "See! I told you these guys were with the rebellion, didn't I? I mean look at how they're dressed!"

"And you are?" GG pressed.

"Well, we were calling ourselves the SLA, the Soul Liberation Army, but I guess we'll need to think of something else now. I'm Don," the one with the bangs waved.

"And what is it you do?" GG asked with a tone of voice that suggested he was working at a frayed conversational string here.

"We're part of the rebellion! To get rid of the demons!" the one with the head tie replied with enthusiasm.

"You tell him, Mitch!" Puke added.

The one now successfully identified as Mitch's shoulders slumped a little bit, "Puke, are you just going to tell them all of our names? I thought we agreed on code names, I don't call you Bobby, do I?"

"Hey! I didn't tell them Leonard or William's name, did I?" to prove his point he stabbed his finger at one man wearing a waistcoat with a bristling white beard and another wearing a billowing poet's shirt.

"Until now that is," Mitch practically hissed.

"Oh yeah, sorry Mitch," Puke/Bobby said after he realized what he'd done.

Devin seeing the tension building between the little revolutionary clique tried to lighten the mood, "So, have you had any success?"

Mitch's face lit up, "Well, we liberated this conference room!"

"Yeah, that cleaning staff couldn't wait to get out of here when we showed up," Puke enthused.

"So....umm how do you know that there's a revolution at all?" Dillon asked cautiously.

"Oh yeah, that's easy. My buddy Adam had to go on a mission for them and he needed my help," Mitch supplied.

"A mission?" GG asked with the same tone as Dillon.

"Yeah, he told me all about it! He said he needed me to cover his desk while he was away. He never did come back, so I figured that with the loss of Adam the revolution would need recruits. That's when I convinced these guys," Mitch explained. "Already we're winning, just yesterday we liberated this conference room from our demon oppressors!"

"As long as they don't come back for it any time soon," GG and Dillon thought in almost total unison.

Devin's eyes got a sudden twinkle in them, "Don't tell anyone, but we are here to free someone from a powerful demon. We could use some help."

"All right! I knew it! Anything at all!"

"We need to go to the records department so we're carrying official paperwork. You could take us there," GG explained.

"I don't know man," Puke said suddenly turning cagey on them, "it ain't far, but how can we know we can trust these guys."

"Of course, you could just lend us your papers if that would be easier," Devin supplied smoothly.

Any distrust the group of revolutionaries might have had about the three of them paled in comparison to their inherent fear of being without their paperwork. The mere thought of giving it to someone else sent shivers down all of their spines. Just the thought of filling out those questions...." Where do you see yourself in five years?" "What do you think is the biggest asset you bring to hell?"

"Ummm...." said Puke.

"Ahhhhh...." Leonard added.

"Errrrr...." William concurred.

"Ehhhhh...." Don reiterated.

"The archives it is!" Mitch concluded emphatically. The look of relief that spread over the faces of the other revolutionaries was noticeable. Upper management, the bane of uprisings everywhere had done the work for Devin more easily than martial law.

"All right, we're decided, you guys go first of course," Devin said quickly hoping to catch them off balance.

"Why us?" Puke asked quickly, showing more intelligence than Devin had given him credit for.

Dillon rode to the rescue, "Well, we've never been to this part of hell before obviously. This is your home turf, we wouldn't want to hog the glory of the mission, would we? What kind of guests would we be if we did that?"

Devin looked at the kid with admiration, stroking their egos never would have occurred to him. But looking back at the five-member underground he saw it was working. The fear that their faces had shown just a moment before was being replaced with the same gung-ho psychopathic expression that seemed to be Mitch's base state. Not only would they go for being human shields, now they were going to actually be into the idea!

"Good thinking!" Mitch grunted. Turning to his compatriots he said, "All right men, we're out in front, remember, don't make eye contact with anyone in the halls if you can help it, if you kick a demon right behind the hoof, they tend to slip giving you valuable seconds to flee, and if we do run into a demon this mission is boned so get back here as soon as you can!"

There had been better battle plans, and war cries than that, but it seemed to have the desired effect on his troops, such as they were.

Chapter 14

"Do you know what sounds like an exciting career?
OFFICE WORK!"-absolutely no one, ever

Back out in the hallway, Dillon was impressed. Devin had managed, with a little help, to manipulate the revolutionaries into being an advanced warning system for them. Not only that, they hadn't even thought to ask to look in the bags the three of them were carrying. Four of the five revolutionaries had ranged out in front of them looking for potential trouble. For some reason, Puke had decided to hang back and was currently trying to chat up Dillon.

"So yeah man! I was there, Tompkins Square man, right in the thick of it!" Puke enthused.

"You mean the yuppie park in Manhattan Mumford and Sons did a song about?"

"What?"

"I don't know what it's about, I mean I don't listen to hipster old-timey music, but yeah, they did a song about it. I think it was a love song," Dillon shrugged.

"It's not about the riots?"

"What riots?"

Puke looked crestfallen, "Wow man, that and being in a band had been the two biggest things in my life... I mean I was there in 88..."

"1988? But you wouldn't be that old? Wait, how did you die?" Dillon asked in surprise.

"Don't want to talk about it," Puke mumbled.

"Aww c'mon, how bad could it be? Anyway, why not tell me, it's not like it can be any worse than being stuck here, right?"

"I got kicked in the head by a horse."

"Where?"

"In NYC."

"Ok... how did you get kicked in the head by a horse in New York City?"

Puke was quiet for just a moment before answering, "You know those carriages they have in the city that go around the park?"

"Ummm, yeah," Dillon responded with a horrible foreboding as to where this was going.

"Well, I thought it was cruel to keep them like that, so I went to liberate one. So, when the driver was off getting a can of Sprite from a vendor, I slipped in through the reins behind the horse and....."

"Kicked in the head by a horse in New York City...." Dillon breathed.

"Yeah," Puke said quietly.

"Noble cause?"

"Fuck horses," Puke spat.

They walked in silence for a bit, there seemed nothing that Dillon could add to that conversation. How do you even respond to, "Fuck horses"? Do you try and slip a joke, like, "Literally? Ha-ha!" Would you be willing to leave it there without the "Ha-ha" so they knew you were joking? Dillon decided to just let it lapse, which was probably smartest.

The other four had vanished around a corner just a little while before. Dillon was just speeding up to catch back up with them after falling behind in contemplation of the horse quandary when suddenly Mitch burst around the corner running at full speed. He was soon followed by the other three in short order.

"FUCK!FUCK!DEMONS!RUN!FUCK!" he yelled as he whisked by them.

Before Dillon could react, Puke had whirled and was running off in the direction of the others. In the distance, they could hear an enormous clopping noise coming towards them from around the corner that could only be the aforementioned demons. Or horses, in which case, fuck them.

"In here," GG said with unperturbed calm as he jerked them towards a large nearby closed door. Before Dillon could even begin to form a protest, GG had dragged them through the large double doors to their right.

When he recovered his footing, Dillon could only gape at what was in front of them. Filing cabinets rose up massively, continuing upward until they vanished from sight. It seemed endless in every direction as the rows of filing cabinets vanished in the distance. Around the walls of what he could see of the endless chamber, enormous piles of paper rose to the sky, meticulously stacked, rising up quite possibly all the way to the next level of hell above them.

"Idiots walked right by it," Devin grinned.

"Quickly, against the wall by the door in case the demons look in," GG pointed to one of the empty spaces on either side of the door.

Dillon was still in awe of the place, forcing Devin to grab him and drag him along with them. Dillon stumbled a bit as Devin released him. His arm windmilled for a second to try and regain his balance until he bumped into one of the enormous stacks of paper. He looked up to see the whole thing begin to teeter away from them.

"Oh...." Dillon breathed.

"Shit," Devin added when he saw what was about to happen.

The sound as it crashed away from them was loud but thankfully muffled slightly by the nature of what was crashing. There was a brief moment of silence until the next stack fell, and then the next, and then...... there were a lot of stacks here is the general drift the author wants you to get. They stood there in shock as papers fluttered down around them, staring with disbelief at the twenty-pound copy-ready carnage they had just created.

GG broke the silence, "Quick, get under some of the paper, those demons that were chasing the others are bound to check on this!"

Shaken from their shock Devin and Dillon followed GG's lead and dove into what had been an enormous stack of papers moments before being reduced to a massive heap. They hunkered down in the muffled cocoon, waiting while the increasingly further away booms continued. Dillon was fighting off a sneeze, all of them were suffering from numerous paper cuts but short of jumping into a filing cabinet, this was the only shelter available.

They heard the door creek open and light came in through a crack.

"Bless it all to heaven Plogg! I told you those steel boots of yours were a dumb idea!" a voice came from the crack.

Another voice slightly further away said, "What does that have to do with anything?"

The first voice let out a sigh, "They shake the blessed halls when you run! You set off a paperlanche!"

"Maybe it was one of the guys we wuz chasin'?"

"I can still hear them running down the hall and they don't land that hard. Naw, it was those big stupid boots of yours!"

"What are we gonna' do Alezbron? I don't want to get in trouble again! It'll be the tar pits for me for sure!" the further away voice practically wailed.

"You wanna' get blamed for this?"

"Of course not!"

"Well then, here's what happens next. We, are gonna close this door, and we are gonna go chase those souls far away from here. If anyone asks, we were nowhere near records. When they find it, well some poor suckers are gonna have to reorganize everything, we just need to make sure it ain't us."

The door shut with some finality. Over the booming paper avalanches in the distance, they could hear the heavy tread of the one demon's boots fading away. GG spoke first, "Well, I do believe we shall have no issues finding a few stacks of paper in here, so that's a positive outcome at least."

Zach had dumped his demon by the side of the road somewhere in the wilds of Milford PA. He had found a place where there were plenty of trees so he could drag him back a bit from the road where he had parked at a pull-off near a small stream. He thought he was being a decent person leaving the thing near water in case it woke up thirsty. The guy looked thin enough as was.

In the other vehicle, Hannah now suspected Nate of having a much better sense of humor than he let on, since he insisted they dump theirs near the former town of Foul Rift New Jersey. It was an ideal place to get rid of their cargo, it was absolutely the middle of nowhere, and Hannah couldn't help but laugh when Nate informed her of where they were.

They had returned to Nate's house to spend the night. Mainly they watched TV, nobody really wanted to talk about what hovered over all of them like a shroud. There was no way to talk about it without letting their fears getting the better of them, there were just way too many fears to choose from, one was bound to sneak through. It was also hard to bring up easily, you can't just say, "Boy I hope they aren't being tortured by demons at this exact moment," without coming off like Debbie Downer.

Today they were going back to Lambertville. Nate wanted to wander around a bit to reassure friends that while yes, the fire was tragic, once they had a new building, they had enough stock stashed back at the house that they were sure to want to reopen. The oddball little shops and their owners formed a community being next to each other all day every day, and when a store closed, it was like a death in the family. Nate couldn't bear the thought of his friends worrying on his behalf, so he insisted they head over to let his fellow shop keeps know he was fine.

Going from store to store felt like being the survivor of the tragedy. Hugs, promises to call, "If you need something" and somber tones of voice. At one point Zach leaned over to Hannah, "Well, so far I feel about as useful as tits on a bull."

She shrugged, "That's kind of a good thing though, right? I mean if we have to leap into action, things have gone really pear-shaped right?"

"Point."

They were standing outside of one of the shops, Nate was talking to a few of his friends when Hannah suddenly gripped Zach's arm. "Hey buddy, who do you see over there?" she asked pointing towards someone walking casually across the street.

"Uhh.... why do I doubt that is Jason Mamoa again?" Zach said slowly.

"Yeah, and I doubt it's Dillon either, I was just about to start screaming at him for coming back and not telling us," Hannah nodded. She tugged on Nate's sleeve while pointing with her other hand, "Nathaniel, do you see who it is across the street?"

"Dan?"

"We gotta get out of here, right now," Hannah said stalking off with Nate and Zach in tow.

"I guess absence really does make the heart grow fonder," Zach said as he followed along.

"What do you mean?" Hannah demanded.

"You saw Aquaman yourself a few days ago."

It had taken a while to clear the dust off of themselves and to stop the worst of the bleeding from the paper cuts before they were ready to set out again. Now that they had what could be considered the ultimate camouflage in this level of hell, lots of paperwork, they were ready to bluff their way the rest of the way out of here. They had officially joined the drone set, and hopefully, nobody would look any further than their armor of neatly stacked piles of paper to think that normal worker drones shouldn't be dressed like that, or be carrying backpacks and duffle bags.

GG assured them again before they opened the door. "I know it seems stupid, but as long as I've been carrying paperwork, I've never even been so much as asked a question up here."

"If it's stupid and it works, it isn't stupid," Devin agreed.

Dillon was shocked at how well it indeed had worked as they started walking down the carpeted halls again. GG had been exactly right. The most they were getting from anyone were those sheepish facial expressions that translated in every culture to, "Work. It sucks, huh?" The body language had changed, the souls on this level reverted to their base states of enforced disinterest, even further than your average office. Soul crushed, humorless, but trying to make the best of it. Most coffee mugs and the attempts at humor they have on them are driven by this damned demolished state of the human soul. Anyone who has seen a coffee mug emblazoned with the phrases, "Wake Me When Its Friday" or "Work Coffee Sleep Repeat" instinctively knows that the owner of said mug is profoundly damaged inside by that point and that they don't even cry anymore, they don't see the point.

One thing he had noticed, they were zigging and zagging through the offices, they hadn't gone in a straight line for over 100 yards since they'd gotten out of records. He decided to ask, "What's with all the turns?"

"We're trying to avoid the offices," GG replied.

"Isn't this all offices? I mean that's the point of this level of hell right, an eternal office job?"

"I think he means private offices, as in, likely to hold a demon supervisor. Which lends all new terror to being called into the boss's office, you know?" surmised Devin.

"Exactly right. Right now, we pass the smell test to the other drones as just additional tormented souls. I don't want to risk that subterfuge under the watchful eye of a demon. One would be sure to spot that at least you two are fully alive eventually, no matter how slow it was on the uptake. I would probably confuse it, in fact, I'm not sure what my status is truly," GG lectured.

As if on cue, they turned another corner and almost walked directly into exactly the kind of demon they'd been trying so hard to avoid all this time. The monster looked at first to be dressed in some form-fitting leather armor, black as night, with lines like the fibers of muscles carved into it. It wasn't until closer examination that you realized, that was just its skin. Dillon would have guessed it was wearing an equally black horned helmet, with a smooth visor covering everything but a slit for the mouth and eye sockets that flames roared out of. But again, on closer examination, it was just the things head right down to the enormous curling horns that angled from the temples ending in razor-sharp points. For some reason, it was wearing a red, and blue checkered tie. It was also carrying a coffee mug that said, "You Don't Have To Be Damned To Work Here, But It Helps!" The sight of the mug made all of them shiver with fear.

"You dopes lost? You don't look like any of mine," the thing hissed while looming over them.

GG was the one who recovered first, he kept his eyes averted as he stammered out, "We are working for our demon lord, Danasdius. Our mission is of some importance, so if we could just be on our way, we'll stop wasting your precious time."

The thing chuckled, it sent little puffs of fire out of its mouth as it exhaled in amusement, "Moraspus finally made his kid do some blessed dishonest work? I'll be canonized and double dipped in holy water!" The creature laughed some more at that before he continued, "Well, sorry to break it to you, you work for me now!"

"What?" GG gasped.

"If that kid hasn't learned the rules about turf enough that he's sending souls into my sector, he deserves to be understaffed for a while. Don't worry, he wants ya' back he can come see me about it, little punk won't have the guts. Nobody messes with Furstatius, or as you can call me Master. Now, come with me, I won't be having my souls dressed like fucking bums!"

"Ummm Furnace Face?" Devin said with his back partially turned.

"WHAT DID YOU CALL ME??!!!!!" the demon bellowed causing GG and Dillon to stumble back.

"Fuckface McGillicutty," Devin said turning back to the demon. There were two puffs of air, not unlike the sound when Devin had snuck up behind the demons at the gate. "You were boring me already."

Furstatius gawked at them in disbelief for a moment. Then he looked down at the two tufts sticking out of his thick leathery hide. "You little prick...." he began, before he slowly and ponderously fell flat on his face. The flames began to shoot out of his ears, they had turned a sickly green.

"You shouldn't waste those," GG chided.

"This would have taken all day, it's already taking us forever to get where we need to go and we haven't gone through one damned level yet," Devin shrugged.

"Will that work on any demon?" Dillon asked as he began to try to move around the prone form, who was snoring loudly.

"Nope, this guy and the ones at the gate are pikers, this one thought he was hotter shit than he was," Devin explained as he put the gun back into his jacket. He set down his stack of papers before saying, "Hold on a second."

Before GG or Dillon could say anything, Devin walked quickly back the way they had come. Dillon was about to call after him when he vanished into one of the multitudes of cubicles. They could just hear a muffled argument taking place a moment later. It was followed by the sounds of a scuffle that caused both of them to start in that direction. There was a loud smacking noise that caused both of them to consider running when Devin suddenly reappeared grinning widely.

In his hands were a black sharpie marker and a stapler. He reached down and scooped up a sheet that he'd been carrying, put it against the wall, and quickly wrote something on it that Dillon couldn't quite make out. A moment later Devin bent over the demon and stapled the paper to the thing's back.

Dillon looked down before they left. In large black letters Devin had written, "Demon is taking a lengthy drugged nap. HOURS AT LEAST. Completely helpless at the moment. Do NOT stab, kick, bury, mutilate, run through a paper shredder, slice bits off of with a letter opener, set on fire, pee on, poop on, or in any way damage this demon, since he will not be able to do a damned thing about it. - The Resistance"

"Oh, that is mean," said Dillon as they hurried on their way.

"Funny though," Devin replied.

"Oh, I'm not saying it isn't, just making an observation that it was also mean."

Moraspus watched as his legions consisting of the demons and the damned marched across the territory of Abbachak the Perturbing. He was not at war with Abbachak. It was just that when Moraspus and Tunsil the Hefty had agreed that the only way to finally decide who owned the ornamental lava fountain that touched both of their properties was an enormous war involving thousands of souls being driven forward by demons to be ground up in a bloody conflict. They had also decided that it would be pretty stupid to have that war in the area where their territories touched, since that was where the fountain was and it would probably be destroyed in the conflict. Which of course would make the whole thing kind of pointless really. What they had further agreed upon through emissaries traveling between their palaces was that Abbachak was a bit of a dick, and who cared what happened to his lands? The conflict on earth that Moraspus had been interested in had wrapped up pretty quickly, so thank his Satanic lord and father that Tunsil had popped up with this. The universe existed to provide Moraspus these little amusements, at least in Moraspus' opinion, and frankly, he had no time for anyone else's, especially not Abbachak's.

Currently, he was in his tent watching his various demonic underlings amuse themselves by tormenting the poor soul Abbachak had sent round to complain about Moraspus' troops setting his veranda ablaze. This had gone about as well as Abbachak's previous calls for them to "Not have your stupid war here." and his request that Moraspus' troops, "Stop eating the horses from my private stables." and the one asking if they could "Please stop raping my fish, koi fish are quite difficult to get in hell you know and very sensitive." Frankly, this was exactly WHY they were having the war here, so they could do all those things on someone else's property. You don't want to risk doing that kind of thing to your own war horses, just common sense.

Moraspus was beginning to consider that it might be time to get back home. Tunsil had agreed a month ago that the fountain was probably Moraspus' after looking at the maps again. At this point really what they were doing was tormenting Abbachak for the fuck of it. And while that was enjoyable, that had to be admitted to, he worried about the hunt for his son, and how it would progress without him constantly manning the whip. It wasn't that he didn't trust his underlings...well no, it was exactly that he didn't trust his underlings. This was hell, nobody was down here for being a stand-up and trustworthy kind of guy, and demons were just built underhanded, it was in the job description.

He was loath to admit it, but he was also worried about his son. He'd sent demons to search for the boy, there had been some results, and then he'd been called away on business. OK, maybe it was also pleasure for him, but that was the business he was in. For all he knew the kid could be sitting at the palace right now, awaiting his wrath. And it would be a hell of wrath, within reason of course. You couldn't obliterate the very essence of kin, demons didn't breed easily, it would be wasteful. But that little mister would learn a lesson about leaving hell without permission and not telling anyone where he was going. It would be millennia until that kid even got let off the grounds if Moraspus had his say, and he absolutely was going to have his say. Moraspus wasn't ready to admit, even to himself, that he worried about the kid because he cared for his son, but he would share with everyone his feelings on being disobeyed.

No, wars were fun and all, that's why they had them, but he had other irons in the fire almost ready to plunge into flesh. He would have to wrap this up and head for home soon. He still wanted to see if he could get Abbachak to tear his horns from his head in frustration, so give it a couple of more days. His neighbor had a collection of blasphemous works of art and literature going back centuries, Moraspus was wondering if there was a way, he could steal them and get the lot blessed back on earth by a Priest or a Cardinal and maybe have the more blasphemous phrasings reworded into children's nursery rhymes before he gave them back to Abbachak and turned for home. The screams from the annoying demon would be legendary.

There had been plenty of more offices to wander through after they left the demon. This section that they were going through now was clearly an older one. What they were seeing now was that instead of cubicles there were large steno pools, vast rooms where people were forced to sit at typewriters. Dillon was kind of in awe of it, really in his entire life, he had only ever seen an actual typewriter when it had been for sale at the flea market.

He'd never seen the clunky-looking black phones that people were using.

The clacking noise of the typewriters being patiently hammered was so intensive and numerous that it managed to fill the air like a swarm of very angry bees. Phones rang. People moved mainly from desk to desk, and rarely in the halls at this point. The demons themselves ensconced themselves in offices attached to the large open areas, their names stenciled and etched onto frosted glass in burning fire, separating them from the souls in their care.

"Wow, it's just like an old movie," Devin said smiling, "I keep expecting the whole thing to turn into black and white."

"What are you talking about?" GG asked with a flustered tone.

"This type of stuff is before me and the kid's time. I've only seen this kind of thing in pictures and movies," Devin shrugged.

"They were in black and white," Dillon added helpfully.

"So, I gathered," GG sniffed, feeling very keenly that all of this "stuff" was all futuristic from his view of time and the world.

"I wonder who all those phone calls are even from," Dillon asked.

"I'd bet telemarketers mainly," Devin replied.

It had taken far too long to even get through this one layer of hell, there was still one waiting for them between where they stood and where they needed to go. This type of conversation was the type you have in that situation, it means nothing, just idle banter to keep your mind off what it really wanted to focus on. Which in this case was part wanting to get on with the task at hand and part turning around and running for the exit in the distance behind them.

While they had been walking GG led them around another corner. This led to a more or less empty hallway with a wooden door at the end of it. A sizzling and popping sign hung over it, it spelled out -X-T, since the E and the I had burnt out.

"Well, here we are at last," GG actually smiled as he headed off towards the door.

The door opened into what almost looked like a hotel lobby. There was wood paneling, white and black checkered tile floor, even potted plants that were dead. What caught Dillon's eye was the elevators directly across from them, Dillon exclaimed, "All right! Elevators! We can just skip the next level and head straight down!"

"No, we can't. We'll be taking the escalators down to the next level, which we will then navigate through to the next set of escalators that leads towards our final destination," GG replied.

"But why can't we take the fast way?"

"Because it isn't the fast way at all, is it?" Devin interjected. "They break down, don't they?" Devin had years of experience dealing with demons, he had begun to see how their minds worked. He was positive from just looking at the sealed elevator doors that it was a trap to catch the lazy out with. You'd be tempted into them before you probably got stuck in the damned things for millennia, slowly losing your mind.

"Indeed," GG nodded. "Without a pass from a higher demon, anybody who uses them soon wishes they hadn't. They exist to provide a false hope for an escape from this place, so they're doubly cruel. They even have "Earth" on one of the buttons, that gets you stuck the longest. Thankfully, if we have to leave the hard way to get out of here coming back, well we'll have an actual demon with us, won't we? I had a pass, which my Master had not rescinded yet to get up here faster, but I would expect he has corrected that oversight by now."

"So why are we willing to trust the escalators?" Dillon demanded.

"Well, if escalators break, they become stairs. We can still get to where we're going," Devin shrugged. "All right, let's hop on our slow train to hell. Well, deeper into hell at least."

As they walked through the lobby, it immediately became apparent that there was some sort of optical illusion going on here. The space was much longer and larger than it first appeared when they walked in. First, they passed an enormous set of stairs going down, the wood for the banisters looked ancient and black, Gargoyles perched in place on either side. Thankfully they were just statues, and not the real things, which would have been one more inconvenience in an already inconvenient trip.

"Huh? Guess he didn't make it all up after all," Devin said pointing at the stairs.

"Who made what up?" Devin asked.

"Carved into the one banister."

Dillon read the words aloud, "Dante era qui?"

"Dante was here," GG supplied.

"A vandal," chuckled Devin, "good thing he was already in hell at the time."

GG just shrugged and lead them on further into the echoing hall. He paused near the elevators themselves where a clacking wooden escalator vanished downward, "Even I know there are more modern designs for these things than this, but it is hell, never put off until tomorrow what you can avoid fixing today. Shall we go gentlemen? And you might as well sit down, it's going to be a long ride down. Still, this beats the steps."

Chapter 15

"Keep on riding me and they're going to be picking iron out of your liver. And, and potassium out of your pancreas, yeah, and Vitamin D out of your spleen.... look, I forgot where I was going with this." - Wilbur Cook, "The Mallomar Falcon"

Everyone was relieved when they were finally back at the house. The entire ride they couldn't shake the feeling that there was something evil following them. Nobody argued it when Hannah had demanded they leave town immediately. After seeing the succubus at her work and Hannah had rapidly explained what she was sure it was, that was more than good enough. Nobody had talked much on the drive home either, each of them was working through their shock at seeing the thing so close to home, each seeing something different in their own way. They had thought maybe there might be a problem while the rest of the group were in hell, but deep down, all of them doubted that Nate would be an important enough loose end for hell to bother with. Seeing the creature so close to the store was serious. The thing might not be here for Nate, but it was so close to the house and had been right by the store, so you almost had to assume it was. It was like having your boss staying at the same hotel you were at for a kink convention. You don't know that he's going to find out why you're there, you don't know he suspects you, but you're already frustrated and checking out anyway.

"What are we going to do?" Zach demanded, his voice showing clear annoyance at this new hellish intrusion.

"Well, I for one, am not sitting around like some lame-ass damsel in distress here," Hannah huffed. "There has to be something we can do to stop her, or it, or whatever you want to call it."

They both looked at Nate. In theory, he was their charge here, they were basically supposed to be keeping him out of trouble. Of course, he was the one who had actually been in hell, so he had the best cause to want to avoid any entanglements with hell's minions now. Even annoyed as she was, Hannah was probably willing to concede that getting into a fight with a succubus might not constitute keeping him out of trouble. It was in reality; she was further willing to possibly admit that it might be viewed as kinda' the opposite of that. The more Hannah thought about it the more she wished she hadn't put Nate in this position by declaring she wanted to do something.

Nathaniel smiled slightly, "Well, Devin didn't take all of his magical weapons with him. I mean they left us stuff to protect ourselves with, didn't they? Why don't we rifle through them a bit and see if anything suggests itself?"

"How long is this going to take?" Dillon asked after what felt like a glacial epoch of listening to the steady clack of the escalator and the even lighter than the originals muzak versions of Christopher Cross songs playing in the ether around them. They had spent the length of three whole Peter Jackson films at least, maybe even the full

LOTR plus the Hobbit on this escalator already, which hadn't even gotten them through the cloud cover below them that completely shrouded the next layer of hell.

"Well, that should speed things up considerably," GG replied.

"How so?" Devin asked.

GG sighed, "Hell's sense of humor, you get used to it."

"Sense of humor?" Dillon pressed.

"While these escalators are meant to be functional and ferry demons and souls between layers of hell, it's still hell. Things have to be as weird and as almost humorously dysfunctional as possible."

"Like Florida," Devin smiled.

"I'll have to take your word for that. Anyway, as soon as the ride reaches high levels of annoyance, and only then, do you finally start actually approaching your destination, which will still be a comical distance away," GG explained.

"OK, more like the Jersey turnpike then," Devin smirked.

GG just gave him a sour look.

"So, what's this next level of hell going to be like," Dillon changed the subject.

"Yeah, what kind of demons do we have in store for us?" Devin asked.

GG was quiet for a long moment before saying, "None."

"What?" Devin and Dillon demanded in unison, which is one of those things that happen in life but most people are embarrassed by when it does. (though it happens a lot in this book for some reason-editor)

"You owe me a beer," Devin said punching Dillon in the arm lightly.

"We will have to be exceptionally careful and stick to alleyways and stay out of sight," GG said in a level voice.

"Huh? I thought you said there weren't any demons?" Dillon looked confused.

"There aren't, but there are also no rules. None, nothing is enforced, there is no governance, no rules, no regulations. The souls of those who used rules and regulations to bully others are trapped there with no rules at all. Demons only ever make an appearance when there is some attempt to create some form of governance so they can snatch away the offenders who lead the push. So instead of demons, which are powerful to be sure, you have lifelong repressed human beings completely free of every shackle they ever imposed on themselves, and completely unable to impose them on others. The most they are allowed is gangs," GG explained with a sick expression on his face.

"Sounds neurotic," Dillon said.

"More psychotic, and pretty damned dangerous," Devin added. "So, what's the game plan here Sparky, we just run like hell?"

"I hate to say it, but yes, mostly. Stick to alleys, stick to shadows, this is why I asked you to bring real guns. They're useless against demons, but hopefully, they have some effect on the souls of the humans trapped here."

"And if not?" Dillon said with a worried expression. Demons were one thing, they had rules that you could use against them, as convoluted as they could be. And so far, they had been able to use that to their advantage. Humans with none...

"If not, well then I suggest we learn to run faster," GG sighed.

They had left Patrick back in Dan's rooms to play video games. After an initial rough start, the man seemed to have become quite addicted to the things and had ended up being better than Dan at most of them. Dan actually felt kind of bad about that, those things weren't everywhere down here yet, they weren't that dated. They would be, oh they definitely would be, but how many of them would ever find their way into guys like Patrick's hands was still up in the air. Considering that Patrick had been brought in as a bait human for a demon prince to torture meant he probably didn't rank too high in the hell hierarchy. After Dan left, poor Patrick would probably completely lose access to his new love. In a weird way, long term, Dan had managed to torment Patrick after all.

Dan was walking the grounds with Thomas and Adrianna. It would look to the casual observer, and Dan had no doubt there were many of them on the grounds out of sight, that he was just taking his pet humans on a tour of the grounds. To a degree that was exactly what he was doing, they were pleasant enough company, and he needed to get out of the house anyway just to leave his room if for no other reason. It might look weird to the demons spying on him that he was being pleasant with them, but not remarkable or in need of reporting on in any way. They would probably decide that Dan could be trying to get their guards down only to crush their fragile souls by betrayal later, that was pretty standard demon stuff. It made a decent cover, because what they were really doing was venturing forth to spy around a bit. He needed to be absolutely certain as to what kind of spell was holding him in place specifically. It had to be specific to him, you couldn't operate the grounds if everyone was locked inside, so that narrowed down his choices as to what type of spell it was, at least that was a bit of help. Seeing it clearly at the edge of the grounds would tell him the rest.

Dan did not want to be here when his father got home, it promised to be unpleasant.

To make absolutely sure that he wasn't, he needed to know how to blow this spell, which meant understanding it. He had no doubt that it was Blurglesoth's spell, especially now, seeing it up close as he pretended to point out things of interest to Thomas and Adrianna as they went. Unfortunately doing what he really wanted to do, pounding Blurglesoth into a green slimy smear on one of the walls wouldn't undo the spell, it had been cast, it would live long after its caster was back down in the vats being reassembled. No, Dan needed to actually find a way past the spell itself, and if he had time after that then he could find something heavy to assault that smug prick Blurglesoth with.

The problem with fantasizing about what he'd do to his father's majordomo right now was, it was just that, fantasy. He was pretty sure he knew the spell to let him through the shield around the grounds, and that would be great if he had had any of the ingredients to make it. Higher demons normally didn't even need props or tools to do things, you wished it, and boom, there you go. There were limits and levels to what you could do depending on where you were in the hierarchy of hell, and the theory should go that a princeling, one of the royalty of hell like Danasdius, should be able to nuke anything the slug had come up with. Problem was Blurglesoth had known that, and he'd used tools to craft this spell putting it outside of even Dan's natural powers. But still, where there's a will there's a way. Now that he knew what he was up against, all Dan had to do to beat the spell was get on the other side of it to get the things he needed.... and as any hillbilly mechanic would say in this situation, "Well there's y'all's problem right thar!"

"Bet you could get rid of this spell with the right stuff, huh?" Thomas said as if reading his mind.

"Whu?" Dan came out of his thoughts with a jolt.

"Don't look so surprised, I've been here for a while, I know how these things work by now. Well, some of it. I got a lot of time being tortured by demons, you don't spend that much time being assaulted by magic, you don't pick up a thing or two," Thomas said looking straight ahead at the lightly shimmering shield.

"Fat lot of good it does me though, I could get out of this easily... if only I could get out," Dan grumbled.

"Well, I ain't trapped in here, none of us are, just you," Thomas chuckled, "we could go get what you need if you tell us where to find it."

"Why on earth would you do that for me? I mean... I'm a demon?" Dan demanded astonished at the suggestion.

Adrianna interrupted, "Not much of one really, you don't even look like one most of the time."

"That's the truth," Thomas added, "if I didn't know you were a demon, or why we'd been given to you, I'd think you were just one of the nicer souls I've met down here. Mind you, that's a pretty low bar, let's face facts, it's no surprise why most of the people down here came to be here."

"And you two, do you feel that you deserve to be here?" Dan asked, his voice dropping in volume as he asked.

Thomas actually chuckled, "Well, guess that depends on your definition of deserve I suppose. When I was young, well, I was young, and young men do a wonderful job of making fools of themselves. Bandits would ride into my village and the surrounding ones, and to my fool brain they seemed the bravest and the strongest men about since the men of my village fell all over themselves giving them what they wanted. Well, being a young fool, I tagged along one day when they rode out of town. Before too long, I figured out that what they really were, were just bullies, but the damage had been done. I might have saved myself if I'd repented, even to myself, but I just told myself that riding with them was only part of growing up and I didn't need to feel sorry about it. You live and learn.... well, not live, in point of fact. Guess it would be, die and learn."

After Thomas had finished talking, both men turned and looked at Adrianna expectantly. She managed to blush, which is a strong impulse to follow through with when you don't technically have a living heart, "Oh, very well. I discovered early on that I liked married men better than young ones. Stop yourself before you have any thoughts about lust. I might have liked it sometimes but that wasn't the goal. It was strictly mercenary; I most certainly coveted and took what wasn't mine."

"But why?" Dan asked, showing his innocence here.

"Well, they're housebroken by then, aren't they? They have the experience to know what impresses a girl, and the funds to do it with. Men my own age had nothing and only wanted one thing, and they fumbled about even doing that. A married man will buy you things, and the right things, they often even know the right things to do once they get you home. A girl needs to put food in the pantry and a roof over her head somehow. I was doing quite well for myself. Until, of course, a jealous wife got me drunk enough so she could chain me up and wall me in. Kept calling me 'Little Miss Fortunato' the entire time. Have to give the woman credit, she made a damned fine wall."

"So, you see," Thomas chuckled, "we have every reason to deserve to be here. But instead of the normal routine, torture, beauty product pyramid schemes, forcing us to work in customer service, and then blessedly back to physical torture again, you've actually treated us like friends. Well, at least not like victims, which is close enough if you ask me. So, yes, if you need some things from out there, we can go get it for you."

To prove their point Adrianna walked through the shimmering shield and stood on the other side, before quickly darting back.

Dan grinned widely, "Well all right then, let's go back so I can write up a list."

They had finally come through the clouds, which had soaked all of them to the bone, sticking with that, "Massive annoyance" theme that hell seemed to be operating under. Dillon wondered at that, they already tortured the souls down here, petty annoyances seemed so beneath the purported dignity and majesty of hell. Even the concept of hell seemed diminished with these low-watt grievances. But then, he considered, maybe the low watt annoyances brought you back to yourself enough that you could really appreciate the full-blown torture again instead of being able to lose yourself in white-hot pain being a constant. Maybe the comparison gave you the full effect of the actual tortures. Equally possible was that the demons running things were petty little shits.

What they were coming down towards looked for all the world like a regular city. Well, maybe not a regular city, maybe more of an overhead shot from some kind of crime-noir film from the forties, just not in black and white. It was like the whole "dark and dirty who knows what lurks here" city aspect was being played up considerably. The walls were stained with the grit and grime of a place that had never seen a pressure washer but had seen a lot of people, also, maybe there was a bit more trash than normal, that kind of thing. But other than looking a bit rough around the edges, it looked just like a normal city. A very empty normal city, even though it appeared to be daytime here. There were very few cars being driven anywhere, there were almost no pedestrians either. Like everyone was in hiding from something.

Something caught Devin's eye, "OK, this is definitely hell."

"You mean other than the fact that we know we're in hell? Some reason other than that?" Dillon joked.

"Yeah, look carefully at the cars," Devin pointed.

It took a minute for Dillon to spot what he meant, but when he did, it seemed so obvious. It also fit into the low-watt annoyance pastiche the place had going. Just about every car that he could readily identify parked on the streets had been manufactured somewhere between around 1973 and 1990 and they were all some of the worst cars that humanity had ever managed to produce. There were Yugos, Chevettes, Pintos, K Cars, Leyland P76s, Polonezs, Le Car's, and Cimarrons. At least, those were the ones Dillon had identified from scanning the multitude of parked cars, there were probably a plenitude of eastern European ones he didn't recognize. He could see why, to Devin especially, the automotive nightmare spreading out before them alone was a pit of hell in and of itself.

"Maybe that's why there isn't much traffic, none of them will start," Dillon shrugged.

GG nodded, "Partially, they will run eventually, but only after the driver has been reduced to tears trying to get it to work. But the reality is the people stay in because it's safer that way." He turned to look at his companions, "Have you ever fully considered it? No rules at all? While most people don't do horrible things because they just don't want to do horrible things.... many.... well, having rules and penalties are the only things that keep them from atrocities. Now imagine the kind of person who is so obsessed with rules and regulations that they make life hell for everyone around them. Maybe there was a reason for the obsession if you get my meaning. People stay inside because they know what evil lurks in the hearts of men, and they fear it. Demons would be redundant on this plane of hell. Things get repaired by magic, it always returns to what you see here, but sooner or later violence will erupt in the streets. I promise you that right now behind many of these closed doors, personal violence is erupting while we look at the walls that hide it."

"So, not a good place to look for real estate is what you're saying," Devin nodded.

The escalator was descending into another lobby area like the one they had left in the level of hell above. Unlike that lobby, this one looked like it belonged inside one of your less stylish flophouses. Graffiti covered all the walls, and trash rustled around the filthy abandoned tile floors. The door to the elevator had been ripped off to expose the empty shaft which glowed a baleful red even at this distance.

"Just like the last level, the way down from here and the way up from here are in completely different places. Hell is nothing if not inconvenient," GG said standing up to get ready to get off the clacking escalator as it jerked its way towards the floor.

"What I don't get, is why don't the denizens themselves leave the level they're cursed to?" Dillon asked as he got up himself.

"Simple, every soul here is convinced that as bad as it is here, the adjoining levels are worse. Rumor is quite popular here, but in this case, there's some truth to it. When a soul is caught on a level they shouldn't be on, they are brutally tortured and maimed. Instead of the healing process, most souls get so they'll be fresh for new torments later, those souls are left maimed and deposited on their original plane of hell, a miserable wretch trying to convince someone to finish the job so they can be put back together in the pits."

"A, 'get out of line and see what you get' living testament," Dillon nodded.

"Exactly."

GG led them off the escalator and hurried off to one side of the lobby, beckoning them to follow. Once he'd crossed the distance, he pressed himself against the wall indicating they should do the same, putting them out of the line of sight of the doors that led out. That was important because just like the elevator doors, these were each barely hanging from a hinge and wide open. There's just something about a lack of rules that makes people take it out on doors. A basic resentment in the mind of the lawless towards the concept of being kept out of somewhere always manifested itself. Either that, or it looked totally bad assed when you kicked them in, could go either way.

A series of gunshots rang in the distance, immediately followed by screaming.

"100 feet from the doors and across the intersection there is an alley. I suggest we run like hell while they're busy shooting at each other," GG said to them pointing at something they couldn't see from where they were behind him.

Before either of them could answer, GG was sprinting out the door. Dillon and Devin looked at each other in shock for a second. Devin shrugged and they both tore after the fleeing alchemist. Dillon was surprised to find that the building that housed something as important as the connection between levels of hell looked like nothing more special than a rundown tenement. He was also kind of surprised to find that Devin was leaving him in the dust thanks to his quick glance back. Re-focusing on running as if his life depended on it, which according to GG it did, he looked to see where the man could be headed and put on a little more speed to catch up with the bookseller.

Diagonally across the intersection they'd exited into, Dillon could just see GG's head peeking out of an alleyway that ran behind the buildings across the street. A moment later his arm waved at them, a gesture that was clearly telling them to hurry the hell up. Dillon might not have been a track star, but now that he knew where he was actually going, he could muster a decent turn of speed, so he kicked the afterburners on. If the native to hell's behavior was anything to judge by, he didn't want to stay in the open any longer than he needed to. If GG was acting scared rabbit about the place, well, he'd been here before.

As he ran, Dillon looked in every direction to see if their sudden appearance out of the building had risen any alarms from the locals. What he saw was actually kind of eerie, he didn't see anybody at all. It was like a movie set, or a zombie film, just empty streets. No vendors, no dog walkers, nobody. It was creepy, and it made him wish that he hadn't thought of that zombie analogy. Dillon did notice he started to run a little faster though right after he thought it, funny how inspiration works.

Un-bitten by any unseen lurking zombies the two slid into the alley where GG waited. Before they had even had a chance to catch their breath the alchemist said, "Come on, we better keep moving. I wouldn't be shocked if someone spotted us running across the street and is calling it into one of the local gangs."

"Shit," gasped Devin before getting his hands off his knee to follow.

"Agreed," Dillon....well he agreed, all right? What do you, the reader, want here? Concurred? It just doesn't work here! Sorry, but this is really hard some days.... just, never mind us, this book has some issues it's working on, back to the story.

They tried to stay to one side of the alley under the fire escapes of the buildings they passed. It wasn't much cover, but considering how GG had described what they were up against it was better than none at all. The alley itself was rank with a host of smells, each worse than the next, but in that, it wasn't all that different from alleys all over the earth. People put things in alleys so they wouldn't be seen and noticed by the rest of the world. Often as not those things smelled bad, dumpsters, trash cans, dead bodies, patchouli, that sort of thing. If everything GG said about this level of hell was to be believed, most of the trash they were walking by probably wasn't even real trash, it was just here to give the alley the proper ambiance.

Dillon couldn't help but notice that Devin kept looking up as they went, "What's up? More specifically, what do you keep looking up at?"

"That's just sick," Devin said pointing up.

"What? .... Oh, yeah," it had taken a minute for Dillon to really see what he meant. What Devin had pointed to was the fire escapes they were moving under. They all looked perfectly normal until you looked at them carefully. Once you did that you realized that all of the ladders that were supposed to drop the last twenty feet to the ground had all been welded in place.

Just like in the level above, GG was taking them on a circuitous route. Whenever an alley branched off of the one they were in he took the branching. It struck Dillon curious that there weren't more main streets. It seemed like everything was alleys here, which sort of defied the idea of an alley, which was usually a little half streets between buildings facing out to main streets. There had been main streets when they'd first come out, but since then, bupkiss. He'd have thought it inconvenient except he had seen what passed for cars here, most of them were small, and who really wanted to be seen driving one of the things? A Trabant not only fit in an alley, but it was also the best place to drive it, fewer witnesses to your humiliation.

They passed another branching, breaking things up by staying in the alley they were on for a change. The end of this alley was awash with light, suggesting that it might finally come out onto a major thoroughfare. As they made their way towards it that light started to fill up with dark shapes. At least five of them. Somebody was coming down the alley towards them, probably with ill intent. The shapes were getting bigger very rapidly.

"Run," GG gasped before whirling back down the way they'd come.

Devin and Dillon took just a moment to ask if he was sure, but by the time they'd turned the alchemist was already past the most recent branching off and picking up steam. Both of them turned to follow when Devin suddenly grabbed at Dillon to pull him back.

"What?"

Devin just pointed. Already five more men had started filing in from the side branch, effectively cutting them off from GG. They weren't particularly big men, one of them was, but it was a gym teacher sort of big, former linebacker in college gone to fat big. It went well with the buzz cut the guy sported. The other four were generally kind of weedy-looking. Two were short men who had facial expressions that suggested a permanent grudge against the universe for making them so short. The other two were both tall and thin almost skeletal. All of them were dressed in the kind of suits that suggested gangsters, pin-striped affairs. On the bulkier one, it fit so poorly that it looked like any moment he might send a button flying just by taking a deep breath.

"C'mon!" Devin grabbed Dillon dragging him back away from the group that was lining up to fill the alley from one side to the other.

"Where in the hell are we going?"

"We've got to get inside one of the buildings, we can see if we can lose them there."

"What about GG?" Dillon asked as he flowed along in Devin's wake.

"Last I checked, he isn't the one trapped, he was making good an escape, now come on we gotta do the same!" Devin didn't hesitate from there. He walked directly over to one of the alley doors and yanked on the handle. When it didn't budge, he kicked at it with all his might. There was a crack, but the door still wasn't open. Next, he threw his body against the door only to have it fly open at the instant of contact sending him stumbling inside. Another hell, "ha-ha" joke.

Devin crashed to a halt before turning back to Dillon, "Hurry the hell up kid, I don't think they want to ask us if we've found Jesus and would we be interested in getting copies of the Watchtower, let's haul ass, huh?"

Hannah watched Nathaniel like a hawk from her uncomfortable place at the bar. In point of fact, normally they wouldn't even be in the bar if Nathaniel hadn't vouched for her and made her promise to only drink soda. The promise was unnecessary, she wanted every ounce of alertness. Nathaniel was sitting across the room from her and Zach by himself at a table. He looked great. Despite his normally bookish and frumpy attire, it turned out he did know how to cut a dashing figure when it was called for. It was a surprise to discover that he had a closet full of clothes that were just elegant fashion personified. It made Hannah think that she should hang out with Dan and Nate after this was all done. Clearly, they had a more interesting life than first glance made her think.

Nathaniel was bait. A well-dressed, single, older man would be too much for the succubus to resist. That was, if she came in here. This was one of the most popular hook-up spots in the area, it was either this or the personals and tinder, and all of them had agreed that somehow this felt more natural. Also, none of them could figure out how to write an ad that specifically attracted succubi. "Rich sugar daddy with no loved ones who will ask after him seeks lonely soul-sucking sex demon." would get lots of responses, but they had no way of filtering out the ones who were just perfectly normal run-of-the-mill money-grubbing gold-digging perverts from the soul grubbing pervert demon. Somehow, "Serious inquiries only," probably wasn't going to do it for separating out the chaff. They had spent hours preparing for this, the last thing they wanted to do was wasting their time getting rid of pervs. (this book came close to saying "beating off pervs", but.... we got a hold of ourselves! ...OK, we'll stop now)

A few people had slid up to him as he sat there smiling with a drink, listening to the band that was playing on a small stage nearby. It wasn't a huge surprise, Nate was still an attractive man for his age, and with the cost of his tailoring, well it attracted positive attention. Hannah was not someone who went in for silver foxes, and Nate really had very little silver, but even she could see the attraction. None of them looked quite what she was expecting from their target. For one thing, they took the polite brush off well, and went and sat somewhere else. Hannah figured if the succubus had found its mark it wouldn't be that easy to shake off.

She was looking back along the bar towards the front of the building when someone caught her eye. Why that person caught her eye was because of the way they flickered from one appearance to another instantly in response to the eyes viewing it. One moment a petite dark-haired girl, the next a buxom blond, the next after that a powerful bodybuilder man. That was a good thing, it meant the hours they'd spent pouring over an ancient-looking book that Devin had left with them as a spotter's guide had paid off, they could train themselves to see the succubus for what it was. What it really was beneath the flickering kaleidoscope of appearances was not particularly attractive at all, and even then, only to a specialized kink set. It was a withered old woman, covered in gray-green skin, including a tail that came out over the top of her skirt. The first succubus might have been hot according to Dillon and Devin, but this one had been working this scheme for a very long time and it showed. The sunken eyes saw Nate in the distance and in an instant, the overlying shape became something that looked almost, but not quite like Dan.

The succubus leaned in and talked to Nathaniel for a moment before he nodded. The creature took the other seat at the table with a wide smile. Hannah quickly turned away so it wouldn't be as conspicuous when she took out her phone and typed out a message, "Succubitch is here and with Nate."

Chapter 16
"Silver is definitely not this girl's best friend." M. Monroe succubus

Mishthala couldn't believe her luck, she'd barely gotten done draining the last sucker, and here was another one just waiting for her that looked lonelier, and better yet, richer. Judging from his suit she could probably set herself up quite well for some time while she enjoyed her freedom from hell. He didn't look bad either for an older guy and most importantly he looked healthy. That last guy had been old enough that he had practically been shooting dust the whole time she was turning him into dust. After she was done with this new one, she could take control of a nice young girl and use all of the sperm she had stockpiled to create some lovely half-breed demon babies. Just the thing to bring the overall evil quotient up in the world. Normally that kind of thing took an incubus, but Mishthala had been doing this since cavemen had gotten hot and bothered by a girl with a little less brow ridge, she knew all the tricks for getting around the rules.

She kept the glamour on as she sat down with him. He immediately offered to buy the man she was posing as a drink. "No thank you, as nice as you look, I'd look like I was looking for a sugar daddy if I took a drink yet. Let's get to know one another first, maybe we can buy each other a round at some point," Mishthala replied, enjoying the bass rumbles the voice of this appearance brought with it.

The man chuckled, and almost melodic sound, "As you wish, I'm enjoying being out. So, what do you wish to talk about?"

"Well, I suppose the starting point here is, tell me about yourself."

Over the course of the evening, Mishthala learned that the gentleman was named Nate and that he had been a CEO who had retired early to one of the little farmsteads outside of town. He'd felt more comfortable here, especially since there was still a locker room white hetero atmosphere on Wall Street no matter how many people like Nate succeeded there. Once he'd made his money, he felt happy to leave, he found he didn't have that drive to make more money than he'd ever need any more. Also, Mishthala learned that Nate must have a powerful mind, because there had been attempts to glamour him further making him suggestible to leaving, to wanting Mishthala more than life itself, and so far, Nate was still happily sitting there sipping with gentility on a Tom Collins as the band worked their way through their set. Nate seemed perfectly content to be enjoying his night out with his new friend "Mike" and in no hurry at all to go anywhere.

Mishthala was actually discovering exhilaration at having to lure this one in with simple human charms. It had been centuries since she'd had to work so hard to interest the prey, so long she'd just taken success for granted. And frankly, the man had an easy-going charm, a comfortable manner that made her think of warm fires on a winter night lying on a rug while classical music played. Mishthala found that she was almost going to regret draining this one, but a body had to feed and do the work they were created for, a biological imperative as it were, your very being wouldn't forgive you just because you were nice. And that wasn't the only thing that wouldn't be forgiving, you didn't want to find yourself back in hell explaining how you had decided to forgo the whole creating half-demon babies thing to spend a romantic getaway with your new beau. She might technically be on vacation, but succubi were expected to take working vacations. Going for romance over production was how even a succubus could find themselves on shit shoveling duty for a millennium or two. She knew she was already pushing her luck with this whole impromptu vacation, no point in pushing that luck any further.

She was still surprised when the man leaned over and said, "Look, it's getting late. I was thinking of heading home for the night. You can come too if you'd like. I think I'd like that at least."

SCORE! There would be no shit shoveling for this lil succubus!

Keeping her composure Mishthala replied, "If that's what you want. I think I'd like that too. Do you want me to follow you?"

"Or we could just take my car, I mean, that way we could keep talking while I drive," Nate said with a charming smile.

"That's taking a lot on trust," Mishthala smiled, playing coy.

"Isn't all of life that way?"

The car they arrived at when they walked down the street was an older one, but it was not a bad looking one by any stretch of the imagination, it looked sexy. Mishthala had no clue as to car manufacturers or anything along those lines, "So, what kind of car is this? I don't think I've ever seen one before."

"Believe it or not, it is a Studebaker," Nate smiled as he unlocked the doors.

Once Mishthala's door was open the succubus climbed in saying, "If you don't mind me saying, this car does not look like that name sounds."

"Imagine how many of them they would have sold if it had been built by Chevrolet? But that's what makes it so special, it proves that none of us have to be what we're named, not at heart. A Studebaker can be sexier than any old-fashioned Mazda, even though it has a name that makes you think of a dear old widower Aunt. I like to think it shows that all of us are in control of what we really want to be, no matter what we're born with," Nate smiled again as he fired up the perfectly tuned motor and let it growl for a few seconds to warm up.

"What a quaint notion," Mishthala smiled back softly as they pulled out onto the empty street and into the dark night.

Nate's house was outside of town a little way, which was all the more perfect really. One of the old-time farmsteads fit Mishthala perfectly as a potential base of operations. Paramours tended to wear out ever so quickly, and neighbors in an actual town might notice if you were constantly digging up the back yard for the bodies. Sure, the river was right there in town, but Mishthala was more than a little dismayed that the "mighty Delaware" was also "mighty shallow" and the chances of any body dumped there staying undiscovered for any real amount of time were practically nil. She had more than enough of driving down River Road looking for suitable burial spots.

Now there was only the matter of breaking through Nate's defenses. It almost made Mishthala worry that the poor man was impotent. Of course, if he was impotent then it was anyone's guess as to why he had decided to drag Mishthala out here. He certainly didn't look the serial killer type, and anyway, Mishthala was a demon, that level of evil would be setting off all kinds of proximity warnings. True evil knows its own, like recognizes like and all that. No, the succubus was pretty sure that Nate had been caught checking the front of Mishthala's amply stuffed jeans a few times and had plans for what he suspected was there. Like casually glancing, the man hadn't been like, actively ogling or drooling or anything, he had far too much class for that. Even wanting to score tonight, a succubus had standards as to who would get the honor of being drained. At least these days, back in the old days if you wanted to score yourself a Prince or a King or something, with the inbreeding and all, you had to be prepared to accept a bit of drool.

Even with all of the slow movement of the encounter the demon was more or less positive that sex was on the agenda for tonight. While Nate had been able to force Mishthala to resort to simple charm and good looks rather than simply mesmerizing him, the succubus was sure of one thing, once they were knocking boots Nate's very soul was as good as hers. The demon might have regrets about it, but occasionally having to drain one you liked was a small price to pay for having one of the most fun jobs in the entire host of demons.

Mishthala was pleased even further when the demon got a good look at the farmhouse itself. It was quaint, remote, and the inside was tastefully decorated. After the evening's festivities were over and it was in the succubus' hands it wouldn't even need a makeover really. Now that she'd seen the place, impatience was overcoming Mishthala, it was time to seal this deal. It had been a nice night of simple courtship, and that was a sweet change of pace, but nice is nice and it don't feed the demon.

As Nate was showing the succubus around the ground floor Mishthala interrupted, "Nate, you didn't just ask me out here to talk, did you?"

"Well, I was certainly hoping to talk some...."

"But that's not the main reason, is it?"

Nate was silent for a moment before he said, "No, I suppose it isn't."

"Well, the night's still young, we can always talk later, can't we?"

Silence again, and then a smile, "Would you like to see the upstairs? The bedrooms, the..."

"I think I'd like that very much," Mishthala smiled.

Mishthala was practically breathless with anticipation by the time they made it upstairs. So, this was what a real seduction was like, no wonder the humans wrote so many books about it. The room they entered was tastefully decorated, including an exquisite four-poster bed. The walls were lined with books that fit perfectly with large dark wooden dressers and end tables that looked to be real mahogany. After all the succubus' years in service to Moraspus on the trash level of hell, Mishthala had truly begun to appreciate the finer things in life in ways mere mortals never could.

Nate turned and smiled, "Would you care to sit next to me on the bed? It's been years since I've done this sort of thing, and well, I'm a little rusty."

SHOWTIME!

Mishthala confidently took a place on the bed next to Nate, enjoying the comforting softness of the mattress and the comforters. This was going to be great! A large soft bed fit for a King and a Queen, a conquest the succubus had actually had to work for, and a handsome rich man to boot. When Mishthala had first walked into that bar the demon would have been happy with anyone really, just someone to suck dry to keep in the game. But not, tonight Mishthala had really hit the motherlode!

There was an audible snapping metallic click from the floor.

Then the closet burst open!

Mishthala gasped, stunned at the young woman who had come bursting out of the closet wielding a baseball bat. The succubus turned to Nate in shock, "Nate what...."

Nate took the succubus' hands in his own for a second, "Mike I'm sorry, but it just won't work."

There was another click followed by a ratcheting noise. The succubus didn't have to wonder now, she knew exactly what was holding her...SILVER. The demon made to leap off the bed only to discover what the first noise had been, silver manacles. A moment after making that discovery the succubus ungracefully landed flat on her face on the floor. The world warped for the demon, becoming a dull and distant thing as the silver dulled and poisoned her perceptions.

Mishthala could hear people moving about and sensed them standing over her. A muffled male voice she didn't recognize said, "Well now that we've got it trapped, what in the hell do we do with it?"

The demon growled into the fine Persian rug, "When I get out of here, I am going to...."

"But, dear demon, you won't get out of here at all, we know what you are," Nate interrupted.

The female who had burst out with the bat said, "Well, we do know where there's a gate to hell and all. I mean how hard could it be to just leave her at the door?"

"I'll drive," replied the voice under the bed.

They were already going up the first few stairs when Dillon thought to ask, "So what's the plan?"

"We gotta find an empty room or something to hide in, if this is anything like what it's trying to look like there'll be some empty apartments or something," Devin responded, his feet clanging on the steps as he flowed up them.

"How about finding a front door?"

"You don't think there's more of them waiting for us to do just that?"

"That's the plan? Hope we find an empty room to hide in?"

"Yeah, I like it better than the alternatives, get worked over in the alley, or getting trapped on the roof and thrown off it. Though if it makes you happy, I did consider them and dismissed them," Devin called back.

"At least you did due diligence I suppose," Devin conceded as he rushed after him.

Devin kept moving past the next floor. "Aren't we checking those?"

"Too obvious, they'll check this floor. We'll do the next floor."

Just as they reached the third floor, they heard the door below them slammed open. "Shhh," Devin hissed heading down the hallway quickly and softly.

Dillon followed behind him, he could hear the men's voices echoing around the stairwell as they debated what to do. That they would be following them he had no doubt, he could only hope that they intended to be methodical about it. The fact that they had waited to regroup before following suggested they might be. Also, he was hoping they might stick together giving them time to find somewhere to hide. He kept his ears peeled for footsteps coming up the stairs from below as he followed along behind Devin who was trying doorknobs.

"Kid, try the ones on the other side of the hall, we ain't got all day here," Devin whispered.

Dillon nodded and made to comply. This brief respite gave him a chance to really look at the building they were in for the first time. Whichever demon had designed this level of hell had definitely loved forties gangster flicks. Just like the town itself, the interior was yet again an obvious film noire homage where even someone Dillon's age could recognize the scene. The place looked directly out of a Jimmy Cagney film in what was supposed to be a "seedy part of town," dim lights showing peeling wallpaper, scuffed hardwood floors, and radiators with cracked paint over them probably sending lead fumes into the air if they ever heated up, which was doubtful. Following that train of thought, for the first time, he wondered about that word, "seedy." Do granaries happen in bad neighborhoods? Were there roving gangs of pigeons in Hell's Kitchen back then?

Across the hall from him, he heard Devin bang a door open. As he turned to join him, Dillon heard a voice from inside the room, "Jesus Christ Elsie! Didn't I tell ya' to lock the damned door? We're being robbed again!"

A shriller voice came from deeper inside what must have been an apartment, "Oh that's some crap Barnie! You were the last one outside and you know it! Anyway, how do you know they're robbing us."

As this was going on Dillon crossed over the hall, and whispered to Devin, "We going in?"

Devin shrugged and stepped inside, followed by Dillon who closed the door behind him.

"You know how I know they's robbin' us, Elsie? How many other people come in your living room you didn't invite in in this neighborhood that ain't robbin' ya'?"

"They could just be lost," presumably Elsie replied.

"Then they would have kno-...holy sweet mother of pearl, one of 'em's got a real gun!" said Barnie, who Dillon could finally get a good look at. The man was sitting there in boxer shorts and an old stained undershirt stretched to capacity. To Dillon's shock, the man had sock garters on, something he considered to be just a movie joke. His slippers were readily visible as well since he had crawled halfway up onto his torn and ragged lazy-boy at the sight of the gun.

An older-looking woman in a robe with her dyed red hair in curlers came in from the other room, "Barnie stop talking stupid talk, I heard the bang earlier too, it was probably a car, nobody down here has.... oh, my!"

Devin looked surprisingly calm about the whole thing, "OK, look, I would prefer not to use this thing. You live here, so you have to know about the gangs. They were about to jump us for our things, we'd kind of prefer they didn't do that. We have our things, because we need our things. It would kind of be an inconvenience if you get my drift."

"Hi," Dillon waved gently behind him.

"Holy shit on a shingle, you're running from the Dalton gang and you hid in my fucking apartment? Are you fucking nuts? Jesus, just rob us!" Barnie spluttered, he looked for a second like he was going to get up and confront Devin directly before he remembered the gun and slumped back down causing the dim light to glint off his shiny bald head.

"Please, we don't want to hurt you at all, or get you hurt, we just need to lay low for a little while until those lunatics decide we left the building," Devin explained patiently.

Barnie shook his head, "Won't work, they'll tear the building apart. They probably got sniffers on you all ready."

"Sniffers?" Dillon asked.

"How the hell would some random souls get a hold of sniffers?" Devin demanded.

"I don't know, I try to keep my head down for the love of Pete. But I know they got one, the Jones gang has one too!"

"Well look, we'll use the fire escape, I know it doesn't go all the way down, but it'll get us close enough," Devin replied. "Ummm...Miss....uhh Elsie, is it? Could you look out the window? Carefully, don't make it too obvious. Could you look to see if someone is still in the alley?"

There was an uncomfortable silence as Elsie went off to check. A moment later she came back, "Well there were at least a couple of guys down there."

"Well, a plus, this place is defensible," Devin shrugged.

"Oh, hell no!" Barnie spluttered.

"Hey Barnie, does Holy Water work on damned souls? I haven't had a chance to try it out yet," Devin said flatly, his eyes boring into the fat man's eyes.

"Ummm...."

"I got a bunch of it in my bag, won't even have to use my gun. Say, I got a great idea, why don't we all sit down to watch TV for a little bit, and hope for the best?"

"Yeah, great idea, take a seat," Barnie said with defeat and waved to a dog-eared plaid couch, his face showing that despite his words, he did not consider this a great idea at all.

"Love to. Dillon, where are your manners, let's take a seat," Devin said with a charming smile.

"So, what's on?" Dillon asked politely as he took a seat on the couch, followed by Devin who still had the gun in his hand.

"There's one channel, and they're running, 'Homeboys in Outer Space' so I hope you're in the mood for it," Barnie grunted settling himself back in.

"I thought all copies of that were banned as a war crime," Devin replied.

Dillon thought about it, "Well, think about where we are."

"Point."

Both of them were caught between trying to ignore the horrific attempt at sitcom humor and being drawn into it. It was just so amazing to think the thing had ever been made in the first place that you couldn't help but be fascinated, the temptation was to crack jokes of your own based on how bad it was. Unfortunately, or fortunately, just as it was getting to a "good" part their evening entertainment was interrupted by a hand trying the knob on the door to the apartment.

Devin was already on his feet and crossing the room when they heard a voice through the door, "Look, we ain't sure what you got in them bags, but the rules around here say we get to see and keep what we like. And hey, be decent about it, we done all the work of tracking you down. Now in a minute we're gonna break down the door and you're gonna be just as screwed, except it's gonna be even worse because we're gonna' be annoyed. So why don't you just open up and hand it over, huh?"

Devin yelled out, "Look, we're nice guys. We were just minding our own business. Just leave us alone!"

"That ain't the way things work around this neighborhood pal and everyone knows it. I don't even know where you get off trying to run stuff through here."

Devin took careful aim and then fired the gun through the door.

There was a scream of pain, followed by, "Jesus Christ! That was nice? You fucking shot me! You seriously called yourself a nice guy and you do that shit?"

Devin shrugged, "I asked you guys to leave us alone nicely."

"Oh, I swear I'm gonna..." Whatever the thug was going to do was broken off by some kind of commotion outside the door. Within moments the sound of a fight broke out that could be heard clearly.

"What in the hell is that about?" Devin turned back to Barnie.

Barnie snorted, "Must have been the Taylor gang. They must think that the Dalton's already got something important, and are holding out on them."

Devin rushed past the surprised Else into the other room and took a look out the window for himself. The scene had changed dramatically, for one, there weren't any thugs in it anymore. What was there now was right under the fire escape sat a truck, they could easily jump down into. Better yet, standing next to it was GG! Devin waved trying to catch GG's attention before calling back to Dillon in the living room, "Kid, come on, our ride's here."

"What?"

"Just come on, I figure we better hurry before the psychos in the hall join forces."

It took a second to force the window next to the escape open because it stuck, of course, it did, but eventually with both of them shoving it open exactly wide enough for them to slip through. Just as Devin was handing the bags out to Dillon, Barnie called from the other room, "So what should I say to those thugs if they ever stop beating each other's heads in long enough to break down my door?"

"Tell 'em we got raptured," Devin called back as he slid out the window onto the fire escape.

Seeing them, GG hopped back into the truck and maneuvered it so the roof would be directly under the fire escape. Dillon froze at the bottom of the steps to the floor below where the escape stopped. The truck made the jump less than it would have been, but that still meant it was further than he really wanted to jump. It was a metal bed down there, and he was willing to bet he'd break before it bent.

Devin came up behind him, "Look kid, I can't make you jump, I wouldn't do that. But let me say, remember your fifth-grade gym teacher? Yeah, he's probably down here on this exact level of hell. Imagine what he'd have done to you kids if it was the Purge. Because those guys back there are gonna do that to us if they catch us."

In a matter of moments, the pair of them were clambering into the cab, and GG had it in gear saying, "I am so happy to see the pair of you again."

"Where the hell did you go, and for that matter, how did you get the truck?" Devin demanded as they sped off.

"Well, since I wasn't going to be much good to you at that moment, I ran off in the other direction, obviously. Having been here before, I knew how much the gangs distrust each other. They also have an agreement to share out any weapons that might hurt demons if they should make it onto this plane. So, I ran through the streets yelling that there was a cache of it being hoarded in that building," GG smiled.

"OK, that explains the fight outside where we were hiding, but it doesn't explain the truck," Dillon pressed.

"Informants scattered like mad to get to phones to call it in on the few payphones that were in operation, one of them left his truck running. Now if you don't mind, I don't have a lot of practice doing this, so I should probably concentrate on the driving."

"How do you even know how?" Dillon wondered.

"I'm very observant, I was considered a genius in my own time you know."

Chapter 17
"I left out a lot of bits."- Dante

"Are you ready to leave?" Adrianna asked, breathless at the whole concept. In all her years in hell, or whatever measure of unit you chose to use for time, hell was still timeless, she had never been part of such a blatant thwarting of the rules as this. It was like watching your most hated teacher getting chewed out by the principle in the middle of class. It was like the end of Ferris Bueler's day off when he gets away with it all. Wow, that was a dated reference, wasn't it? Still, it was a good solid analogy, so it stays.

"Not exactly yet," Dan said as he finished setting up the final few ingredients in a brazier.

"What on earth could be keeping you?" asked Patrick who had stopped playing video games when he discovered what they were up to.

"Well, I want to make sure we aren't followed, don't I?" Dan said with a grin. For the first time since they'd known him, all three of them suddenly remembered they were in the room with a demon, it was that type of grin. "Just wait here, I'll be back in a little while." Seeing their expressions, he quickly added, "Don't worry, I save this side of me strictly for other demons, they always have it coming, they're demons."

Blurglesoth was not having a good day. No, if anything, this would go down as one of his worst days ever. Not the worst he would ever have, he was pretty sure of that. This was hell, he worked for one of Satan's actual children in Moraspus, worse was always possible, probable even. That day was most likely coming very soon, as in as soon as Moraspus got home. He was positive that would be the worst day of his existence, Moraspus would see to that. What the kid had done to him was bad, surely, what the father would do when he found out how badly Blurglesoth had blundered this would be so, so much worse, he was sure of it. What the kid had done had certainly proven that he had some of his father in him and that the majordomo had underestimated him, that was absolutely apparent now. Recent events had taken serious sadism and ingenuity that Blurglesoth had never suspected the boy capable of. Blurglesoth had completely forgotten about the industrial-strength, gigantic meat grinder in the torture chamber, the thing hadn't been used for years and was more of a novelty piece from back in the Bosch days of torturing souls. He had forgotten about it right until the kid pushed him into it and set it to work. The kid had even upgraded it, giving it both a motor, turning it into more of a blender really, and he gave it a puree setting.

Blurglesoth was currently residing in a very large jar down in those very torture chambers. The lid, was on.

Yep, this was definitely not the best day he'd ever had.

The truck banged and clanged as they sped through the mostly abandoned streets. The loose bolts rattled loud enough they could be heard by the truck's occupants even over the busted exhaust, which was no small feat considering it sounded like it was leaking from the manifold as well as the pipes running right underneath them. This, was not a healthy little truck. In fact, saying that they sped through the streets was frankly stretching the definition of the word.

"What kind of truck even is this?" Dillon asked. He considered himself an expert of all things terrible in the automotive world, so not recognizing something this awful was odd. The Beast had made him into a connoisseur, he spent time on the net looking up the worst cars in automotive history if only to remind himself that there were much, much worse options out there. Many of those much worse options he'd already seen on this level of hell.

Devin answered, "This, is a 1970 Dodge Dude. Supposedly a sports package, they overbuilt the body to the frame and they were notoriously fragile, not a trait one wants in their farm truck."

Dillon shrugged, "Considering every other car we've seen down here, I am not at all shocked by that. In fact, I'm grateful it isn't French. Question is, will it hold up long enough for us to get out of here?"

"We're close anyway," GG interjected not taking his eyes off the road for a moment, "so it doesn't have to go much further."

As if on cue, the truck sent a huge belch of black smoke out of the tailpipe. This was immediately followed by a horrific clanking noise that began to come from the engine. Whatever was happening to the engine must have cut a coolant line as well, judging from the eruption of white smoke from the front making the air in the cab suddenly taste sweet from the anti-freeze. It was joined by an ungodly grinding noise coming from the transmission directly under their feet.

"Dear Lord turn it off and put it out of its misery before it throws something through the cab!" Devin screamed over the din.

"Well, what now?" Dillon asked when the noise had subsided to the occasional ping and pop of cooling metal.

"Original plan, I guess. We hoof it," Devin shrugged as he opened the door, which now squeaked loudly, this was only interesting in that it hadn't before when they got in.

As before, they made for an alley across the way that was heading in the right direction. Just as they were about to turn down it, what they had all mistaken for a pile of rags, moved and spoke, "Spare a nickel for a fellow American who's down on his luck?"

It stood up and held a huge hand out towards them. GG squinted at it and then his eyes went wide accusingly, "Wait a second, you're a demon! You're not supposed to be on this level!"

The thing was wearing a ragged trench coat and had an elderly fedora pulled down low, the shadows hiding its actual face. Even with the shadows, there was no disguising the eyes themselves, which glowed red in the gloom, "Look, keep it down, willya? The humans on this level find out I'm here, I'm toast. Look, I'm just an honest demon looking to lay low for a while, I don't want no trouble."

"Lay low for a while?" Devin interjected quickly.

As much of the face as they could see looked embarrassed, or maybe it was the posture it took that just conveyed it to the shadows under the hat, "Look, Moraspus is kinda pissed at me last I heard. But then again, who ain't he pissed off at? I mean it was a long time ago and it was an honest mistake. I thought, mold bad. Right? I'll spread a bunch of mold around. How the hell could I know it would cure a bunch of stuff? It was an accident, could have happened to anyone. I don't know if that Fleming guy ended up down here, but I'd love to get my claws on him."

Devin started to chuckle, "You know what? For your accidental service to humanity...GG, give him the keys."

GG shrugged and dug the truck keys out and handed them over to the demon, "But it doesn't even...."

Devin held up his hand, "There's a Dodge truck back there, broke down on us, but I don't know, maybe you can push it around and keep your stuff in it."

"No foolin'? Wow! Ain't nobody done nothin' as nice for me as giving me a broken-down truck before! Anything I can do for you guys?" the demon enthused so much that he tilted his hat back and they could see his face. Now that they had, they all wished they could find a tactful way to tell him to put his hat back how it was, tentacles AND fangs was just overkill.

"Maybe you can get us to the escalator going down unmolested?" Dillon inserted himself in, clearly seeing a way a demon could help them now.

"No problem," The demon replied with a grin, which *really* made them miss the shadows of the hat.

They said their farewells to the demon outside of the building that housed the next escalator. To Dillon this particular crossroads of hell looked like nothing so much as it did something sinister and foreboding directly out of one of the old Batman movies, or better yet, the games. Like, that serious Gotham art deco menace, sharp lines, plenty of gargoyles looking over everything, lots of shadows. Since in theory demons were banned from this level of hell, Dillon had to assume that they were just decoration and not the real thing. Being that it was hell though, it could go either way.

Inside it was silent, except for the distant, almost mournful clacking of the escalator. The arched ceilings were invisible in the gloom of the place looming somewhere high overhead. Instinctively they kept to the walls where various ash trays, newsstands, and just odd ball junk was available to hide behind at a moment's notice. This turned out to be a damned good thing, they were halfway across the lobby when the elevator suddenly dinged.

All of them fought back sneezes from the dust they disturbed as they scanned the opening doors from the shadows. Inside were wedged two demons, both bulky creatures who had somehow managed to get inside together, this might have taken grease. Oddly, one of them wore glasses and a suit that went splendidly with his briefcase, but maybe not so much with the hissing snakes he had for fingers.

"Finally! Now let's deliver this report and go home!" he gasped, starting to tumble out.

The other demon's enormous, clawed hand slammed him back into place, "Not so fast there, Spanky! I know what level we're on."

"Oh?"

"Dis the only level dat the souls hunt us we go out of dis building without a work order," the other demon grumbled.

"Fuck."

"Yep, that just about covers it. Guess the doors only opened to fuck with us."

As the demon finished speaking the doors slammed violently shut, almost catching one of the business demon's snakes in its trap.

"See what I said about never taking the elevators?" GG grinned.

After another long, boring, and completely skippable by this narrative trip down another escalator, they began to get a good view of the next level of hell. It was more or less a sea of trash at first glance. But not at second glance. It looked like a landfill, sure, but it was like a landfill made out of all the crap that became outdated or was just a stupid idea to begin with on earth usually still in the box. In reality, it smelled less like rot from above, and more like.... like that plastic smell something has when it's fresh out of the package.

"The land of the covetous, the thieves, the adulterers, those who spend their whole lives wanting what others have. Here they have everything after the world has decreed it garbage, always knowing that whatever they receive is dated and hated in the world above. Commercials run on every TV, on every computer, on every radio advertising the things above so that they know that everything here is an inferior version. It is where Moraspus rules, and here that Dan was certainly spirited away to," GG intoned.

"Well, that was a little bit of an ominous soliloquy now, wasn't it?" Dillon looked shocked.

"What? I thought you wanted to know what we were getting into," GG protested.

"Not like that! You made it sound all creepy and stuff," Dillon complained.

"Well, it is hell you know," GG sniffed.

"He's got a point kid," Devin concurred.

"Still, I don't want to get psyched out before we get there, "Dillon shrugged. "I know where we are. Maybe point out the positives, like, 'Hey! You can still get crystal Pepsi down here,' or something."

"What's the demon situation on this floor?" Devin changed the subject.

"Significant, but they really only torture souls randomly. People wander around all the time without being bothered. Even so, I would make sure we all know where our weapons are at all times, I doubt we get off without having to use them."

"Oh, swell, something to look forward to," Dillon said flatly.

Dan led his little group into his secret den under the mountain. It was the first time he'd seen the place in many, many years. He was struck by the changes that had happened in the time he'd been gone, GG had made the place clean and orderly, it looked like a classy bachelor pad. It humored him to see it. The him that left Hell all those years ago would have been furious at having his sanctuary tidied like this, the him that he was now actually approved of the orderly flow GG had achieved with the place. It would seem that aging on earth had actually matured him more than he thought. Or, equally possible, having a husband who would yell at him about it, taught him that socks belonged in the hamper. Patrick had already discovered the television and the ancient gaming system and was lost to the world, that left Dan alone with Thomas, and Adrianna.

"So now that you've escaped, now what?" Thomas asked.

Dan really hadn't thought it through that far, but now that the question was asked, he just gave the first answer that came to him, "Well, I've got to go back to the mortal world. There are people there that I'm sure are worried about me. I could probably manage to take the three of you with me as a thank you. I might have to make a couple of trips, but still."

Adrianna shook her head, but it was Thomas that spoke, "That's nice of you, and don't think for a moment that I don't appreciate it. But, the way I figure, hell turned out to be real, and if it is, maybe the other side is real too. Maybe one day they get around to a bit of that mercy and forbearance towards us that book was always on about. Maybe they look at some of the souls down here and say, 'All righty, you've served your time, we think you learned the lesson.' I wouldn't want to sneak out and lose all that time I've already served here."

"I know you mean well Dan, but also, there are so many who suffer down here and so many more that have given into the evil that got them here and embrace it. I think we'd both rather stay and help those that aren't too far gone, maybe make it all a bit more bearable, maybe if there is forgiveness, saving them might help us too. Even if it doesn't, I'm sure the need is there all the same," Adrianna added.

Dan was stunned for a moment; it had never occurred to him that there might be some in hell that became angels of mercy. He was ashamed after that, hadn't they just helped him escape from his Father's clutches, and with his Father, "clutches" was the exact type of dramatic term to use. Finally, after he had processed what he'd heard he said, "Well, if that's what you want...I mean....it kind of proves to me that maybe you shouldn't be here, but...well, you can have this as a base of operations."

"We thank you for that, we truly do," Thomas smiled. "Maybe Patrick will even be able to help us some if we can ever tear him away from those games you've shown him."

"No, thank you for all your help, I hope I'm worth it," Dan smiled softly before he performed the spell that sent him back to earth.

The first thing they realized as they left the ancient stone building that housed the escalator was that there were buildings, even streets down here, but they had been built from what at first glance looked like junk. The building materials were things that even denizens of hell wouldn't use and pine away for the newest version of. Many, many,

many of those things had been built by a company called Ronco. The streets were uneven and bumpy, but that was all right since almost none of the cars actually ran. Most of them provided building platforms for homes and businesses.

"I'm surprised really," Dillon said as they tried to stick to the shadows as they moved.

"About?" Devin asked.

"I would have thought there would have been more George Foreman grills," he shrugged.

"You kidding? Those things still sell like crazy. Bet you we can find a ton of Sega Dreamcasts though," Devin chuckled.

"A what?" GG and Dillon asked in unison.

Devin gave Dillon a long hard look for a moment before saying, "Well, now I just feel old."

"Think how I feel," GG sniffed.

They continued on their way listening intently as they went for some kind of alarm or trouble. For Dillon it was an education, he didn't know what half of the stuff was that made up the construction of this level of hell. It was like watching the failures and the various moments of obsolescence that made American Consumerism on a grand scale. You could even date it as an index fossil going from the foundations up older to newer. Really looking at it all, really taking it in, Dillon was struck by one thought. As far as he could tell people would buy all kinds of stupid shit. Worse, they would invent and market stupid crap not knowing what they were dumping on these poor wretched souls down below. Every terrible thing that ended up down here, somebody had thought it had been a brilliant idea.

"I wish I had some room in my bag," Devin broke the silence.

"Why on earth would you? Most of this stuff is crap," Dillon looked shocked.

"Yeah, but back on earth, it's collectible crap. A lot of this stuff is in mint condition. Stuff my bag full of it, become the king of eBay for a month," Devin replied, his eyes roaming the walls around them covetously.

Dillon's reply was cut off by the sounds of a scream coming from around the next corner. Heedless of Devin waving him to stay still he moved up cautiously to see what it was.

"Be careful! It's almost definitely something involving a demon," GG hissed at him.

GG had been absolutely correct in his guess. Dillon looked around the corner of a building composed entirely of boxes of Lawn Darts to witness what could only be called either a torment of the damned, or bullying with demonic strength involved. The demon in question looked almost like a bright red Minotaur. Almost, because instead of a shaggy bull head, it had normal skin (also bright red) and its features were more of a cross between the cartoon cow from the milk containers and a human face, the big eyes, the wide cow nose, combined with normal human features but still with the massive bull horns coming out the side of his head. What it was currently doing was twisting a soul's arm behind its back. Dillon could see from where he was that that arm had done a couple of circuits already like a rubber band that had been twisted on a little balsa airplane. He could also see that if it was twisted much more it would just be torn completely off.

"Say it! Say, 'I want you to hurt me Daddy!'" the beast growled.

The screaming man paused only long enough to gasp out, "I want.... you to.... hurt...me Daddy!"

"All right, I'll hurt you, but only because you asked nice. Say 'I only wish I was wearing a frilly doll dress for this!' G'wan!"

Something in Dillon snapped. He had been holding back and letting the others take the lead the entire time they'd been down here but he just couldn't stomach this. He had pictured demons to be delivering carefully thought out, insidious tortures to the deserving damned. What he was getting here was a Jr. High School bully with a glandular problem and a low IQ catching the nerdy kid after gym class. He stepped around the corner, wielding both of his guns. In one hand he had a tranq gun the same as Devin had used repeatedly since they'd been down here, in the other was a super-soaker. More importantly, it was a super soaker filled with holy water, and Dillon was feeling vindictive towards the demon in front of him at this moment.

"Hey horn head!" he bellowed and immediately regretted it. Not getting the demon's attention, he wanted that, but "horn head" was a really lame insult, and he was sure he could have thought of something better, given some more time to think about it. Maybe calling it Otis the cow would have worked better, there were a lot of possibilities, and he had chosen the lamest one.

The monster turned to look at him, still holding the poor tormented soul's arm. "You want some of this too little man?" it growled.

"Sure," Dillon grinned, "but first, why don't you cool off?" OK, that was better than the horn head bit, but still pretty weak.

A moment later the demon was screaming as its skin began to sizzle and rupture where the stream from the Super-Soaker struck it.

"Well hurry up and help me!" Devin barked running past Dillon.

"Help you what?"

"Help me cut him up! If he goes down to the vats relatively whole, he's going to be squealing us out before we make another hundred yards!" Devin barked. Dillon couldn't help but notice that Devin had pulled a pretty sizable machete out of his bag, and was marching up to the demon with grim determination.

A crowd of souls had begun to appear as if they were magical creatures of the forest in a Disney flick and the heroine had just started her big song. Dillon also noticed that the man who had his arm twisted suddenly looked a lot better. He held up a hand as Devin approached. "Hold up now, you look like you got places to go, I don't."

"What?" Devin asked nonplussed.

"Meaning, if you want.... Torgo here has been a pain in all our asses for quite a while now. I think we might be happy to help cut him up a bit," the man said before he put a kick deep into the demon's gut, which set off a fresh set of howls.

"Hey kid," Devin called back to Dillon.

"Yeah?"

"Hit the demon with the tranq gun, don't want any of these fine people to get hurt by that bastard thrashing around like that."

As they left, they could see the mob descend on the hapless demon. Dillon was reminded very bluntly that a lot of these people probably DID deserve to be here after all. Especially considering some of the sounds the demon started making.

Dan appeared in the living room of his house back on earth. This, almost caused Hannah and Zach to have a full-blown heart attack since they were watching TV there while Nathan was preparing dinner.

"Oh, hello, I didn't know we had guests," Dan said with a smile.

"Nate, you might want to pull out one more plate," Hannah called out.

"Oh?" Nathaniel's voice came from the kitchen.

"But actually, make sure you aren't holding one right now," she added.

"Yeah, seeing as how Dan's back," Zach called.

There was a crash as a plate shattered on the floor.

"Told you," Hannah said.

A moment later Nathaniel crashed into Dan's arms. They held each other for a few moments before Hannah cleared her throat loudly. They broke apart and turned to see her worried expression. "What's wrong?" Dan asked.

"Where are the other three?"

"Other three?" Dan looked dumbfounded, well he more than looked it, he was.

"Oh Dear, her boyfriend, Devin, and GG went into hell to get you! Aren't they with you?"

Dan's face went through a couple of different expressions quickly before he said, "I've got to go back."

"Not without me you aren't!" Nate said.

"Make it a full complement, if I don't see my baby boy soon, I am going to have to personally hurt someone," Hannah declared tapping her foot with pent-up worry.

"You aren't leaving me here to guess what happened, that would be total bullshit," Zach concluded the declarations portion of this scene.

Dillon could tell the other two were still annoyed with him about the demon, which he thought was unfair. Devin had gotten to shoot that one on that other level of hell, and the ones at the gates, using Dillon as bait no less, and no more had been said about it. As far as he was concerned, they could be as annoyed as they wanted to be about it, Dillon would have done it again in a heartbeat. They didn't actually have to stick around to dismember the demon, there were certainly enough volunteers for that, so it wasn't like it cost them any time. He had no regrets, because, at the end of the day, one thing Dillon just couldn't stand was a bully. He wasn't surprised to find that hell had an abundance of them, but when he could actually do something about it, no matter how temporary, well it did your heart good to hit that sucker full in the chest with some holy water. If they didn't have to be quiet as they skulked through the stacks of Commodore computers and ET The Extra-Terrestrial Game Cartridges, he was sure he could have talked Devin around to his thinking.

They all stopped when someone hissed at them from inside of a house made of weird automobiles that according to the tag on them were something called Citicars. "Psst!" whoever it was leaked air from the shadows.

They looked at each other dumbfounded for a moment. In their entire lives, this had never happened, and all three of them were unsure for a moment how to proceed, all of them thinking, "Who says 'Psst'? Nobody really says that"

Finally, Dillon said, "Are you leaking air from somewhere vital or do you mean us?"

"Do you see anyone else?" the voice whispered in annoyance.

"Well, no, we don't even see you, but we weren't really expecting..." Dillon waived his hand to indicate this entire situation surprisingly effectively.

There was an exasperated sigh, finally the voice said tightly, "Look, you're looking for Dan, right? So, do you want to wander around here all day, or do you want to actually go where he is? I mean we could stand around here looking stupid, I suppose, but he's been worried sick about you three so me letting you get killed would probably upset him a little."

Chapter 18
"I do NOT have Daddy issues!"-Hamlet

Patrick pulled open the door to the K-Car, "Hurry up, I've got a game of Pitfall paused, and if we take too long Adrianna will un-pause it just to let my guy die."

"We're supposed to...." Devin waved at the car.

"Just go through the car, trust me, I lived here myself for some time it's fine," GG said sliding over the plaid and tan seats.

"God, I never thought I'd find myself behind the wheel of one of these hunks of crap, even in passing. This is the kind of thing that makes me miss my Studebaker," Devin replied following him. Dillon couldn't help but agree with him, the cars they'd seen so far in hell made Dillon feel that he should be more charitable to the Beast if he ever got out of here. At least there was a time that the Beast had been a decent car, even if that time had been long before Dillon had owned it.

Once they were through the relic from the Age of Iacocca, they were amazed to find themselves in a well-lit tunnel. Seeing that there were branching passages made Dillon instinctively move closer to Patrick as he was leading them on. In no way, shape, or form did he want to get lost in a maze of garbage, alone, left to try and figure out how the place remained stable. He was maintaining his composure, but this was one of those experiences where as long as there were other people, and they weren't freaking out, you just assumed everything must be fine, but only for that long. Dillon knew deep down that if he was left alone for even a minute he'd begin to panic, wondering how in the hell boxes of "House of Barbie Shanghai" dolls didn't just collapse, crushing all of them. (the answer that would have made him feel much better was that the lack of weather in hell kept them in a continuous stable condition so that.... or is that taking the fun out of it? never mind, magic, it was magic that kept it all upright.)

Deeper inside garbage mountain they hung a sharp right and entered a room of considerable size. There were numerous souls inside, even some demons, but that wasn't what Dillon noticed. The first, and only thing he saw was, "Hannah?"

And that was all that mattered for a little while. He didn't know how long they'd been in hell when judged from the real world, but he knew that he missed the hell out of his girlfriend (that was a clever joke, c'mon admit it.... OK it was a dad joke, look, the author has kids, those type of jokes just fall out of him) The two of them just hugged for a while with her face buried in his chest, both of them squeezing tightly afraid that the other might vanish again.

Eventually, he broke the hug to say, "But, what are you doing here?"

"It turns out Dan escaped his dad's palace on his own, but then he got back to earth and found out you weren't there... We've been sending out people to look for you everywhere," she explained.

"We probably would still be looking if it wasn't for that incident with the demon," Dan said coming over to join them.

Dillon grinned widely, "See, that was *totally* helpful and not self-indulgent at all! And you guys thought it would get us in trouble."

"Welp, all right then, I'm man enough to admit I was wrong. I'm also willing to concede the demon was a jerk anyway and had it coming. Now that we're all together again we can blow this cigarette stand and joke about it later," Devin said with a grin.

"I'm not going," Dan said quietly.

He had to wait for a little while until the squalls of surprise and outrage settled down before he just raised his hand, "I'm going to fight my father for this part of hell."

"Did you get hit on the head during your escape?" GG barked in shock.

Dan managed to smile at that, "Look, my father is never going to give up if I leave like this. No matter where I go on earth, there will always be a demon a few steps behind me. If anything, I'm surprised, and even a bit grateful Nathaniel and I had the time we did together. But, the only way to get rid of the threat, is to get rid of the source, and that is my father."

"Buddy, I like you, but if you're doing this because you're afraid of your father, you're telling me already that you don't think you can beat him," Devin reasoned with him.

Dan smiled a little wider, "Why not? Most of the souls will be on my side, quite a few of the demons as well."

GG stepped forward, looking worried, and maybe even a little angry, "Danasdius, what is your side? What is this rallying cry you expect a whole level of hell to turn on your father for, enough of them that you can actually defy your father on his own ground?"

Dan turned to him, this time his face showed a little of his demon heritage for only a moment, but it was quickly tamped down to be replaced by something almost angelic, his voice was firm as he replied, "GG, you know we can let you go right? Any time we want? If you've served sufficient penance that we can decide. Or even keep you from coming here, how the rules are on earth keep changing who even gets sent here and a lot of the souls here never would have come here now? We can let you go to whatever reward you've earned. But we don't. Father says that the damned don't deserve hope, but I've seen acts of kindness here in hell. Look at what you did when you were worried about me. Doesn't that deserve giving a soul reconsideration? If people have paid dearly for their sins, and have redeemed themselves in a place where redemption should be impossible, why do we still keep them?" Dan paused as he wound down for a second like a clock spring. In a softer voice he finished "Anyway, that's the cause I think people will rally behind. I'll send all of you back now."

There was silence for a moment, then Devin said, "I'd prefer you didn't send me back at least. Look if it gets tight you can send me back, or I can just go, I have the means. But I've been dealing with the crap that leaks out of hell for years now. I know that not everybody still deserves to be here, or even deserved to get sent here. I've seen a lot of people grabbed off of earth as just innocent bystanders. I wouldn't mind helping before you send me back. Heck, we brought the book, I can send myself back at any time if it comes to that."

It would be kinder to say that everyone, each on their own, and with no prodding at all also said they were staying. That what followed was some kind of noble, Hollywood sort of moment, where each of them says, "I'm in" and "Me too." with firm handshakes and looks of determination. So, we're going to go with that. Picture The Expendables, but with more hair and fewer wrinkles. I mean this book assumes there's a scene like that in there, it's been a while since we've seen it.

Moraspus stepped through the gates of his palace grounds and noted that something was wrong immediately. There were no secrets in hell, fewer when it involved moving an army around. That kind of thing is usually difficult to keep under wraps. "Hey, I didn't notice that mass of armed people going all the way to the horizon there a minute ago, are they new?" is a phrase that seldom has the opportunity to be uttered in earth or hell. There was that one incident when a mountain that an army was hiding behind was washed to the sea back in the early days of man, but to be fair, it was a pretty small army, and they couldn't do much with the element of surprise as they were too busy trying to not join the mountain on its way to the sea. So, if everyone knew he was coming, where the hell was Blurglesoth with word of his son? He considered his majordomo to be incompetent, but then again, he had considered every one of them that he'd ever had to be incompetent. But one thing he didn't consider the ball of slime was being slack in his toadying, he should be here to welcome his master home.

The halls themselves also seemed empty as he wandered around the place. There were servants, and they got right on down in a good prostate of themselves when they saw him, but there wasn't a damned soul in the place that could officially welcome him, or tell him what was happening on the home front. Power attracted sycophants like a corpse collected flies, but suddenly everyone who had any position of power in his household had chosen this moment to vanish. Suspicion ran deep in a demon anyway, but this would be suspicious in any account.

He made his guards position themselves in a way that it would be almost impossible to strike him before he said, "All right boys, topside is half-deserted, let's check out the torture chambers."

It was just a simple rule of thumb, if something happened to his toadies, the first place to check wasn't his chambers or the dining area, it was the torture chamber. Because if ol Blurgy was mobile in any way he'd have been waiting for him bowing and scraping with the rest of them. Actually, he'd be bowing and scraping all the harder. Because he knew for a fact that when Moraspus was upset about something, shit never got a chance to roll downhill. And that was because Moraspus would blow up whoever was standing at the top of the pile. Blurglesoth was a clever, conniving suck-up, no way would he let his master walk in the door without the opportunity to frame whatever news awaited the way he wanted it framed. If he blew off his master's arrival, he was either torturing and didn't know (a good torture could take a while), or someone had decided to get a leg up on promotion and had decided to torture the slime demon.

The door to the torture chambers slammed open in front of him. Chambers was the operative word here. The visible part of the building was impressive even in hell, it was built to be, but that was just the iceberg. The real business of punishment happened below, and it was extensive and lengthy. Moraspus took pride in his vast array of amusements under his palace, on a normal day he might have come down here immediately just to unwind. Today he wanted to know what was happening in his palace, and this was the real assaulted nerve center.

He stepped through after his guards had checked first, and he had his answer.

In the form of a very large jar filled with a green liquid. A green liquid that had eyes.

Moraspus started laughing. That was funny right there, he didn't care what came next, that was worth a laugh. The eyes swam about in their large jar until they were looking at him. "Welcome home Master," a sullen disembodied voice replied, causing further amusement.

When the demon paused in his laughter, which took more than a few attempts, he'd begin to slow down, take one look at the jar and that would set him off again, but eventually, he said, "So, care to tell me how you got yourself pureed?"

There was a put-upon sigh, "Your son tricked me using some of the local souls to acquire him magical accouterments to break my spell of restraint. It ended with him putting me in a very large dicing, grinding, and blending device. Which, oddly enough he had no problem locating on the grounds."

"Hmmmmm," the demon lord nodded, "I didn't even know that thing had a puree setting. Still, I didn't think the kid had it in him."

"If your magnificentness could find your way clear to opening this jar...."

The demon chuckled, "Naw, I think I kind of like you right there Blurgy, you're nice and handy this way. I might find out later how you spread on toast."

"It pleases my lordship to jest...."

"Who said I was kidding?"

Of the group of them, Devin had turned out to be the most surprisingly useful. The surprising part was because Devin had once been ordained as a priest at some point in his life, therefore giving him the ability to make things holy. When pressed on how this had come about, he had responded with, "Hey, I deal with evil books and demons in my line of work, it seemed like a solid life skill to have." No one was really able to argue that or get more out of him.

Which was probably a good thing, faith is important in things like that, and it would have been seriously wounded if they had known about it coming from a correspondence course he had ordered after a night of drinking. If it worked, nobody needed to know that he'd found the ad in the back of an old issue of High Times.

While Devin was blessing cases of Aspen soda, the rest of them worked on the other preparations. One of the main ones being organizing volunteers, of which there was a hefty amount once word got out. The other was organizing actual defenses. Dan had been right about how many would rally to him, even the hope that some of them might be able to finally move on from here had been enough to mobilize masses of souls. That wouldn't be enough, Dan still knew deep down that even with the steady stream of souls, and a surprisingly large number of demons, they would never be able to hold up to Morsapus' own army in an open battle. Moraspus had been training his troops for eons, they were battle-hardened, highly trained, and chosen for tenacity and viciousness. The goal was to seal off a section of Moraspus' territory on this plane of hell and then to re-enforce it enough to hold it. If they could hide behind walls, they had a chance to send a goodly portion of the demon lord's army back to the pits for rebuilding every time they tried to breach the walls. Moraspus liked action and chaos, a siege might bore him into leaving them be and calling a truce so he could find something more exciting to destroy. That was the hope, and hope was the thing they needed the most of if they were going to pull this off.

It was those defenses that Hannah and Dillon were busying themselves with at the moment. They were supervising two demons named Org and Bestalost as they made a wall out of cars. They had found a cache in one of the huge mounds made up of 1973 LeBarons when they were clearing out the area in front of where their wall would be. With their enormous mass and heavy steel construction, the cars might not have been much to drive and own, but they made perfect construction material.

Org was doing the lifting, he liked lifting. He was an enormous demon, both in height and musculature, so he had been the obvious choice for the job. Despite his ferocious and frightening appearance, his actual temperament was like a Labrador retriever. Whenever he smashed one of the land yachts in place Hannah and Dillon would quickly praise him like they would do a dog that remembered it needed to let go of the stick. As soon as they did, an instant smile that lit up his face would appear, showing his fangs and tusks fully. It was almost childlike. If the child in question had fangs and tusks of course, which is a rarity despite what the Weekly World News has said for decades.

Bestalost was a different story entirely. They had no idea why the demon had decided to join Dan's side, but they also had no doubt as to his capacity for evil. For instance, every time his muscle-bound co-worker smashed another car in place, Bestalost used his unique ability of breathing fire to weld the cars together. At each opportunity, he'd make it a point of clipping his partner with the fire if the bigger demon didn't move fast enough. So, it would go, SMASH, gout of flame, and then slowly Org's big rumbling voice would eventually say, "Ouch." Every time he was chided over it, the fire-breather would grin and wink before saying, "Sorry."

Zach and Nathaniel had the unenviable task of trying to find things in the mounds of trash to arm their army with. Guns rarely made it to hell, well, that wasn't true, they rarely made it into places where human souls could get a hold of them. Demons tended to hide them and hoard them in case the souls trapped here got ideas just like the one that was going on right now. If they did show up, they were usually cursed to jam or even blow up when used. If they found a cache of guns, they'd probably lob them at the enemy in the hope that their foes might make some effort to use the things. The explosions as the things blew up could probably wipe out an entire regiment.

But that didn't mean there weren't things that could be used. Lawn Darts, for instance, were in plenitude. Zach had the great idea of using leaf springs from Ford Mavericks to build various projectile launching weapons as well. But the real key was to find things that had a history of horribly malfunctioning and using that to their advantage. Takata airbags, children's mini hammocks, Kidde fire extinguishers all had potential for re-purposing as long as it wasn't for being an airbag or being hammocks, or as fire extinguishers.

"All right, Timothy, fiddle the nozzle a bit, but be careful, those things can come off real.... oh," Zach had been saying to the Victorian man who had been trying to figure out how to take advantage of the propulsive nozzles on those very fire extinguishers.

"Yeah....maybe we should stash these about out front in the lead up to the wall. Convince the bad guys to try and use them?" Nathaniel said.

"I wonder if Tim's going to be back from the body shop in time for the battle," Zach sighed. He had kind of liked the man that was now lying on the ground in front of them slowly disintegrating around the hole the nozzle had put in in his forehead. Despite his uptight sense of propriety, his learned nature made him a pleasure to talk to. The hole the nozzle had left had leaked that sense of propriety all over everything.

Nathaniel put his hand companionably on his shoulder, "Well, you did warn him about the thing, so, it's not on your head what happened."

"Went right through his though."
"Yeaaaahhh....yeah it did."

"HE DID WHAT?" Moraspus bellowed at the underling who had brought him the news of the now walled-off section of hell.

"It would appear that part of your section of this plane has seceded. From what I was able to gather from souls rounded up near the walls, it's your son who is leading it," the small, oily, scaled demon with horns growing evenly spaced every few inches along the sides of his face said. He was not happy to be the one delivering the news. Before this, he'd been plotting Blurglesoth's untimely demise so he could take his place. He had hoped to be above this kind of thing where he got to be the messenger, especially one delivering unwelcome news. In hell, it was perfectly appropriate to kill the messenger. With his former target for assassination floating in a jar in the throne room, this would seem the perfect time to make his move up the ladder. Having to deliver news like this wasn't helping him make his case for his ascension any at all. You don't maintain a positive association with your employer like this, that was for sure.

The expected bellow in reply didn't happen. Instead, the demon Prince Moraspus slumped back on his throne. His fingers drummed onto the lid of Blurglesoth's jar. A look of consternation was somehow imparted by the floating eyeballs as this happened, but his majordomo decided it was best not to complain. With any luck, his lord might deign to let him out of the jar at some point, and he didn't want to screw up the deal now by interrupting him while his master was deep in thought.

Finally, the drumming stopped. "Well, if it's a war they want, we've got all the troops ready now anyway," he said, his face breaking into a toothy, and utterly frightening grin.

The alarm sounded on the walls, Moraspus knew about them and their revolt all right, and he was bringing an army as had been expected. Some souls panicked at the sight of it and dove off the walls in their fright. It had all seemed so plausible as they'd been preparing, but now that they saw what was coming, they suddenly thought some time in the pits would be better than whatever Moraspus would do to them. Eventually, the din of panic settled calls went out for silence and the commotion gave way to an eerie silence that was meant to give nothing away to the approaching army as to how many defenders to expect. The approaching army on the other hand was making more than enough noise for everybody as they clanked and clanged their way forward.

Suddenly Moraspus' voice cut through everything, booming as if it was the voice of God itself, "Give it up boy and come home! You've had a good run of it, but it's time to do as you're told!"

Dan who was back from the wall a little conferring with his generals, which he had a lot of, hell had a plethora of them for some reason that no enlisted man ever remarked on, sighed, "I hate doing this."

A moment later his own voice matched the sound of his father's, "Not this time! If I fled, you'd only hunt me down again! And I'm too old to come home like a runaway little kid who got hungry. But since I'm here now thanks to you, I should try to fix what I hated about this place so much that I wanted to leave. I should start to behave like an adult! Do you even know what this is about? Of course not, so let me illuminate you. We could send the souls on to the next stop any time we wanted father! One word from their ruler, which is you, and the ones whose sins aren't sins anymore, or who have been punished enough could leave! You have the power, and you refuse. I'm not backing down now, this stopped being about adolescent rebellion a long time ago. You want it that way where you rule, so be it. But I've taken this part of hell, and once we're done here, I'm freeing the ones who should go on to whatever's next as my first act once I'm truly their lord!"

This brought a ragged cheer from the souls behind the wall. It was interrupted by Moraspus' chuckling, "Are you? You and what army?"

In the silence that followed Dillon hissed to Zach next to him on the wall, "Are they in range yet or not?"

Zach carefully poked his head over the top, "You know, I think they are."

"FIRE!" Dillon barked.

Thousands upon thousands of lawn darts arced into the skies of hell gracefully. Dan yelled across the eruption of screams from below, "The one I have manning these walls!"

After that nobody had much more to say and it started getting kind of messy.

Moraspus' army of souls and demons was a professional army, so it came as a surprise to everyone what a frightened fortified force of amateurs could do given the right motivation. That amount of damage was added to by the fact that Moraspus hadn't brought siege engines, he told his generals that he didn't think he'd need them, because arrogance is a properly evil attribute. The real fun began with the next volley from the improvised catapults. Aspen soda bombs, cans, and two liters arched into the sky that would have blotted out the sun if there had been one. Holy Aspen apple soda, thanks to Devin's blessings. The carnage they caused even made those demons on the walls on Dan's side wince a bit.

For a little while, Dan even entertained the idea that his father might give up. He was feeling confident enough he didn't do what he'd been secretly planning to do, which was send his living friends back to earth the second the fighting began. Instead, they continued on with their tasks. Zach watched over the catapults, Hannah and Dillon kept supplies moving to the front to replace those that were fired at the enemy, Devin kept finding things to bless, and Nathaniel and GG stayed with Dan himself helping advise him back at their headquarters.

Everything had been going too well, so in a way, it was almost a relief when Dillon rushed into Dan's former hideout that had been transformed into the command center. "They've changed tactics! They're just swarming the walls as a mob in concentrated spots!"

Dan sighed, this was the part that he'd been hoping to avoid, but if he wanted to protect his friends, he had no choice. He got up, nodded, "Stay here, I'll send a runner to get the rest of you back here, but I want you all here so Devin can just take you back."

"But-" Dillon began.

"No buts, I should have sent you back myself by now but it almost looked like it was going to work. This is between my father and myself, and that's how I suppose it was always going to be settled," Dan said before heading out the tunnel.

Dillon started after him, but it was Nathaniel who put his arm on him, "He'd really prefer if as few people as possible saw him look like he's about to look."

As soon as he stepped out of the K Car Dan began to change. He was not just a demon, some creation made to carry out hell's work. His was of the bloodline that could be traced back to the founder of hell himself. Call him the Devil, Old Scratch, the big guy, Beelzebubba, whatever you wished to refer to him as, Dan called him Grandpa on those rare occasions he had ever seen the fallen one. Mere underling demons could shrink, they could change appearance, but they could never grow so large as to challenge one of the true rulers of hell. Those rules didn't apply to Danasdius or his father, they were the true royalty of the abyss and Dan was going to have it out with his old man right now. If Pop didn't want to quit this, Dan would put him on his ass and make him quit.

His skin was the first noticeable change. Since he'd been in hell, he had become pale and pallid in skin tone, it went even further now, turning an almost translucent blue. A tail sprouted, long and barbed, his legs became the legs of a goat, ram's horns grew from his head flanking the white hair that erupted and flowed down his back. That hair sat between wings that had sprouted out of his back, not the expected leathery demon wings, but the wings of a white bird that spread out behind him, hinting at his angelic origin. All of this happened as he grew in size, larger and larger, until he was mountainous, towering over this plane of hell.

While he had been changing the entire group had reassembled in the mouth of Dan's headquarters standing outside the K-Car. Zach stood next to Nathaniel, "So that's ummm your husband normally?"

Nathaniel smiled, "Even when he's in his true form, god he's sexy."

Hannah blushed a bit before asking, "So when he's like, normal human size, does that stay, you know, proportional to how it is now?"

Nathaniel just gave her a knowing smile.

"You must be very happy," she forced herself to mutter, her face turning scarlet.

Further discussion was cut off when Danasdius, Grandson of the great and mighty Lucifer bellowed in a voice so loud it shook the earth, "Come, Father! Let's be done with this! Come and face me, or let me wipe your armies from the ground!"

He didn't have to wait long; across the battlefield, his father grew to a size that matched his own. Where Danasdius looked like a cross between folklore faeries and the angelic, Moraspus went more for the classic devil. Considering his age and importance in the ranks of hell, Moraspus could indeed have been the demon the stereotype came from. No one asked him how he felt about that, which would be odd considering what an obvious question it was. The reason was probably that most people had heard about what had happened to the last demon who asked him about his close resemblance to the cartoon devil of lore. You can insert a Hellraiser joke here to describe what happened to that demon on the suffering scale.

"Well, boy, come and do what you're going to do!" the giant cartoon demon roared. (don't mention that the book said that if you ever meet Moraspus in person, but we're willing to bet if you do, your mind will be preoccupied)

They both lumbered towards each other, oblivious of the armies beneath them that were frankly taking quite a stomping at the hands of the gigantic demon lords. More of a squishing really, and at their feet, not their hands, we probably should have clarified that better. In moments they were standing in front of each other, oblivious to the various troops that were now running vigorously from their lords if they were still able.

Father and son eyeballed each other for a moment, until Moraspus had the audacity to stick his chin out! He was daring Dan to punch him, with a mischievous twinkle in his eye no less, like this was all a big joke to him! Dan gawked at his father for only a moment before he fulfilled his father's wish. He hit Moraspus flush in the chin with his right fist. As the demon lord jerked back from the force of the blow Danasdius followed it up by burying his left fist into the gut as hard as he could.

Time seemed to stand still. His father arched backward landing with a resounding rumble. It was far past a crack, or a boom, this was full-blown earthquake rumble going here. The air was still being rent by the aftershocks as Dan strode forward to stand over his father, daring the older demon to get up, white steam rising from his furious form. He looked down at the father who raised him as best he could, for a demon prince of hell of course, which has an assumed amount of negligence in that equation. An upbringing that had vacillated between pampered and tormented, but still, it was his best. It wasn't as if Danasdius had exactly wanted for much except the things you couldn't put into words or put a price on. For just a moment Dan felt guilt about what he had just done. He was considering trying to help his father up when suddenly one of the older demon's eyes snapped open. And then Moraspus winked at him!

As shocked as Dan was, he didn't have anything on the watching audience of souls and demons, especially not once both behemoths vanished a moment later.

Chapter 19

"I love it when a plan mostly comes together in some way or another."-John "Scipio" Smith

Dan was only a little shocked when they re-appeared inside Moraspus' palace. After being knocked down like that, he suspected his father would want to be away from prying eyes, he just hadn't expected his dad to bring him along. Dan's eyes went everywhere looking for something he could brain his father with while the demon was possibly still woozy. "Why are we here?" he demanded.

"All right," his father said simply.

"What?"

"Keep it, go on vacation to earth if you want, keep the part of hell you've carved out though. At some point you can carve some more from your neighbors like a proper Prince of Hell," Moraspus shrugged, a very large glass of something appeared in his hand. "Scotch? Good stuff, I have it imported in from the past, before the big commercial distilleries took over."

"Keep it? I only hit you once, it couldn't possibly have rattled your brains that much," Dan couldn't believe what he'd just heard. His father never gave up!

His father sighed gustily and then smiled, "You're going to have to be quicker on the uptake if you want to rule in hell boy. You have spent eons here in hell, most of your life, happy and content with luxury, sloth, and whatever scraps I let slip off my table."

"Only because you...."

"That isn't how hell works my son. You want something you have to take it and be prepared to bloody the nose of at least twelve upstarts who want what you've got. And that was what you finally showed you were capable of. You didn't run away and hide, you didn't give up, you took what you wanted and you fought to keep it. This could be considered a test, and no one was as surprised as me that you passed. But it was the last test before I let you out the door," his father said taking a long pull of scotch. "Sure, I can't get you one?"

Dan shook his head in disbelief, dumbfounded by what he heard, "You know what? Yes, yes, I think I would like one. Make it a double." A moment later a glass appeared, alcohol fumes still rising from the pour.

Moraspus watched him take a sip and continued, "If you weren't under my watch and guard, out there, and not prepared to be the demon you're capable of if the need arose, do you know what would have happened to you?"

"I can guess."

"If you guessed that you'd be in a stew pot while one of my rivals sent me bits of you to inspire me to pay ransom for you, you got it in one. Now, word will get around, you popped Moraspus one right in the kisser and planted me firmly on my ass. The other lords will decide that you, and the little bit of this plane I'm giving to you to try your little hippy-dippy experiment on, isn't worth that kind of bad business. In short, you finally grew the heck up. And if you think I'm having my adult son slumming, cluttering up my palace for the rest of eternity, you sir have another thing coming. Now finish up your drink and get the heaven out of here before I change my mind," the Prince of Hell grinned.

"I love you too Dad."

"Don't you ever say that again in earshot of anyone, you understand me?" his father snarled.

"So that's it? We just leave?" Dillon sputtered, still shocked at what he had just heard.

"More or less," Dan shrugged.

"I just can't believe it," Zach agreed.

"What can I say, it's a rite of passage that nobody mentioned. Which is pretty par for the course here, if you think about it. He'd never let me go until I proved to him that I could take care of myself."

"So, what happens now? I mean, you're staying in hell after all of this?" Hannah demanded.

"No, no I'm going to continue my life above, starting right before the book got stolen," Dan smiled at them. "Patrick, Thomas, and Adrianna will set things up in my realm the way I want them while I'm gone. I'll pick some demons to work with them of course. The nice thing about Hell being eternal, it also can reach anywhere in time that I really want. Right before the book got stolen, in that golden time when my business hadn't been torched to cinders sounds like a good spot to go back to."

"Will we remember all of this? I mean I'd be kind of bummed to have done all this and...." Dillon asked.

"Unless you don't want to. I'm sure I could find a spell that could blank you if that was what you really wanted."

Devin who'd been quiet up to now piped in, "Our time passed. We've done all the things we did; they're written on the ledgers of our souls. We can't undo them just by popping out at a different spot in time."

"Seriously, what about the people we interacted with in that time? That your father's demons did? I mean things got affected by all of this!" Hannah demanded.

"Well, since Dan's father isn't looking for him anymore, that timeline kind of breaks off to wither and die. Some people might have some bad karma they don't know about, but otherwise, it doesn't count," Nathaniel explained from his spot leaning against Dan. "Dan explained it to me before, when he suggested we go back to my time when we were planning to leave the first time, and I informed him bluntly that even if it was bad TV in hell, I'd seen TV. No way was I going back to not even being able to find a book to read let alone watching My Mother the Car reruns. The timeline on earth will come up with something believable to mend itself. Timelines do that, they heal when there's been a disturbance involving mortals."

"Do you honestly think your father will keep his word?" Zach asked.

Dan smiled, "I think, what he really wanted was for me to become my own man and stand up for myself. He's reverted to being a dad to a degree since we had our talk. He even invited me to lunch, I believe the cuisine was going to be majordomo smeared on crackers."

"I'm going to stay," GG said quietly.

"What? I thought for sure you'd want to come with me!" Dan jolted upright.

"Forgive me my friend, but I think I have some karma to work off of my own. You'll need a majordomo for your kingdom, won't you? Who better to guess your wishes than me? Setting things up so souls can be unbound from their eternal torment.... maybe it might free my own one day. I think I'd rather like to see what happens next down here," GG explained.

Dan slipped free of Nathaniel and hugged GG tightly, "I think with that attitude one day you will be free of here." Letting him go to look at him he added, "Now I'll still come down and check on you of course."

"I would expect no less from a Demon Prince," GG smiled gently.

"And if I do somehow slip through? When my mortal body on earth perishes, what if I don't come back here? What if I go wherever there is after it all?" Dan asked.

"Sometimes the good you can do is its own reward."

"Speaking of which, I suppose it's time I take these lovely people home," Dan said.

Devin had the book in a satchel as all of them left the bookstore. It was bittersweet, as a group, they had been through so much, and now none of it existed anywhere but their minds except the ending. The Beast was in town parking now, the timeline had fixed itself that the world believed they had come to the store instead of shopping first. Zach would have to ride home with them since now the world believed he'd come with them for the day.

Devin turned towards his Studebaker which was exactly where it had been, parked in front of the store when this all began. Hannah, Zach, and Dillon had turned the other way to go home. Dillon suddenly paused, telling Zach and Hannah to wait for a second, he jogged down the street to catch Devin just as he was opening the car.

"Before you go," he panted.

Devin's eyebrow went up, "Yes?"

"Could you...you know.... teach me more about the stuff you know?"

Devin chuckled, "Had a taste and you want more, huh?"

"Could you just go back to boring normal after seeing what we've seen?" Dillon demanded. "No, wait, never mind, obviously you never could go back to normal once you'd seen it before. So can you blame me?"

"Your girl going to be happy? You messing around with the 'black arts' like that?" Devin asked making the hand gestures.

"You know how I'm going to tell her?"

"I can not even begin to imagine."

"When she starts bugging me about it in three days when her own curiosity gets the best of her. And trust me, it will," Dillon grinned.

Devin nodded, he pulled out a small silver case that he clicked open. He handed a business card to Dillon, "Call me, we can work something out. You'd be amazed as to how often things like this pop up, and I'm not too good for myself that I wouldn't say yes to help."

When Dillon was back with Zach and Hannah, Hannah put her arm around him and snuggled close as they walked. She leaned in and whispered, "Please tell me you got his number so he can teach us some of that crap. I can't see Dan doing it."

"Got his card."

"Oh, you are so smart, knowing your lady's needs and all," she grinned widely at him.

"We need to make sure your dad never finds out."

"He would shit, and he would yell, but that's OK. Suddenly, I don't think I have the worst Dad on earth. I've almost broken him of his complaints about us living in sin, after he finally gives that up it'll be gravy."

Dillon turned to look over at Zach and felt bad about him being the third wheel for a shopping trip. To engage his friend a bit he asked, "You OK over there?"

"You got Devin's number, right?" Zach replied.

Epilogue

"I feel lost without him after 3000 odd years of close, bitter, enmity, and unhappy association." - Gracilisisis

The thin man was enjoying the local carnival immensely. He had a taste for things that gave the public a sniff of the bizarre, the weird, the dangerous; those things that still existed in a sanitized society that reminded the populace of an earlier more lawless time. His pleasure in this nature of thing didn't fit his career as a school guidance counselor, but frankly, he only fit the job on paper and in overall appearance. Appearances have a way of deceiving, no one knew that better than he did.

That wasn't to say he didn't enjoy his work. He loved the look on the faces of the parents when he pulled them aside and quietly said to them, "You know, the world needs janitors too."

He loved his life overall; it was so much better than the one he'd left behind. Of course, it would be hard-pressed to be worse. As long as he showed up to work every day, a job where he was paid to crush the dreams of Junior High students, there was nothing and no one to bother him.

As he moved through the rows of carnies bellowing out the allure of unwinnable games, he could hear that there was some kind of excitement brewing at another part of the carnival. Excitement in his free time was always good, maybe he could create his own entertainment with what he found when he got there. As he got closer, he could better understand the announcer over the poor-quality speakers as the man described an eating contest. Ah, gluttony, gluttony was always good for a laugh. Maybe he could distract one of the contestants enough that they choked to death.

He worked his way through the crowds to get to the front with relative ease. Being this thin had its advantages, by the time someone had considered his rude insinuation on their personal space, he was already sliding past the next one. He was disappointed when he got near the stage in time to hear the buzzer loudly declaring that time had run out on the contest.

He looked up to see an enormously fat man climb ponderously to his feet as the crowd cheered his victory.

The thin man's face registered shock.

The winner spotted him in the crowd, his own folds creased in surprise.

"Ho....lee....sheep dip," the two former guards said in perfect unison, soulmates, together again.

About the Author

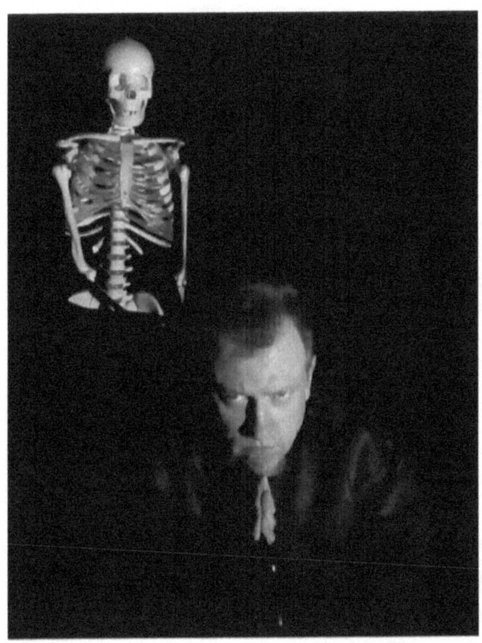

Paul has lived all over the country before settling in Appalachia over fifteen years ago with his wife Leslie and their son. He also has two adult children living in his native Pennsylvania.

He's published over 50 short stories and seven books ranging from fantasy to horror comedy to horror. Paul is a member of the Horror Writers Association, appearing on a panel for horror comedy at the 2021 Stoker Con.

He has a dark and serious horror side, but he has also never answered the question, "Is everything a joke with you?" correctly once in his entire life.

Other HellBound Books Titles
Available at:
www.hellboundbookspublishing.com

The Horror Zine's Book of Ghost Stories

"This collection of ghost stories is fresh, varied, and entertaining. Perfect company for a long winter's night."
– Owen King, co-author with Stephen King of the New York Times #1 Bestseller Sleeping Beauties

Twenty-six brand-new tales of ghosts, spirits, and the afterlife to chill even the most hardened reader to their very marrow. Grand masters and newcomers alike serve well to petrify with stories to keep you laying awake in the dead of night - long after the last of the light has died - listening for that telltale scratching at the door, a soft whisper of disembodied voices, and the icy caress of long-dead fingers upon your ankle…

The Horror Zine's Book of Ghost Stories is delighted to present to you original, never before seen, spine-tingling tales from Bentley Little, Joe R. Lansdale, Elizabeth Massie, Graham Masterton with Dawn G. Harris, Tim Waggoner, and the very best up and coming writers in the genre. Includes a foreword by Lisa Morton.

"An incredibly creepy collection of stories of the recently and not so recently dead, written by some of the finest writers in horror. I suggest that when reading, do so in the daylight, because reading these at night will only make you more aware of your own, unempty house."
– Susie Moloney, author of The Dwelling and The Thirteen

Invasive Species

A monster has come to Maldus, Arkansas, and the residents of the small mountain town are too busy to notice. With the monster comes something even more terrifying and threatening than gnashing teeth or razor-sharp claws.

The monster has brought change.

The residents of the small mountain town are too busy to notice at first. Busy with things such as addiction, racism, work, or land deals. Unnoticed, the change the monster brings in its insidious wake spreads like wildfire.

Unnoticed, the town of Maldus falls prey to an Invasive Species.

VHS Nasty: The Video Nasties

We are proud to present our very first non-fiction "coffee-table" book! A fascinating expose of the 1980's video nasty phenomenon that gripped Britain and led to some of the most draconian censorship the country had seen for decades.

VHS Nasty: The Video Nasties is the definitive, full-colour guide to the halcyon days of the 1980s, when the British government and its nanny state, headed by the self-proclaimed and totally unelected "Protector of Public Morals," Mary Whitehouse, decided it would dictate what the viewing public could-and, more specifically, couldn't-watch in the privacy of their own homes.

The fight to control the voracious, countrywide spread of video players brought about the much-maligned Video Recordings Act 1984, which came complete with a list of "video nasties," horror movies deemed much too disturbing for the delicate sensitivities of the British public, and which were not to be viewed on home VCRs. And, not only were those films banned, producers and directors were prosecuted, video stores were raided by the police, and video cassettes were burned (Fahrenheit 451 anyone?).

Naturally, the act not only blighted the whole video/home entertainment revolution but it also inadvertently created the cult underground movement and a huge collector's market for the iconic films, many of which still change hands for phenomenal sums of money!

I Spit on Your Grave, The Driller Killer, Cannibal Holocaust, Xtro, The Texas Chainsaw Massacre, and *The Evil Dead* were just a handful of the initial 72 titles that made the "must-see" list of the 1980's horror aficionados, all of whom moved heaven and hell to get their hands on a copy!
Tony Newton and David Bond lead us through the history of those dark, draconian days with an engaging, conversational style that makes for simply terrific reading. They also provide a comprehensive, title-by-title list of each and every one of the banned and prosecuted films, along with comments and memories of some of the producers, directors, writers, and actors responsible for creating the whole video nasty phenomenon.

With insightful contributions from: Lloyd Kaufman, Taylor Sprow, Ramsey Campbell, Graham Masterton, Barbie Wilde, Nicholas Vince, John Thomson, Ruggero Deodato (Cannibal Holocaust), Steve Wright, Terry M. West, Richard Stanley, James Cullen Bressack (Blood Lake), Mark Miller (Seraphim Films), Colin McCracken, Eric Weston (Evilspeak), Glenn Criddle, Max Weinstein, John Penney (The Return of the Living Dead 3, Hellgate), and many, many more.

The Horror Writer
"The most definitive guide into the trials and tribulations of being a horror writer since Stephen King's 'On Writing.'"

We have assembled some of the very best in the business from whom you can learn so much about the craft of horror writing: Bram Stoker Award© winners, bestselling authors, a President of the Horror Writers' Association, and myriad contemporary horror authors of distinction.

The Horror Writer covers how to connect with your market and carve out a sustainable niche in the independent horror genre, how to tackle the writer's ever-lurking nemesis of productivity, writing good horror stories with powerful, effective scenes, realistic, flowing dialogue and relatable characters without resorting to clichéd jump scares and well-worn gimmicks. Also covered is the delicate subject of handling rejection with good grace, and how to use those inevitable "not quite the right fit for us at this time" letters as an opportunity to hone your craft.

Plus... perceptive interviews to provide an intimate peek into the psyche of the horror author and the challenges they work through to bring their nefarious ideas to the page.

And, as if that – and so much more – was not enough, we have for your delectation Ramsey Campbell's beautifully insightful analysis of the tales of HP Lovecraft.

Featuring:

Ramsey Campbell, John Palisano, Chad Lutzke, Lisa Morton, Kenneth W. Cain, Kevin J. Kennedy, Monique Snyman, Scott Nicholson, Lucy A. Snyder, Richard Thomas, Gene O'Neill, Jess Landry, Luke Walker, Stephanie M. Wytovich, Marie O'Regan, Armand Rosamilia, Kevin Lucia, Ben Eads, Kelli Owen, Jasper Bark, and Bret McCormick.

And interviews with:

Steve Rasnic Tem, Stephen Graham Jones, David Owain Hughes, Tim Waggoner, and Mort Castle.

**A HellBound Books LLC
Publication**

www.hellboundbookspublishing.com